Every Breath You Take

by

Barbara Lohr

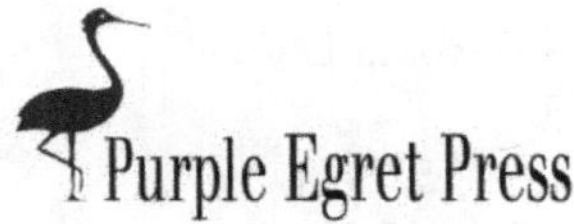
Purple Egret Press

Purple Egret Press
Savannah, Georgia 31411

Cover Art: Kim Killion – The Killion Group
Editing: Bev Katz Rosenbaum

Print ISBN: 978-1-945523-11-3
Digital ISBN: 978-1-945523-10-6

For all the single mothers,

you have the most important job in the world.

Keep believing in the power of love.

Chapter 1

Lindsay was dancing to "Girls Just Wanna Have Fun" when her vacuum sucked up an Oriental rug. She could hear the loud squeal above her earbuds. *Not again.* The roller had jammed. And as usual, she was behind schedule. Her parents were babysitting and she'd promised to be home by noon to take Rebecca and Susan to Silver Beach.

And now this. Yanking out her earbuds, Lindsay dropped to her knees and grabbed the rug. Rich people and their fancy fringe rugs.

Flipping back her pigtails, Lindsay gently tugged on the red and gold carpet. Even with a breeze from the open porch door, she'd worked up a sweat. Some of her customers were fussy about their electric bills so she never turned on the air conditioning. Thank goodness there were ceiling fans and one whirred above her now. Still, perspiration trickled from her hairline. Her pink tank top clung like a damp rag.

The vacuum gave up the rug a few threads at a time. One final wrench landed her on her back. Lindsay pulled herself up. Some of the fringe had ripped right off the rug. Great. Next time she came, she'd bring a needle and thread. Who had Oriental rugs in a beach house? The red and gold sofa flanked by gold velveteen chairs gave her the creeps. Furniture from the 90s crowded the place. Gilded mirrors and framed prints went with the heavy mahogany side tables.

The square coffee table held magazines like *House Beautiful* and *Vogue*, none of them current. And it didn't get better in other parts of the house. The long dining room and breakfront conjured up images of white linen and formal dinners. Not a scratch on the shiny surfaces. But the lampshades with gold fringe were the real kicker. The dining room chandelier dripped with crystals.

Built high on a bluff, the house would have had a great view. Like the inside, the landscaping needed work. Bushes and trees had been let go and she couldn't even see the lake. She wiped a hand across her sweaty brow. Time to get back to work.

Her thumb was on the vacuum switch when a door slammed somewhere. Lindsay froze. She'd started to work in the guest rooms at the front of the house. Yanking sheets from the beds, she'd jammed them into the washing machine, along with the towels from the shared bathroom. The laundry room was just off the kitchen. She hadn't reached the master suite in the back yet.

Was someone there? Edging toward the kitchen, she grabbed a knife from the magnetic strip next to the sink.

Sometimes squatters jimmied up a window and crawled inside a summer house for a couple days. They might be on their way from Chicago to Mackinac Island. Or they could be local kids, horsing around. Oh great. Lindsay's pulse pounded in her throat. Steps echoed on the hardwood. The squatter wasn't being shy, that's for sure. Did he have a gun? With the exception of burglaries in empty homes, Gull Harbor hadn't had a crime since she could remember. But these were crazy times.

Her grip tightening on the knife, Lindsay backed against the kitchen door. She fumbled with the knob, eyes trained on the doorway to the master suite. If she could just get outside. But where had she left her car keys?

Her heartbeat thrummed in her ears. The footsteps sounded louder. Closer. Bigger.

"What the hell is going on?" The guy was tall, ripped and frowning. Barefoot with a two-day beard. Yep, he looked like a drifter all right.

But he didn't have a weapon.

"I already called the police," she lied.

"Good to know." Yawning, he slumped against the doorframe. Unzipped jeans slid lower on his hips.

"They'll be here any minute." Her hand worked the door knob.

"Really? Why?" Pushing off from the door, he held out a hand. "You better give me that knife."

"Like heck I will." Lindsay took a fierce stance she'd seen on TV. "You're in real trouble, mister."

"Hand it over before you hurt yourself." But he stayed put.

"Don't come any closer. I warn you." She made a shaky circle with the blade. "I'm dangerous."

The guy didn't look convinced. "If you're going to stab me, you better take the safety case off first." He ran a hand over his two-day stubble. Was he laughing at her?

She dropped her eyes to the knife, its blade shrouded in hard plastic. "Oh."

Meanwhile, a musky male scent rolled over her. Lindsay had forgotten that men could smell so yummy. She swallowed. Her knees weakened. This was so wrong, given the circumstances.

"Look, I own this place."

Lindsay almost dropped the knife. "Mr. Phelps?"

"Right. Tanner Phelps. And you must be…" He waited.

Her lips opened and closed. It shouldn't be this hard to get out her own name. "L-Lindsay. Lindsay Swanson. Your cleaning service. I sent you an email saying I'd start today." Sliding the knife onto the counter, she wiped a damp palm on her cut-offs.

"I don't check my email much." His jeans were slipping again and Lindsay swung her eyes to the skylight. But she'd always had good peripheral vision.

"Lindsay, Lindsay." He snapped up her direct mail piece from the counter. "Lindsay Swanson? Beach Vacations cleaning service?"

"Right. You mailed me a key."

"Oh, right." His long lean frame straightened. Was he blushing? "Excuse me. I'll be back in a minute."

Lindsay enjoyed watching the muscles in his receding back make the cobra tattoo over one shoulder move. *Snap out of it.* Dashing back to the rug, she tucked the ripped fringe out of sight. Everything else looked pretty good.

Then Tanner was back in khaki shorts and a pale blue polo. His short hair had been slicked back. "Would you like to sit down?" He nodded to the stools at the counter.

Perching on the red leather stool, Lindsay wasn't feeling real comfortable. He sat down next to her. When she crossed her legs, she felt his eyes sweep from her pigtails to her tennis shoes. Chills rippled up her spine.

He sniffed. "What's that smell?"

"Air freshener. Cinnamon apples." Okay, maybe she'd overdone it.

"Good God." Jumping up he made it to the kitchen door with three long strides and tore it open. The cool outside air filtered into the room. Tanner glanced back, his eyes sweeping the area. "Did you see an inhaler anywhere?"

"What color?" She'd cleaned the kitchen counter. Anything that looked important had gone into the desk drawer.

"Beige. A cylinder." He pushed open the screen door and stumbled outside.

Heart pounding, she yanked open the desk drawer. The inhaler was right there, next to an extra set of keys. She rushed outside after him. Cripes, this could be serious. The thought of giving Tanner Phelps CPR made her own throat seize up. Grabbing the inhaler, he locked his lips around its edges, pressed down and inhaled.

"Sorry, so sorry." What had she done? Had he returned her questionnaire about preferences, including allergies? Dashing back into the house, she struggled to pry open the windows. Some gave way, rattling with resistance. Others stayed stuck.

When she returned to check on him, Tanner was sitting on the back stairs. It looked like they'd made it past the CPR stage. Every breath he took brought his shoulders lower. Why hadn't she checked the garage to see if anyone was here?

Lindsay stepped into the sun. "What can I do?"

His head whipped around. "Don't you have any environmentally safe products?" The teasing tone was gone.

"Not many but I can get some. I don't remember you requesting them on the questionnaire."

"There was a questionnaire?" His forehead wrinkled.

"With a self-addressed envelope." She sat on the slab across from him.

His wrinkles eased. "I'm sorry. My life's been kind of crazy lately. But I'm serious about the cleaning products. I have a lot of... allergies." The last was offered with an apologetic note.

"Be right back." Going inside to the purple caddy that held her cleaning products, she grabbed the notebook of client preferences. None were listed for Phelps so she dug a pen from her purse and went back outside. Tanner was looking better and the inhaler had disappeared.

"So tell me about your personal preferences?" Pen poised, she flipped the notebook open and tried to channel Mercedes, the epitome of corporate cool.

"Look, I just like things tidy."

Tidy. She started writing.

"So, is your hair always braided that tight?"

"No." *Tidy and a smartass.* She tapped her pen on the notebook. "Anything else you want to mention?"

"Everything in its place. I hate messes."

Anal idiot. Scribbling on her pad, she tried to look efficient. *Anal and hot.* How had she ever missed this guy? Gull Harbor wasn't that big.

Then it hit her. Tanner was new. This might be a good chance to make the pitch she'd worked out with Mercedes. See how it went. She looked up to find those maple syrup eyes studying her.

"Um, um." *Pitch!* "My partner and I are starting a new business. Don't you wish you could optimize your revenues during the winter?" She searched her mind for the talking points they'd worked out.

"What revenues?"

"Aren't you going to rent out your property?"

Tanner tipped his face to the sun and closed his eyes. "I haven't decided. Just got here last night."

"Well, uh. Wouldn't additional income generated from your winter rental be a comfort?" *A comfort?* What was she, an air conditioning repair man?

"Maybe." Squinting one eye open, he looked adorable when he smiled. "Tell me why."

She needed more practice. The business was a half-baked idea, still in development. "Many people like to come here for snow skiing in the winter. We get a lot of snow," she added in an undertone.

"Oh, I know."

That sexy purr? She lost her train of thought. The sun was directly overhead. Noon. Rebecca and Susan were waiting for her and she wanted to stop at the office. "And then there are the Notre

Dame football games. People stay in Gull Harbor. Plus, we have a lot of fun Christmas activities."

"Notre Dame guys can be a pain. What Christmas activities?"

"A Christmas parade with Santa." The girls loved that parade.

Tanner looked at her as if that was the lamest thing in the world. "Santa?"

"Children enjoy sitting on Santa's lap."

The noise he made wasn't very polite. "No kids. Not in this house. And no pets either."

"What?" She felt offended. "You don't like children?"

"No. Definitely no kids, cats or dogs."

"Wait a minute. You're lumping children with cats?"

"That is, if I decide to rent out the house."

"I see." Had he signed the contract she'd sent? This client might be more trouble than he was worth. Continuing her notes, Lindsay scribbled, "Idiot does not like children or dogs." She put a box around the word Idiot.

"With those qualifications, you might not meet the needs of a lot of people who rent up here."

"Doesn't matter. Like I said, my plans for the fall are...fluid." When he frowned, Tanner looked pretty fierce.

She clicked her pen. "But you want cleaning services, right?"

"Yes. That's what I saw on your card."

"Direct mail piece."

"Exactly. Direct mail piece." The sun brought out a golden glint in his eyes. "Anyway, I figured I could use some help."

For a quick second he seemed lost. But it wasn't her place to ask questions. Besides, this idiot didn't deserve any sympathy. "Have you lived here long?"

"Yes. But I was away. Active duty. I don't know how long I'll be here." He was being purposely vague.

"You have family or friends in Gull Harbor?"

Tanner glanced over as if gauging whether he could trust her with world-class secrets. "Family. Had."

The past tense wasn't lost on her. "So sorry."

His jaw shifted. "My father. He was the only one left."

Lindsay sat back. After all, she recognized loss when she saw it. "I'm so sorry." But she'd already said that. He was rattling her and it was time to leave.

Jumping up, she yanked on the cut-offs that suddenly seemed too short. He followed her inside where it felt blessedly cool. The aerosol smell was gone. "I'll be getting out of your way. Hope I did okay today."

His eyes swept the area. "Looks fine to me." Luckily, he didn't notice the rug.

Tanner sniffed. "The air seems to have cleared."

"I didn't make it to the master bedroom yet."

His lips twisted. "Plenty of time for that Friday."

She gulped. "Do you want me every week?"

"I most certainly do." His level look seared her. "Every Friday."

"Okay, sure." More work for her. Just as long as the idiot wasn't around.

Clearing his throat, Tanner looked away. "I mean, bring your supplies and do whatever it is you do." One hand motioned toward the laundry room. "But with, you know...."

"Environmentally sensitive products." How amazing that she got that out.

"Exactly. I'd appreciate it."

"Me too. Don't want you to pass out. Heck, that could be bad for business." What was she saying?

His laugh was belly deep. *Now* who was the idiot? She had no filter. Her brother Finn always told her that.

Grabbing her cleaning caddy, she ran back to the Jack and Jill bathroom between the guest rooms for her bottles and sprays. When she returned, he was standing at the open back door. "Next week then?"

"Next week. Sure." One guy? Piece of cake. Since he was anal, he was never going to mess this house up much in one week. "I never know the actual time."

"Doesn't matter. I usually get up a lot earlier. I'll be out of your way."

"Oh, I'm not worried."

Liar, liar. The thought of having Tanner Phelps watch her clean made her skin prickle.

She had to get out of here. It always took two trips to get everything to the car. She'd parked on the driveway. A basketball hoop hung over the massive garage door, now closed or she would have seen his car. Finally she had everything tucked in the trunk of her dad's old Gran Marquis when Tanner appeared at the door, her notebook in his hand. Lindsay's stomach plummeted.

"You forgot this," he called out. Had he read her notes? His stone face revealed nothing. She tripped on her own feet on the way back. When he handed it over, she couldn't even look at him. Now clutched in her sweaty palm, the notebook was open to the page with her comments about him.

"Thanks so much, Lindsay," he said in a clipped tone.

"You're welcome." Feeling mortified, she couldn't get out of there fast enough.

Despite the fact she was already late getting home, Lindsay had to stop at the office. She wanted to check with Mercedes and see how their campaign was going. Her new partner kept spreadsheets, which Lindsay thought were overkill. Did Mercedes think she was back in New York, booking TV time for one of her international clients?

Parking in the small lot alongside the building, Lindsay headed for the back stairs. At one time the green building had been Michiana Thyme. Vacationers enjoyed orange ricotta stuffed french toast and then wandered into the dress shop to pick up a sun hat. But the owner had retired and moved to Florida. Cole Campbell, Mercedes' brother-in-law, had bought it as a temporary public relations office for Gull Harbor. Taking the steps two at a time, she wondered when they'd be able to replace this patched up carpeting.

"I only have a minute," she announced entering the dimly-lit office that still looked like an abandoned store. Empty hangers hung in recessed walls. The three desks were banged and chipped, hauled in from back offices and clustered together like survivors from a storm.

Looking up from her desk, Mercedes smiled. "That's what I like about you, Lindsay. Always a dramatic entry."

Her gorgeous sister-in-law had already changed from her cleaning clothes to one of her designer suits. The only way to deal with Mercedes was to come right back at her. "So did you mop the floors wearing that today?" Lindsay didn't try to hide the laughter bubbling in her voice.

"So, I look ridiculous?" Face falling, Mercedes ran a hand down the lapel of a suit she probably couldn't afford anymore. "A girl can dream, can't she? You'll see. People will be coming through our door in droves this summer, wanting to sign up for the Premium level of Beach Vacations."

"Sure they will. We better clean the place up before we have visitors." Dropping her purse to the floor, Lindsay sniffed. "Hey, Mercedes, do you think I smell like industrial cleaner?"

Leaning closer, Mercedes inhaled. "A little. Why? I mean, that's what we do on Fridays and Saturdays."

So I reek. Frustrated, Lindsay grabbed one of the mailers from the desk. They had a couple thousand left and she planned to distribute them in local stores. Tapping the piece against her lips, Lindsay thought of Tanner studying her design with that unreadable smile. "I ran into one of these this morning."

Mercedes eyebrows went up. "What's with the dreamy look?"

"Nothing. I was cleaning the house of a new client up on Sleepy Hollow Lane. The place was supposed to be empty. Suddenly this guy comes down the hallway. Scared me half to death."

Her heartbeat picked up remembering Tanner's long, lean body. The close cropped hair that was strangely appealing. The soft denim slipping from his hips. "He was wearing jeans. Sort of."

"*Sort of?*" Mercedes leaned her chin on one hand. "Why do I think there's more to the story than just a strange guy in a cottage?"

"House." Lindsay corrected her. "The place is furnished like a year-round home. Not *House Beautiful* or anything like that. Kind of old fashioned."

"In a shabby chic way?" Mercedes liked to categorize everything.

Tilting her chair back, Lindsay had to think about that. "No, more in a plush, overdone red and gold way. The house dates back. It's not the average rental cottage."

"Don't do that, Lindsay." Mercedes waved toward the chair. "You'll crack the legs and fall right over."

Like it would matter in this dump. She let the chair down with a thunk. "Sometimes you sound like my mother."

"Sorry." Her new sister-in-law ran manicured fingers through her blonde hair.

Lindsay chuckled. "Mercedes, you are so New York, you kill me."

"You say that a lot." But Mercedes was grinning. When she had come back to Gull Harbor last fall, Lindsay's older brother Finn snatched her up. A total geek in high school, he had adored Mercedes back then. In fact, he'd insisted that Lindsay hire her to help clean cottages. Sure, Lindsay needed the help but she'd hated Mercedes' uppity ways. How she'd enjoyed taking the uptown girl down a peg or two. With time Mercedes kind of grew on her. Finn was persistent and they got married on Valentine's Day.

"Mercedes, have you ever heard the name Phelps?"

"Hmm. Sounds familiar. Is that the new guy?"

"Right, but I sure don't remember him." Lindsay couldn't help her smile. "And he is definitely unforgettable."

Her sister-in-law lifted a delicate brow. "Tell me more."

"He's weird. Doesn't like kids. Doesn't like dogs or cats and lumps all three together."

"Hardly sounds like a match for you."

"I am not looking for a match. I'm fine." Grabbing a stack of mailers, Lindsay shaped them into a neat pile. "I'm just..."

"What? I don't want to pry, but what do you see in your future?"

Gulp. "My future?" She'd been a widow for three years. Even so, she wasn't looking for a man. Her life was organized around Rebecca and Susan, with her parents and Finn as backup help. "I'm fine."

"If you say so." But Mercedes didn't look convinced. Turning back to her desk, she pulled up a spreadsheet. "The summer business is picking up."

"You mean, the Economy level of Beach Vacation? The level that only includes cleaning?"

Mercedes hated to be teased. "Go ahead, mock my packaging."

"Packaging." Lindsay repeated. She loved all these marketing terms. They helped her believe in what they were building with Beach Vacations. "I would call it your pizazz. But seriously, what are we going to do?" Mercedes was the marketing genius. Their third partner, Mercedes' sister Kate, was expecting a baby and she hardly came into the office anymore. A miscarriage last fall had made Kate extra careful.

"It takes time, Lindsay. You don't just build a business by wishing."

The patronizing tone rubbed Lindsay the wrong way. "I'm totally willing to do my part."

The yapping of dogs broke into her thoughts. The two women exchanged a look. "Finn," they said together.

The back door banged open and in scampered two Jack Russells, followed by Lindsay's hunk of a big brother. "Don't you ever go anywhere without those mutts?" she teased.

"Not if I can help it. I like being leader of the pack." Coming closer, Finn bent to kiss Mercedes.

Lindsay fought a twinge of what sure felt like jealousy. "Okay, okay. Enough of the PDA."

The two broke apart but that lingering look cemented the uncomfortable feeling in Lindsay's chest. She felt like a third wheel with Finn and Mercedes.

Blushing, Mercedes turned away. When she was around Finn, she lost her haughty demeanor—a definite improvement. "Come here, Elvis and Wiggy," Mercedes crooned. The dogs pushed forward, their tails wagging right off their brown and white spotted coats. While she scratched between Elvis' ears, she said, "Lindsay was just telling me about a run-in with one of her customers today."

"A run-in?" That got Finn's attention fast.

"Relax." Lindsay searched for the right words. "He didn't

expect company so he was still in bed."

"He didn't come onto you, did he?" Finn leapt into his big brother mode.

"If telling me to only use environmentally conscious cleaning products is a new dating tactic, then yes. He did."

Relaxing, Finn snorted. "I thought usually your customers weren't home."

"They're not. He didn't tell me he was coming this week. Or I goofed up again."

"Don't be so hard on yourself, Lindsay. You're always on top of things." Mercedes came to her defense.

Flipping her calendar open, Lindsay slotted Tanner in for next Friday. "Anyway, he's not sure if he wants to rent out his house. And there may be limitations. He doesn't want kids or dogs."

"No kids? Must be some kind of creep." Finn adored Rebecca and Susan. "What's his name?"

"Tanner Phelps. Used to live here or so he said."

Something clicked in Finn's eyes. "That cocky kid? From what I remember, his dad sent him off to military school. Tanner had gotten into trouble. Coach Teegarden was crushed. Tanner made the varsity basketball team when he was a freshman. He had winning season written all over him. Then he was gone."

Lindsay tried to put those pieces together. "So he's a bad boy?"

"Might be a good idea to stay away."

Lindsay bristled and Mercedes leapt to her defense. "People can change, Finn. You know that."

Her brother's shoulders relaxed. In high school the kids had called him Goofy for some cartoon character. But those hours he spent in the computer lab had paid off big time for him.

"What's his gig now?" Finn asked.

"I have no clue. He's in town. That's all I know."

The two dogs had been sniffing around. The place looked bad enough. Lindsay didn't want it to smell bad too. Finn followed her glance.

"Elvis, come." Finn snapped his fingers and just like that Elvis trotted over and settled at Finn's feet. Wiggy followed. "Tanner's dad used to own Phelps Realty. Their signs were all over. That's about all I know."

"We were just talking about our business strategies." Mercedes made an obvious effort to change the topic. Lindsay wanted to hug her.

She felt hungry and her stomach growled. Sitting open on Kate's desk, a box of cheese crowns from The Full Cup was calling her name. "So we sent out a few thousand mailers. But the phone isn't really ringing off the hook and emails aren't blowing up our inboxes." Thank goodness there was a cheese crown left. She'd never been much for sweets until she started hanging out in this office. She reached for one. Having The Full Cup right across the street with their fresh pastries was a job benefit.

Biting through the sweet icing and pastry layers, Lindsay figured this was as close as she came to sensual pleasures these days.

For the next fifteen minutes, they talked about their marketing plan. They were going to take packs of mailers to merchants and restaurants along Whittaker and Red Arrow Highway. Posters would be ready soon.

"It would be nice if we could partner with a realty company," Mercedes threw the comment out like a fish hook. She wasn't fooling Lindsay. "Does Tanner's family real estate business still exist?"

"I haven't seen their sign in a long time, now that you mention it."

Brow furrowed, Mercedes tapped a pen on a notepad. "Let's look into that."

The bottom drawer of her desk stuck when Lindsay hauled out her tote. "I've got to get home. Mom's watching the girls and I made some promises."

"Need any help? Their favorite uncle is always ready to fill in." As a big brother, Finn got a gold star.

"Nope. Got it covered." Sometimes Lindsay felt guilty about all the support her parents and Finn gave her. Some of the older couples in town took off for Florida. Not her folks. They were ready to baby-sit twenty-four seven since her dad took early retirement.

Saying good-bye to Finn and Mercedes, Lindsay headed home. Spring was in the air. Birds twittered in the trees and sand grated underfoot wherever you went. She loved it and rolled down her window to drink in the fresh air. But this summer would be way more than beach time, at least for her.

How could she persuade Tanner Phelps to rent his place out this winter without seeming desperate? Of course, there were some barriers. Like the notebook sitting open on the seat next to her, the word "Idiot" so large he couldn't have missed.

Lindsay had to work at being more subtle. Keep her thoughts to herself. But subtlety had never been her strong point. She turned up the radio, hit the accelerator and belted out "Girls Just Wanna Have Fun."

Chapter 2

Watching Lindsay drive away in her Gran Marquis, Tanner had a
lot of questions. But he hadn't asked them. Maybe because she had
the most unnerving gray eyes he'd ever seen. Maybe because she
was all hot and sweaty and he'd liked the sheen of her skin. Or
maybe her adorable confusion left him speechless. Lindsay
Swanson was a welcome distraction.

Leaving the sunny morning, he reluctantly went back inside,
grabbed his coffee from the Keurig and did a quick walk-through.
The place looked clean. He sniffed. Hardly a trace of noxious
fumes since Lindsay had opened the doors. Tanner ran a finger
over a side table, as if he were back in military school. All he
needed was the white glove. Yep, not a speck of dust. Tanner liked
that. He'd liked her, with those cute pigtails.

Then he remembered the notes in her little book.

Idiot? Really? He chuckled.

It might be easier to sort out this house than it was to figure out
Lindsay. Going into the kitchen, he snapped up her mailer. Lindsay
Swanson. Peeling a *Say Yes to Michigan!* magnet off the refrigerator,
he tucked the card under it. Too bad it didn't have her picture on
it. He was being juvenile. Tanner took a swig of coffee, hoping the
caffeine would clear his brain.

Back to sorting. From the master bedroom to the living room, this house had way too much stuff. Probably a result of the Reign of Ursula, as he referred to his father's second wife. From the shelves bulging with his father's books to the hideous furniture that made it hard to breathe, the place was packed. He remembered the day Ursula had moved in. She'd ordered the movers around as if she were Patton. His new stepmom had paid them to take his mother's furniture to Goodwill. He fingered the inhaler in his pocket.

Only one remedy for the sadness that could overtake him if he didn't pay attention to the signs. Slipping on his tennies, a T-shirt and shorts, he left the kitchen for the cool garage and hit a button. The wide door rattled up. Sure enough, a basketball was still stuffed in a corner behind a filing cabinet where he'd always kept it. Fifteen minutes later he was dribbling and shooting balls into the hoop above the garage door. His dad had installed the basketball hoop right after Mom died, mainly as a diversion. It worked. Hour after hour, Tanner would work the driveway, slamming the ball against the backboard until old lady Driscoll next door complained. None of the other neighbors said anything. After all, they'd liked his mom a lot. If they got the flu or a cold, she'd be on their doorstep with homemade chicken soup.

The cool June morning smelled like pine trees. He'd missed that. Staring up at the stars in Afghanistan, he'd tried to picture Gull Harbor but it's hard to recreate a smell in your head. All he sucked in was the smell of the desert— sharp and dry and heavy with diesel fuel and smoke. Definitely not home.

Thumping the ball on the concrete got his blood pumping, or maybe it was the thought of Lindsay in her shorts and clinging top. He dribbled faster, trying the tricky moves he'd taught himself after studying the Globetrotters on TV. Under his legs and around his calves, he bobbled the ball as he ran up and down the driveway.

At first, he felt rusty, like a tank that hadn't been used for a while. But he kept playing, taking the deep breaths he knew were crucial. The rough texture of the basketball felt solid and familiar in his hands. When he pivoted, leapt and shot, the ball hit the backboard with a pleasing thump and swish. He smiled. His aim got better with every shot.

Since it was early June, the weather hadn't turned blistering hot. This sun felt just right. June eased Michigan into warmer weather, like the relative you'd almost forgotten but happily welcomed. He'd thought a lot about Michigan weather while bouncing through the desert in an open jeep or marching with a sixty-pound load on his back in the unforgiving sun.

Going up for a layup, he missed. Maybe he'd concentrate on Lindsay and not the past. Didn't take long before his shirt was soaked, sticking to him like a second skin. He'd play until his legs felt wobbly. Somehow they'd found a basketball in Kabul. The men had played almost every night unless they were sent out on a mission. The brotherhood of basketball. Chest heaving, he held the ball against his waist, wishing he'd brought water out with him.

"Hey, you're good."

The ball fell from Tanner's hands, and he reached for his rifle as he pivoted. But of course he had no firearm. Didn't want one ever again.

A little boy stood by the bank of four mailboxes at the end of his short driveway. The kid's grin made his narrowed eyes more evident. Downs was the word that came to mind. His head of carrot red hair was a mess, as if he had just rolled out of bed. But it was noon.

"Hey." What did you say to kids? "Nice day, huh?"

The little boy flung his arms wide, like he was hugging the world. "It's beau-ti-ful." Tanner smiled at his enthusiasm.

"What's your name?" The kid looked young to be alone.

"Red." His attention was focused on the basketball.

"Where do you live, Red?"

One hand motioned toward the Driscoll place. "Over there. My mom's real busy." The door was open and the kitchen curtains were pushed back, as if she might be checking on him.

"Right." So she let him wander around? Yanking the edge of his shirt up, Tanner mopped his brow. "How old are you, Red?"

"Six." Then he pressed a chubby hand across his open mouth. "Oops. I'm not supposed to talk to strangers."

At least she'd taught him something. "But I'm your neighbor. I live right here."

"What's your name, neighbor?" Red thought his own comment was hilarious. His belly laugh made Tanner laugh too. Who could resist?

"Tanner."

The kid's nose wrinkled. "That's a weird name."

"So is Red."

The boy got quiet. Damn. Tanner thumped the ball a couple times. Had he hurt his feelings? Then Red threw his head back and chuckled. "That's a good one. Tanner."

Feeling out of his league, Tanner turned and sent the ball arcing through the clear summer air, air without sand or diesel fuel, air you could breathe. It slammed the backboard before swishing through the net.

"That's so cool." Red's mouth hung open.

Retrieving the ball, Tanner held it out. "Want to try?"

"Can I?" He wiped his hands on his shirt.

"Sure."

So Tanner took him through bouncing the ball. Progress was slow, but Red's laugh kept him going. Kids were supposed to laugh. It was natural and nice. In Afghanistan the kids had been hollow-eyed and scared most of the time. After a couple minutes Tanner knew there was a lot of work to do with Red. But he didn't mind. Squirrels chattered in the trees. Sounds of the gulls filtered up from the beach. Playing with the ball out here brought back normal. And he hadn't felt normal in a long time.

"Red!" A woman's voice sang out. She stood waving at the back door of the house next door.

"That's my mom," Red told Tanner with a roll of his eyes, as if her worries were ridiculous. But kids should have moms to worry about them. Mothers who could comfort them. "Coming, Mom." Hitching up his jeans, Red scurried off. Then he turned. "See you later?"

"Sure. Later." Tanner watched the kid scamper home. Would

his mother be mad? But at the door she stooped and hugged Red, who immediately began filling her ear. Tanner could only guess what he was telling his mother. He went back to the ball, the hoop and his game.

But he couldn't get Lindsay out of his mind. Those darn pigtails came swaying through his head, like the swish of the net. Did her deep gray eyes turn silver in the sunlight? Maybe he needed his house cleaned more than once a week.

~.~

Lindsay heard the girls arguing before she even opened her parents' kitchen door.

"Wait until Grandma sees what you did," Susan said in the whiny voice often used with her older sister.

"I'm the oldest. I get to do what I want."

"But it was my turn to lick the beaters."

"No, it's mine." The tone and comment almost made Lindsay smile. She recognized herself.

But this wasn't funny. Lindsay pushed the door open. "I'm back!"

Her mother's kitchen was a disaster. Chocolate had splattered everywhere —from the cabinets to the girls' clothes. A two-tiered chocolate cake was tucked safely under the cabinets, but the kitchen table had become a battleground. Half-frosted graham crackers were scattered on the wooden surface. Perched on chairs, the girls faced each other, red-faced and angry.

Lindsay slammed the door behind her. "What is going on?"

Tears filling her eyes, Susan stabbed a finger at Rebecca. "She started it."

"I did not." Rebecca brushed a chocolate-smeared cheek.

"She wouldn't let me lick the beaters!" Susan wailed. "She kept doing this."

Before Lindsay could stop her, Susan lifted the hand mixer and pressed the switch. The beaters whirred and chocolate splattered Lindsay's face and top. "Stop! Give me that." She grabbed the mixer and turned it off. Susan cried harder.

"Lindsay, is that you?" Pink rollers in her hair, her mother appeared in the doorway in one of her flamingo caftans. "Oh, I thought I heard your voice, sweetheart. Oh, my." She glanced around in surprise.

"Mom, will you just look at this mess?" Lindsay held her frustration in check. Sometimes her mother could be a space cadet, but she didn't want to blame her. Rebecca and Susan should know better. Mom shouldn't have to be with them every second.

Patting her rollers, her mother said, "Tonight's the bingo bus. I had to get ready."

"I know, Mom. The girls should have known better. They may be too little to use the mixer alone."

Every Friday and Wednesday night, Lindsay's mother climbed aboard the bingo bus headed to Muskegon farther north. Lindsay could only imagine what happened on that bus during the two-hour ride. Twenty women, a few flasks and a woman named Irma who led the singing. What's not to like?

"Time to clean up." Grabbing two sponges, Lindsay wet them in the sink. Then she handed one to each girl. "First clean each other up. And be nice. Then the table." She'd do the cabinets herself. For some reason, she thought of Tanner and his comment about children. At the time she'd been offended. Now she snorted. He had a point. Kids were messy.

Whisking the bowl from the table to the sink, her mother said. "Sorry about this, Lindsay, but they seemed fine together when I left."

"Don't worry about it, Mom. It's all fixable." Lindsay kept wiping down the cupboards. After all, her parents provided free babysitting. Paying a sitter would eat up all the money she earned, which wasn't much. She sure hoped Beach Vacations took off. Rebecca and Susan maintained a stony silence while they dabbed at each other. Her mother hummed some tuneless song, usually her fallback position when she got nervous.

When things were set right again, her mother said, "I thought you and the girls were going to St. Joe this afternoon."

"Right, with Dad. Rebecca, Susan and I."

Five-year-old Rebecca crossed her arms. She looked so much like Lindsay in the old family photos. "I told you, Mom. My name is Becky now."

Lindsay managed a stiff smile. "Okay, Becky. Now let's go home and change. You don't want Grandpa to see you like this."

After herding them into the car, Lindsay drove the two blocks to her own cottage. After Rich was killed in the war, she'd lived with her folks for a while. But getting their own place made her feel independent, even though some months were a stretch.

While the girls changed in the bedroom they shared, Lindsay

pulled on clean jeans and a pink hoodie over a white tank top. Then they headed back to her parents' place.

Her father had just pulled his silver SUV into the garage when they arrived. "Guess I'm just in time." He held up a bag. "Replacement parts for that running toilet. How are my favorite girls?" A warm smile creased his face as he came to help them out, his navy jacket slung over his shoulder. Since he'd taken early retirement, he'd been doing a lot of odd jobs around the house.

"Poppy John, Poppy John," the girls clamored at his elbow. "We're ready!"

The nickname turned her dad to mush. He glanced over at Lindsay. "First, I need a hug from my little girl."

"I thought *I* was your little girl," Rebecca said, pouting a bit.

Dad turned a stern eye on Rebecca and Susan. "Don't you ever forget that your mama is my little girl."

"Oh, Daddy." Lindsay drank in Bay Rum, the aftershave he'd worn forever.

"You are my little girl and don't you forget it," he whispered.

She sighed. "Yes, Daddy." For a second Lindsay was five again, safe in her father's arms. Secure in the belief that only good things would come her way.

Then he turned to Rebecca and Susan. Poor Daddy. They climbed all over him, threatening to throw his back out again until Lindsay stopped them.

One hour later, the four of them were whirling on the carousel at Silver Beach. The old fashioned merry-go-round was a huge draw for people visiting towns near St. Joe, Michigan. Lindsay stood next to Rebecca on the tiger, while her father kept a hand on Susan, riding a white horse painted with butterflies. No matter how old she got, Lindsay still liked to whirl on that carousel while the calliope music played. The gaily painted circus animals rose and fell as they spun. Her father always paid for at least two turns and then he bought them popcorn and cotton candy. Today was no exception. Armed with red and white striped boxes of popcorn and clutching a plastic bag of cotton candy, they walked toward the beach.

"Not many people here in June," her father noted as they strolled along the shoreline.

The sun was setting and Lindsay shivered, glad she'd brought sweatshirts for the girls. "In three weeks or so this place will be packed with tired kids and irritated parents."

"Of course you'll never be like that, honey," her dad told her.

"Sure. Right." But guilt washed over her like one of the waves lapping the shore. Raising two children on her own wasn't easy. This wasn't what she'd planned when she married Rich right out of high school. Oh, back then he tried so many jobs from working construction to selling insurance. But nothing really took for Rich. She'd hoped that once they had Rebecca, he'd settle down. But he kept changing jobs, restless and unhappy. Then he enlisted. Lindsay didn't know if it was the structure or what, but Rich really took to it. He belonged there and with time Lindsay felt a little jealous, as if he'd chosen that life over her. Rebecca hadn't even had her second birthday when he shipped out.

When Rich came home a year later, she became pregnant with

Susan. She was so proud of him that week. Just about everyone in Gull Harbor stopped by her parents' house where they were living. The second pregnancy made Lindsay both happy and sad. Poor Susan. With the newborn squalling in her arms, Lindsay wanted Rich there, although he got in touch with her when he was notified of the birth. Susan never did know her daddy. Rich hadn't kept in touch as well as Jamie Pickard, Sarah's husband, who facetimed his family every Sunday. Every family was different. At least that's what Lindsay had told herself back then.

"All finished." Susan offered her empty popcorn box and half eaten bag of cotton candy.

"Both of you wash your hands in the lake. Go on now." Gathering the popcorn boxes, Lindsay tossed them in a trash can.

"I suppose you're all full now," her father said when the girls returned, wiping their hands on their jeans. "You probably can't fit in any burgers at Clementine's."

"Yes we can, Poppy John!" They raced toward the parking lot.

"They're impossible," Lindsay said with a smile.

"Those girls are wonderful. Wouldn't expect anything else from your children, sweetheart. You're doing a great job."

Now, that brought tears to her eyes. Lindsay was trying and it wasn't easy. How dare Tanner Phelps feel that way about children? Her feelings shifted. No more mooning over tight abs and smoldering looks. What did she care if he became a long term client or not?

They pushed their way into Clementine's. The smell of grilled burgers hung in the air. The place was packed with vacationers and regulars, faces reddened by a day in the sun. After a short wait, they got a booth. The burgers were hearty and tasty, but Lindsay had so much on her mind. "How's business coming, sweetheart?" her dad asked while they were finishing up the sweet potato fries.

"Okay, I guess. Mercedes is working on expanding the mailing list. We're going to post signs in every store window. It takes time. Rebecca, stop teasing Susan or you won't get any ice cream."

"But I wasn't."

"Yes, you were." Lindsay turned back to her dad. "I think we have a good handle on it."

"That's my girl, Lindsay. You and Finn. Always doing something new."

"Right. That's us." Being compared to her superstar brother almost made her laugh. But that's probably how Daddy saw it. So far, giving him grandchildren had been her major accomplishment.

Lindsay sipped her Corona while her father played tic, tac toe with the girls. Had Daddy always had those age spots on his face and hands or did the bright summer light bring them out?

They were all too stuffed for ice cream. The girls colored on the placemats while Daddy paid the check. On the way home, the back seat got quiet when Rebecca and Susan fell asleep, their heads tipped toward each other. Unlike the tourists who took Highway 94, Daddy always took the old Red Arrow Highway south to Gull Harbor.

Her father had grown up in Gull Harbor and met Mom in her polka dot bikini on spring break in Fort Lauderdale. They fell in love at first sight. Now her folks vacationed in Florida for a week every February. Her mother missed the warmer weather. Who wouldn't? Michigan winters meant being socked in by snow and cold that kept people wrapped in wool coats, scarves and heavy boots. Sometimes she wondered if they would move south someday like a lot of the other older folks. But Lindsay pushed that from her mind.

"I think it's time you girls had a sleepover at Grandma and Grandpa's. How about tomorrow night?" her father said when they were almost home. Roused from their food coma, they cheered.

"Can we play with Mom's Barbie dolls?" Susan asked.

"Why, of course."

Her parents kept her old Barbie doll collection for special visits.

"I hear you're holding Barbie and Ken hostage," Lindsay murmured with a chuckle.

"Gotta have a drawing card."

"Right. As if you need it." Rebecca and Susan loved spending time with her parents. A night to herself sounded wonderful. Time in the tub, maybe a pedicure and then curling up with a good book. "Love you, Daddy."

Her father laid a hand over hers, warm and reassuring. "Love you too, sweetheart."

But when Saturday night came and the girls were safely at her parents, each with their Frozen roller bags packed full, Lindsay felt restless. Walking through the small two-bedroom cottage, she straightened up. Put the dirty dishes in the dishwasher and was about to set her self cleaning oven when she ground to a halt. The place seemed too quiet. Hadn't she done enough housework this week?

So of course she headed for the Mangy Mutt. Her brother's restaurant was her second home. Finn let her pick up lunch hours when the girls were in school. Although she didn't spend much time in bars, the Mangy Mutt felt safe because the restaurant belonged to her brother. Finn was often there, along with Mercedes.

When she got there, the place was jumping but not crazy busy, like it would be in a month. Once the boat people pulled into their slips down in the harbor, the line outside the Mangy Mutt would extend down the street. Dressed in jeans with her favorite western boots, Lindsay slid onto a bar stool. No use taking up a table for one in the eating area. Her blue and white striped sweater was new and she adjusted the boat neckline in the mirror in back of the bar.

"What'll it be, Lindsay?" Nick, the bartender, asked.

"My usual." She glanced toward the restaurant area where families were filling the booths and metal tables. While Nick drew a cold Corona from the tap, she grabbed a lime from one of the bowls.

"Here you go." After Nick set the beer on a napkin, Lindsay circled the lip of the frosty mug with the slice of citrus. Yeah, this was beginning to feel like summer.

Then she saw him. Hunched over what looked like a burger and fries, Tanner Phelps looked like a guy in hiding. Maybe he was on the run from the single women of Gull Harbor. There weren't many, not since Carolyn took off for Santa Fe and Diana married Will. Everyone was pairing up except Lindsay. She had too much on her mind to date and she didn't need the complication. She pivoted slightly on the leather stool so Tanner wouldn't find her staring. From her new angle she watched him in the mirror.

His short hair accented his high cheek bones. With the collar of his jacket turned up, Tanner looked like he was going incognito tonight. So she stared and sipped.

Control yourself, Lindsay. Her juvenile behavior brought back Sunday afternoons when the girls filled the picnic tables at the Swirly Top. Giggling and elbowing each other, they'd watch the boys snap rubber bands at each other. The girls used pocket mirrors to dab on lipstick as if they did this every day.

Had she even worn lipstick tonight? One glance in the mirror answered that question. She was getting careless. Makeup had become optional, something she rarely had time for. Grabbing one of the menus she knew by heart, Lindsay flipped it open. Fish tacos were always her first choice even though the Mutt had "burgers to remember," or so the summer people wrote in their Trip Advisor reviews.

Her eyes kept drifting from the menu to the mirror along the back of the bar. Right between the Makers Mark and Tanqueray, Tanner swirled his fries through ketchup with long fingers that matched his height. Somehow that flick of his wrist stirred something inside. Must be that overhead fan. She adjusted her sweater just as he looked up. Their eyes locked. Lindsay brought her mug to her lips so fast, she nearly took out a tooth.

Finn came up behind her, squeezing Lindsay's shoulders. "Hey, girl. You out on the town? Mom told me they had the hellions tonight."

"Rebecca and Susan are *not* hellions. Just a handful." She liked it when Finn teased her. "Just you wait."

"That sounds like a threat."

But Finn and Mercedes never talked about having children. Sometimes Lindsay wondered. "Just kidding. Of course my kids are model children. Like their mother." She ran her tongue over the throbbing front tooth.

Finn reared back. "What planet did you grow up on? I watched you climb from your bedroom window more than one night. Maybe I should bring Rebecca and Susan up to date on their mother."

She swatted at his hand. "Look who taught me everything I know."

He shrugged. Elvis and Wiggy, Finn's two Jack Russells, pattered up and sat, eyes pinned on the man they adored. "I love my nieces. Did I complain when Rebecca wrote her name in crayon on a leather bar stool?"

Lindsay pointed a lime slice at him. "She's Becky now, for the time being, and she was only three at the time."

Finn looked past her. "That guy at the end of the bar keeps looking down here. Do you know him?"

"That's Tanner Phelps." Her cheeks heated as she checked the mirror. "Stop staring, Finn."

But it was too late. Tanner did an abrupt head nod in their direction.

Finn's eyes had narrowed and he wasn't glancing away. "Yep,

Tanner. Taller and with shorter hair than I remember."

"He served in the military."

Casually draping one hand on her forehead, Lindsay peeked through her fingers. Tanner was nibbling a pickle. Somehow he made that look sexy. "Did you know Tanner well?"

"He was younger. I didn't fraternize with lower classmen."

She snorted and Finn laughed. He'd been such a nerd and knew it.

But Finn showed them all. His amazing tech knowledge became the pillars of his widely successful businesses. And then he began buying up the town. The building that became the Mangy Mutt had been empty for a couple of years before he transformed it.

Tossing some bills on the bar, Tanner stood up. Lindsay dropped her hand and turned her full attention to her brother. Watching Finn's face told her Tanner was coming over.

"Hi, Lindsay." That slow, deep voice? One meeting and she'd know it anywhere.

Working up a look of surprise, she turned. "Oh, hi, Tanner."

His eyes swung to Finn.

"This is Finn, my brother." Did she imagine the relief on Tanner's face? Did he think she had a date? While the two men shook hands, Elvis and Wiggy got busy sniffing Tanner's khaki pants. The horrified look on his face made her choke on her beer. She wiped the foam from her nose.

"I'm sorry." Lindsay couldn't stop the chuckle. "It's just that..."

"Dogs in a restaurant?" Tanner looked from Lindsay to Finn.

"You're in a place called the Mangy Mutt," Finn said with a

grin.

"So the health rules don't apply, right?' But Tanner was smiling. Should she mention his asthma? She had rules about not sharing client information.

"You don't remember me," Finn said. "We were in high school together. I was a year ahead of you."

"And he was a geek. A total nerd." Lindsay's comment didn't bring a smile to Finn's face. Sometimes Lindsay wished she could think before talking.

"I don't remember much about high school." Tanner's face had blanked out.

Finn laughed. "You're lucky."

"Maybe." Tanner gave a curt nod. "Well, nice meeting you. See you, Lindsay."

"Right. See ya."

He moved away but not before glancing down at her boots. The corner of his lips tweaked up. She was glad she'd worn them.

The girls at the reception desk elbowed each other as Tanner walked past with his head-high, military stance.

"The basketball phenom." Finn muttered. Her brother pinned her with a stern glance. "Stay clear of him, Lindsay."

"What?" She hated to be told what to do, especially by her older brother.

"Look, you're a mother with two small kids. You can do better than that." Even her father didn't talk to her that way.

"Are you kidding me? He's a client." Now she was really mad. "And I'm not a child, Finn."

"No, but you've got responsibilities. That's all I'm saying. Don't head for trouble and that's what I remember about this guy."

What was he talking about?

"Hey, you two, am I late?" Dressed in a smart black sundress, Mercedes swept in on a cloud of expensive perfume. Her sister-in-law kissed them both hello.

Lindsay loved Finn. He'd done a lot for her and the children. But he was so used to telling his employees what to do. That attitude didn't fly with her.

What did Finn know about dating in Gull Harbor? Singles weren't flocking to the small beach town. He hadn't been doing so well himself until Mercedes Kennedy came back to town.

"Have dinner with us, Lindsay?" Finn asked, sliding from the stool. "We're going up to the rooftop to watch the sunset."

"Yeah, come on." Mercedes linked one shapely arm through Lindsay's.

"Maybe I'll come up later." She pulled away.

"Okay, we'll save a chair." Finn exchanged a look with Mercedes and they headed for the steps, Elvis and Wiggy pattering behind them. Grabbing her bag, Lindsay slid down to the end of the bar. No way was she eating with her brother after that comment.

"Generous guy," Nick said, picking up Tanner's tip.

"Yeah. Right. I'll take fish tacos." A goofy smile on her face, Lindsay sank onto the warm leather stool. This was so sick. She sat there thinking about the guy who'd created this heat.

Chapter 3

Lindsay went to the office Monday to brainstorm with Mercedes. In addition to posters, they decided on flyers for local businesses. "People have to see something three times before they buy," Mercedes said. "We've got to be out there, girl."

Whatever. Lindsay was happy to follow her lead. Mercedes reached for the last cheese crown that had probably been sitting here over the weekend. She was becoming as bad as her sister Kate when it came to sweets, not that Lindsay was the queen of self control. Over the weekend she'd gone on an Oreo binge with Rebecca and Susan. Every time she thought of Tanner slumped at the end of that bar Saturday? Time for another Oreo.

Seated at her computer, Lindsay saw the email pop up. *Tanner Phelps*. Her heart rate accelerated. Maybe he'd thought about her "idiot" notes. Was he going to fire her? Tell her not to come?

She clicked.

Hi Lindsay,

Wanted to know if you could give me more time. That is, if you're up for it.

Good thing she didn't have anything in her mouth or she would have choked. She kept reading.

This house needs more than a cleaning. It needs to be sorted out. Things thrown away. Does your service provide that? Let me know if you are available and when.
Tanner Phelps

So formal. Did he think she knew any other man named Tanner? *If you've got the money, I've got the time.* Had she said that last part out loud? Guess so, because Mercedes was peeking over her shoulder. "Ah, Mercedes, are you reading my emails?"

"Of course not." Chunks of white frosting fell on Lindsay's shoulder.

" 'Let me know if you are available and when,' " her business partner read out loud, giving Lindsay a sly smile. "Well, are you *available?*"

Closing out of email, Lindsay didn't answer. She told herself the money was the only reason for the excitement spiraling through her body. Tanner was a client. Usually her clients were young couples, hoping to pay for their summer cottage by renting it out in July and August. Or the rental might belong to a widow or a family estate.

Tanner? This was different and Lindsay liked a predictable routine. After three years, she knew how to be a single mother, although it wasn't easy. The chocolate incident had prompted Lindsay to sign Rebecca and Susan up for summer playschool at their church. Her mother would pick them up at noon. That would give Mom and Dad a break in the mornings.

Single mothers had to constantly adjust their schedule. And that was something Tanner knew nothing about. For the most part, her cleaning service and picking up shifts at the Mutt and Rosie's restaurant covered her expenses. But some months, that wasn't enough. If Beach Vacations took off, Lindsay might have the independence she longed for.

Staring at Tanner's email, suddenly she was ravenous. "I've got to have a cheese crown."

"Sorry. I ate the last one." Cheeks bulging, Mercedes pointed to the empty box.

Grabbing her purse, Lindsay took off for The Full Cup. Her heart skipped ridiculously as she made her way down Whittaker. This was crazy. Helping Tanner would just be another job. Head down, she nearly ran smack into the tall wrought iron clock that had stood at the corner for almost a century.

Waiting for the light to change, Lindsay thought back. This was the corner where Finn had rescued Mercedes when her heel broke off only a year ago. Her brother ended up carrying Mercedes into Michiana Thyme. Their relationship had taken off from there.

The light turned green. Lindsay dashed across Whittaker and turned left. The Full Cup offered freshly ground coffee and baked goods. Sarah's family had owned it for as long as Lindsay could remember.

A bell jangled when she barged through the door. Lifting her head from the tray she was arranging, Sarah Pickard smiled. "Lindsay! You finally came to see me." How the woman could be so cheery was beyond Lindsay. Her husband Jamie Pickard had died in Afghanistan three months earlier.

"Cheese crowns," Lindsay gasped.

Laughing, Sarah pushed the tray into the case and reached for a shiny white box. "You're getting as bad as Kate and Mercedes, not that I mind. After all, business is business. Sweet business, right?" She swept tissues into the box and stood waiting.

"Half a dozen," Lindsay blurted out. "Mercedes is on a tear today and Kate will probably be coming in." *And I am going hormonal.*

"Ah, I see." With a knowing smile, Sarah tucked six cheese crowns into the box, the overhead lights glinting off the thick white glaze. Lindsay had to look away. Her mouth was watering, for Pete's sake. Suddenly she realized her hunger concerned more than pastry. Damn. And over an email, no less.

"Got time for a cup of coffee?" Sarah asked after she'd rung up the sale.

The young widow's wobbly smile told her that today Sarah might need company. "Well, sure."

Handing the string-tied box to Lindsay, Sarah bustled to the front to fill two mugs with coffee. Lindsay sat at one of the white metal tables at the window. Something must be up. She glanced through the etched glass onto Whittaker, the main drag lined with family businesses. If she closed her eyes, she would have been able to describe the inside of every shop.

"Always good to have a little visit, right?" Sarah slid two mugs onto the glass-topped table and took a seat.

"Right." Loading her mug with sugar and cream, Lindsay waited for Sarah to take the lead. But she'd never been very patient. "So, how's everything going, Sarah? We don't see much of you. Are the boys okay? Your mother's all right since...?" She'd talked herself into a corner again. And there it was. Lindsay couldn't even say Jamie's name.

Fiddling with her hair, Sarah kept a tight smile. Lindsay bit her tongue. She would wait if it killed her. Then Sarah's smile faltered. When she grabbed Lindsay's hands, she was trembling. "How did you do it, Lindsay? How did you lose Rich and then get up every day and go about your life?"

"Oh, Sarah. Honey. I'm so sorry." Now it was her turn to squeeze. The tight knitting of their hands brought comfort.

"It's bad, I know." Looking back was so painful and Lindsay didn't want painful again.

"Bad? It's terrible." Loosening her grip, Sarah snapped a napkin from the dispenser and blew her nose. "We talked to him every Sunday. Jamie might have been gone but he was somewhere, you know."

"Yes, I do know." For a second Lindsay was sucked back into those scary days. "You get up every day and keep going."

"But I don't want to forget him," Sarah sobbed.

"You don't have to. You won't." But Rich hadn't been as attentive as Jamie. He'd escaped to the war. Lindsay couldn't explain something she'd never understood herself. "It gets better."

"Does it?" Raising her chin, Sarah attempted a watery smile. "You're so pretty, Lindsay. You should date. How long has it been?" Always thinking of others, Sarah had circled back. That was her role in Gull Harbor— dispensing pastries, coffee and comfort.

"Three years. I'm fine, Sarah. My parents have been such a help and the girls are growing up. And of course there's Finn. My life's in order." She exhaled. Some days she wished it were that simple. "Mercedes and I have a new business plan. That keeps me very busy."

"She told me all about it." Settling back, Sarah took a sip of coffee. "My mother's been wonderful too." Like Lindsay's own parents, Lila Wilkins looked after Justin and Nathan. Raising the boys became a family effort. "You're so strong, Sarah. You'll see."

Outside the screen door squealed open. Children's voices chattered. Crumpling the napkin in her hands, Sarah stood and tossed it into the corner trash can. Then she adjusted her long white apron. "Back to business," she said brightly.

A family crowded into the bakery, the children running to press their hands against the glass case. Lindsay was relieved to grab her box and leave. Sarah gave her a wave. When Lindsay burst out into the light, the street didn't seem as sunny. Head down, she rushed back to the office.

"How's Sarah?" Mercedes asked when she returned.

"Fine." Lindsay didn't want to talk about it. Opening the box, Lindsay let the wave of sugar entice her. She grabbed a cheese crown and sat down at her desk. This was way too much sugar and she should stop. Her cut-offs were getting tight. She bit down and almost moaned with contentment.

Bringing up her emails, she stared at Tanner's message. Yep, it was still there. She began to type and then clicked Send. "Mercedes, I may be late Wednesday, okay?"

"Whatever." Mercedes paused. "Would this have anything to do with that Tanner guy? The new customer?"

"Of course not." Lindsay crossed her ankles so that wouldn't really be a lie.

~.~

Her knuckles turned white as she gripped the steering wheel. On the way to Tanner's that Wednesday, Lindsay listed all the reasons why she didn't want to help him sort through his "stuff." Mercedes could probably use more help with the campaign. Her own house needed cleaning. The list of excuses almost made her hit the brake. Then she remembered Tanner in his jeans, and her reasoning unraveled.

She pulled over into the wild grass edging the road in front of Tanner's house and parked.

Looking like he was eighteen, Tanner was bobbling a ball on the driveway in shorts and a T-shirt. Then he aimed, leapt and shot. The powerful shoulders, muscled calves and bared abs sent a shiver through her. Getting out of the car, she adjusted her ponytail.

"Hi, Lindsay." Tanner tossed the ball into the open garage. She caught a glimpse of a black SUV parked inside, the kind Batman might drive.

"Hey." She got a whiff of soap as he came closer, those brown eyes glinting gold in the morning sunlight.

"Good morning. Thanks for giving me some time." Lifting the edge of his shirt he wiped off his face. *Whoa!* She liked the view but blushed when he caught her staring. His eyes rested on her hair. "No pigtails today?"

Self conscious, she ran a hand down her ponytail. "Not today."

So he'd noticed?

He hitched a shoulder toward the back door. "Come on in."

"Tanner?" They were at the door when a wave of indecision swamped her. She enjoyed cleaning empty houses. This felt different and uncomfortable. "You know maybe I can't..."

"What?" They were standing in front of the back door. Smile gone, Tanner crossed his arms, as if bracing himself for bad news.

She wet her dry lips with her tongue. "Um, maybe I can't stay that long. You know, a couple hours."

He blew out a breath. "Trust me. I'll want to quit before you do. The thing is, you know what kitchen stuff is and where it should go. Or even if I should keep it."

Leaving the fresh air behind, they walked inside.

"Wow." She glanced around.

Stuff was everywhere. The Corian counters were piled with mixing bowls, baking pans, sets of dishes and glasses of all colors and sizes. Plastic containers were heaped haphazardly. Small appliances were crowded together—some shiny new and others as old as her mother's meat grinder.

"Yeah, wow is right." A bleak expression emptied his face. "And there's more. Follow me."

The situation wasn't any better in the dining room where soft summer light fell through the large window. The long, shiny table that overlooked the side yard was loaded with china and crystal and knick knacks from the breakfront.

Glancing back as if to make sure he hadn't lost her, Tanner continued into the living room. "You've already seen this mess."

"Some of it, mainly the furniture."

The massive coffee table and square end tables were crowded with figurines, small paper plates and napkins, never opened. Everything from card sets to candle snuffers.

"So, all this is yours?"

He studied it with a grim look. "It is now."

"I didn't realize there was this much stuff when I was here last time."

"Neither did I." He didn't sound happy. "Then I opened the drawers and cupboards."

Of course she hadn't peeked into anything that was closed. Lindsay made it clear to the girls who worked for her that clients deserved their privacy. Besides, most of the cottages she cleaned were owned by people who came from Chicago on weekends. They might have a toaster and a coffeepot. One set of knives and some dishes. Vacationing families often ate out.

But Tanner's house? This looked like a year-round house that hadn't been sorted in a long time.

"Want some coffee?"

"Sure." But she might need way more than coffee. A door to one side of the living room led to a screened porch. She'd dusted and cleaned the glass tables last week. "Do you think we could open the door?"

His face brightened, as if she'd just done his tax return and he was getting a refund. "Great idea." Stepping around the coffee table and chair, he opened the door wide. The unmistakable smell of the lake rolled over her, carefree and comforting.

"Better?"

She looked up to find Tanner studying her. "Yes, thank you."

With that, he struck out for the kitchen with those long legs. She bumped into the dining room table struggling to keep up with him. "Ouch!"

He turned. "Everything okay?"

"Sure, no problem." She'd have a bruise the size of Texas on her thigh.

Once in the kitchen, he pulled open a drawer. "How about raspberry Kahlua? Coconut almond mocha?"

"Plain coffee will do just fine. "

"Good choice. This fancy stuff is old anyway." Grabbing two inserts, he motioned to the island, crowded with mugs. "Take your pick. I'm running a special."

"So many choices." A yellow mug with a ladybug on the handle caught her eye. "Ladybugs are good luck."

"They are?" Tanner popped a k-cup into the Keurig machine. "I could use some of that."

"You haven't had good luck?"

"Hell no." Then he grinned. "That is, until now."

She gulped hard, cupping the mug in both hands. *Don't read anything into this, Lindsay.*

Tanner reached for the mug. She handed it over and he set it under the spout.

Flat brown boxes leaned against a wall. "I think we're set with boxes," he said. "Pens and tape. But most of this is going. Is there a Goodwill in town?"

"Oh, don't throw all this away. We...you could have a garage sale." The words were out before she could think.

"A garage sale?" He said it as if she'd suggested lighting a bonfire in the living room.

"An estate sale," she corrected herself. "After all, this probably is an estate."

"In a way." Tanner still looked baffled. Her coffee was ready and he handed it over.

She hated to probe but of course she did. "This was all your parents' stuff?"

"Kind of." The words came grudgingly. "Some belonged to my mother and father. The rest came with my stepmother. Ursula."

The way he said that name? Lindsay figured Ursula was another Cruella De Vil.

"And they're all...gone?" Another totally inappropriate question. She should stop right here. "I mean, have they all passed on?"

Tanner's eyes shuttered and she wanted to reel back that question. "Mom died when I was ten. The casseroles and endless invitations to dinner got to be too much for Dad, so he signed up for a cruise and met..." Here he paused dramatically. "Ursula."

"I'm so sorry." If something happened to one of her parents? Lindsay couldn't even imagine how that would feel, having a replacement step in so quickly.

Tanner concentrated on the coffee machine. "Once Ursula sank her hooks into him, I hardly saw my dad. Well, until she moved in with us." Suddenly, this man became a hurt little boy. He took a sip of coffee. Tanner poured in some cream and tasted the coffee again.

"Okay then. A garage sale?" he asked. When Tanner seemed to shake off those memories like beach sand, she felt relieved.

"Right, people will come in droves. They pay you and then cart everything away." She had so much going on in her life already with the Beach Vacations promotion and her girls' activities. Why had she ever suggested this?

"Where do we start?" His brown eyes swung her way and clung as if she were Wonder Woman come to save him. Tanner might be over six feet but he could be so darned cute.

But time to get this show on the road. "We're going to need stickers to price things. You can get them at Meijer's up the road."

"I can do that." Opening a drawer, he grabbed a pad of paper and a pen. "When are we going to have this sale?"

That *we* again. "Well, um. We need a big traffic day." Her mind raced ahead while her heart was still pounding from the *we*. "Fourth of July weekend? Is your calendar clear?"

"My calendar?" Tanner snapped up a Gull Harbor Rotary calendar from the counter and flipped through empty pages. With one stroke he scrawled Estate Sale over the week of July Fourth.

It was official. They grinned at each other, suddenly a team. The temperature had ratcheted up. Perspiration prickled along the back of her neck. "Could we turn on the fan?"

"Is the heat getting to you?" His slow smile didn't help. Tanner reached for the switch.

Burning. "Just better for working." She set the mug down so fast, her coffee slopped over onto her white T-shirt. Lindsay reached for a sponge. "Sorry, it's just that there's so much to do."

"Hey, relax." He watched her dab at her top.

Feeling like a klutz, she set the sponge aside. "Well then, let's make up some of those boxes." Anything to break the tension in this room.

Duct tape ripping, Tanner tore off lengths to build the boxes while Lindsay grouped plates and glasses. Then she stood back. "You sure aren't keeping much."

"I have what I need. Just a knife and a fork. That's about all I've needed for the past six years." Straightening, he got this quizzical look on his face. "Well, maybe two."

Men were amazing. "I think that's called extreme downsizing. You might want to keep one sauce pan, a frying pan..." By the time she was finished, he'd put half the cooking utensils back in the cupboards.

If he rented the house out, he'd need a basic kitchen. Then again, maybe he'd stick around. Not rent the house out at all. She felt downright giddy at the thought.

The kitchen had become very small. They were bumping into each other and she felt an unreasonable jolt each time. Needing to put some space between them, she took off for the dining room, lugging a box behind her.

"Are you bailing on me?" Tanner called after her.

"No, just saving time." Heck yeah, she was bailing on him. He was pressing buttons and crossing boundaries. Her own imagination wasn't helping at all. Doing this house stuff together felt way too intimate. A tremor rippled inside her when Lindsay was with Tanner. Maybe earthquake victims felt this right before the ground opened up and swallowed them.

"All this china goes?" She set the box on the dining room table.

His head appeared around a corner. "There's so much of it." Tanner entered the room.

She looked around. "At least three sets."

Fingering the frown between his eyes, Tanner said, "Maybe we should count the dishes in each set. You know...save the set with the most plates."

Okay, now that was anal. "Were all of them your mother's?"

His lips thinned. "No. My mom used the ones with the blue flowers a lot."

"Then we'll save those?"

"Sure." Tanner nipped his bottom lip. Her stomach tightened. "Look, I hate making decisions about this kind of stuff."

"The gold and red set is kind of gaudy." She threw that out there.

"She was."

Lindsay didn't even have to ask. Tanner's feelings about his stepmother were pretty easy to read.

"The three sets are really different." Lindsay had been taught to treat the family china with respect. She never grumbled about washing the plates by hand.

"The women were different." Here he scratched his head. "The red and gold set goes for sure. The yellow flowers are a maybe. Save the ones with the blue flowers."

She grabbed a stack of red edged china. "Guess I'll get to

work."

"Right." With that Tanner returned to the kitchen. The clatter of metal on metal and the hollow thud of baking sheets hitting the boxes made her ears ring. But somewhere in Gull Harbor a woman would be delighted to have this china. Lindsay enjoyed the thought of belongings being passed down. She was sentimental that way and was very careful boxing the china.

When her phone pinged, she glanced down at the message from Mercedes. *Where are you?*

Got a job today. I told you. Well, what the heck. *Tanner Phelps.*

All she got back was *Oooh.*

Lindsay smiled, knowing Mercedes was going to chew on that. Going into the kitchen she snagged another box. The fan wasn't helping the heat. "We could open the door."

Perspiration glistened on Tanner's forehead while he worked. He looked like one of those toned guys in the black and white ads that showed lots of slick skin. Lindsay had forgotten what it felt like to be turned on.

But this wasn't high school.

And she was overthinking this.

Tanner looked over. "What?"

"Nothing."

"You okay?" Coming closer, he ran his eyes over her hair. "Your ponytail's coming loose."

Reaching up, she gave it a good yank. "That better?"

"Yeah," he said softly. Tanner's pupils had this heated golden ring around them. The air between them felt like it could ignite.

He jerked. "That fan isn't doing it. Let's turn on the air conditioning." Reaching around her, he hit the switch.

"I'll close the porch door." Slipping under his arm, she stumbled back to the dining room. She had to shape up. Get to work. After all, Tanner was paying her. She closed the door against the lake breeze and went back to the dining room.

But it took an amazing amount of concentration to sort the silver that was stuffed in drawers and stacked haphazardly on the lower shelves in the armoire. Lindsay felt so distracted. Slipping off her pink hoodie, she worked with steady concentration. Before long, the cotton tank top felt glued to her body, even though the air was blasting. Tanner called out questions and comments from the kitchen. "What about the cookbooks on this shelf?"

"Are you using them?" Lindsay heard the dull thud when the books hit a box.

Teamwork. The word appeared in her mind like a stop sign and brought a halt. The clash of the silver she dropped brought Tanner to the door. "Everything all right in here?"

"Fine. Of course." She waved him away.

Things weren't fine. Not at all. This felt like, well, a couple. The intimacy felt weird and wrong. She'd been alone so long. The single mother. Lindsay knew that role. It fit her and it suited Rebecca and Susan, didn't it? With her parents' help, they'd created a life.

Now something was shifting and it caught her off guard. Trying to shake her mood, she went back to work. But her rhythm was gone. Maybe a change of scenery? But she couldn't go into the kitchen. Tanner was there. So she tried the small study off the dining room. A large desk dwarfed the room. Books were piled on the floor. Taking a few small boxes with her, she began to fill them. Tanner had done some organizing here. History in one pile. Fiction in another.

She filled the small boxes, knowing books didn't sell that well. Although Gull Harbor didn't have a book store, folks seemed to manage just fine. If people came for a vacation and didn't bring the right books, Gull Harbor had a library with dear Mildred Wentworth at the main desk.

Huckleberry Finn. She ran a hand down the spine. Not a paperback, this bound version had gilded letters, now almost worn away. Sitting down on the floor cross-legged, she opened the book and breathed in the unmistakable smell of time. The book was inscribed. *To my Huckleberry boy, Love Mom.*

Now, he'd want to save this one. Lindsay had read *Huck Finn* in high school, but it had been a long time. She was on chapter three when Tanner appeared at the door.

"Found something you like?"

"Oh!" What was she doing? Lindsay scrambled to her feet, as if she were Rebecca, hiding the book behind her back. "Sorry. Guess I just got caught up. I know you're paying me by the hour. Don't worry, I'll deduct thirty minutes."

"Which one is it?" When he came closer, she drank in the scent of a man working hard. Strange yet so nice.

"*Huck Finn.* We all read it sophomore year." Her face flaming, she held it up.

"Oh yeah. My mother read this to me." He slipped the book

from her hand.

"Huck Finn sets off on this great adventure on the river."

"I know. He's with Jim. They're both runaways."

How amazing that he remembered. "Right. They get into a lot of trouble together. Without adults around, I mean."

"Boys often do. Without parents, we can be real trouble." For a second Tanner looked like the loneliest man in the world.

"It's just a book." She only meant to hug him. He looked so forlorn. But Tanner turned into the hug, his eyes huge and searching. The book fell with a soft thud.

"Your eyes are like syrup," she whispered. They swirled, warmer with each word.

"Really?" When he smiled, Tanner's eyes crinkled in the corners.

"I'm being stupid. I should wear a mouth guard," she murmured. Finn always kidded her about that.

"No need. I'll guard your mouth," he whispered, lowering his head.

"Oh, I don't think..."

He silenced her with his lips. She tasted coffee and sweat and something else that was definitely Tanner and very nice. The kiss lifted Lindsay like a giant wave on a windy day.

She lost herself in the kiss, first soft and then sweeter. The kiss felt new. Something she'd never experienced before, like her first time on the carousel at Silver Beach. Had she ever felt like this with Rich? Uncertainty made a sick circle in her stomach. Lindsay pushed her hands flat on his chest. "I have to leave."

Breaking his hold, Tanner looked stunned. "Please don't. I'm so sorry."

Snatching her pink hoodie from the dining room, she streaked to the kitchen, grabbed her purse and was out the door. Tanner followed her outside. "That was totally out of line. I apologize."

At the driveway, she turned. "No, it's not you. Really." Feelings twisted inside her--unruly and frightening. Tanner looked stricken. Lindsay opened her mouth but nothing came out, as if she'd forgotten her own language. So she turned and stumbled to the car.

Thank God her car started. In her rearview mirror, a small red-headed boy appeared. She'd seen him around town with his mother and two smaller children in a twin stroller. A special needs child, or so she thought, and always with a bright smile. Now the boy stood by the side of the road and waved. "Good-bye," he called out as she slowly took off.

Tanner stared after her. Would he chase the boy away? Probably. He hated kids.

~.~

Standing there helplessly as Lindsay drove away, Tanner wanted to kick himself. What had gotten into him? But the kiss had come so naturally. And he was hungry for it. Hungry for *her*.

Lindsay had wound her arms around his neck, so soft and willing. Unplanned, it felt right. Now she probably wouldn't come back. Damn. He'd lost a house cleaner and a garage sale. And he'd lost something else, although he couldn't name it.

Then it hit him. Maybe Lindsay was married. He'd never asked her. Of course she wouldn't wear a ring while she was working. His stomach clenched.

"Pretty lady." Red joined him. They watched the car disappear.

"She is pretty." More than pretty.

"But she sure looked mad." The little boy sounded troubled by that. "Was she mad, Tanner?"

"I guess so, buddy." He ruffled Red's hair. The kid must dress himself. His shirt was buttoned wrong. He used to hate it when Ursula fussed about his clothes. Once he was taller than she was, the nagging stopped.

"Want to play ball?"

"Sure. You bet." Swinging his arms with purpose, Red started for the open garage where he knew Tanner kept the ball.

Chapter 4

What just happened? Lindsay didn't know what to do or where to go. When she got to Red Arrow Highway, she had serious brain freeze. Her lips still tingled. Her parents had insisted on picking up the girls from summer playschool. If she went home to her parents' house now, they'd see she was upset. So she turned her car toward Gull Harbor and the PR office. Lindsay could sit in the office and stare at her computer screen until her heart stopped pounding.

Relief flooded through her when she pulled up and the champagne colored Mercedes was nowhere in sight. Only Mercedes would have a car to match her name. Had she left for the day? That would make things easier. Parking, Lindsay got out of the car. The poster was at the print shop but maybe she'd work on some flyers, or another mailer.

But who was she kidding? She didn't want to design another promotional piece. She wanted to sit and remember how Tanner's kiss had felt. Soft and hot, all at the same time. Best of all, he'd looked as surprised as she felt. Feeling as if she had marshmallows in her shoes, she vaulted up the steps two at a time. Her hand shook as she turned the old-fashioned door knob and pushed. "Mercedes?"

Her sister-in-law swiveled from her computer screen. "Lindsay.

I thought you weren't coming in today."

"Where's your car?"

"Finn took it in for a tune-up." Looking suspicious, Mercedes stood. "What's up?"

"Nothing." Lindsay dropped her bag into the drawer, folded herself into her chair and turned on the computer. The blue screen flared to life but she didn't click on her messages or on Facebook.

Coming up behind her, Mercedes touched Lindsay's shoulder. "Hey, are you all right?"

"Sure. Of course." She clicked on her email program. "Time to get to work."

Perching on the desk, Mercedes crossed her arms over another silk blouse. "Are you going to make me play twenty questions? What were you doing at Tanner's?"

"Well, not that!" Lindsay blurted out.

Mercedes' lips tipped into a Cheshire cat smile. "Well, of course not. I didn't say you were, did I?"

"We were sorting things out. His things, I mean. For a garage sale." But she wasn't thinking of dishes, pans and Tupperware. His lean, muscled arms felt imprinted on her body. The graze of his beard stubble pulsated on her forehead.

That kiss. Lindsay licked her lips.

Mercedes wasn't giving up. "Did he do something weird? Didn't Finn tell us he was kind of strange?"

"Stop, Mercedes, no." She grabbed her friend's hands. "Tanner is not strange."

"What then?" Mercedes waited.

How could she ever explain this? "He kissed me." After all, who did she have to confide in?

Mercedes' lips formed a pleased O. "Well then. You go, girl."

"It came out of nowhere." Lindsay began to giggle. Then her chuckle rolled into a belly laugh until Mercedes was laughing too, smearing her expensive eye makeup. "Even he looked surprised."

"I think we have a winner," Mercedes choked out. "I'd call this chemistry."

"Winner? Kissing a guy you don't even know?"

"What's wrong with that? I mean, he didn't try to rip your clothes off or anything." Mercedes sobered up. "Did he?"

"No." The very thought got her giggling again. "Not yet."

They were off on another roll. Lindsay laughed until her cheeks hurt. She loved it when her big-city sister-in-law let loose.

Finally, they both settled down. Wiped their eyes and blew their noses. Then Lindsay expelled a slow breath. "I acted like an idiot, Mercedes. Ran away, if you can believe it."

"Oh, Lindsay. Why?"

"I don't know." She wasn't going to admit that Rich was the only boy she'd ever kissed. That she had no way of comparing.

"You were surprised, that's all. Not that I'm encouraging to go whole hog slut with him and jump into bed."

Her words sent Lindsay spinning. She felt hot and cold at the same time. Maybe she was going through an early menopause, like her mother.

"You're a woman, Lindsay. And apparently you've been alone too long," Mercedes said with maddening practicality. Standing, she ran a hand down her black suit skirt. "You can make this whatever you want."

"That might be fine with you." Mercedes had a lot more experience than Lindsay. "All I want is to have this job. Help him with a garage sale and then..."

"And then?"

"Heck, I have absolutely no clue."

"Just enjoy it. Right now, he's a client and we need more houses!"

"Right, but he has a year-round home with a fireplace."

"Perfect." Mercedes looked pleased.

"But if he rents out his house this winter, then he won't be in town."

Mercedes' smile slipped. "Right. Not so good for you. But we don't know."

Playing with her ponytail, Lindsay didn't like uncertainty. "The garage sale would have been lots of hours for me."

"Maybe you can mend some fences. I mean, if you want to," Mercedes hurried to add.

"Sure. Right." Chewing on the corner of her lips, she turned to her computer and Mercedes went back to work.

When she clicked on her emails, one popped up from Tanner.

From the Idiot

Her heart pounded as she opened the message.

Lindsay, I don't know what got into me this morning. I can be such an idiot.

Even though he couldn't see her, she blushed at that. That may have been her first impression. But that was before she saw all those dishes. Before she heard about the stepmother. Before she'd opened his copy of *Huckleberry Finn*.

That will never happen again. I promise you. I need your help with this garage sale. I hope you can come back tomorrow. We can take another crack at all the crap in this house. Please. I can't do this alone.

Tanner

Relief made her light-headed, followed by crushing disappointment. It wouldn't happen again? Really?

Hands on the keyboard, she hesitated. Maybe she should wait. Not appear so eager to respond. Cripes, this felt like junior prom. Her hands fell into her lap. All of a sudden she was back in the Gull Harbor cafeteria that smelled like peanut butter and adolescence, waiting for Rich to invite her to the dance.

But this wasn't high school.

She began to type.

No problem. Glad you came to your senses (hah, hah) and realized you really didn't want to kiss me. Harassment in the workplace and all that.

But I do want to help you so I'll be there at eight tomorrow morning. We'll knock that project off in no time. Lindsay

That sounded very adult. Pleased, she sat back and hit send.

"Do we have any cheese crowns left?"

"Two and eat them both, please. Save me."

But Lindsay only ate one. After she got her sugar fix, she worked on a flyer for a while. Mercedes liked the design and they decided to run it past Kate. "I miss having her around the office," Lindsay told Mercedes.

"I know. Me too. But I guess she's in the uncomfortable stage of her pregnancy now. She does a lot of the press releases and announcements from home."

"Whatever works for her." Kate had married Cole Campbell, her high school crush, about a year after she returned to Gull Harbor for a short visit. "See you tomorrow."

And she was off. When she reached her parents' house, the girls were watching TV, and the house smelled like spice cake. Susan grabbed something from the coffee table and ran toward her. "I made this for you, Mommy."

On a piece of green construction paper, Susan had drawn a house. Next to it stood a mother and two smaller figures, with a cardinal flying overhead. "That's us." Susan pointed proudly.

"It's beautiful." Lindsay gave her a kiss. "How about you, Rebecca? Do you have a project too?"

"I don't feel like coloring. That's dumb. And my name's Becky." Her oldest daughter remained glued to the TV. Lindsay decided not to push it.

"You know what, Susan? We're going to put this up on the refrigerator when we get home. How was summer camp?"

"I hate it," Rebecca said, never taking her eyes from the TV.

"It was so fun, Mommy!" Susan could barely contain herself.

Her girls were total opposites. Susan was her father's daughter, although Rich had never seen her. Blonde with Rich's blue eyes, she accepted everything, no questions asked. Rebecca, on the other hand, was all Lindsay. Sometimes Lindsay didn't know how her parents had ever put up with her.

"Hi, sweetheart." Her mother bustled through the door of the kitchen in her polka dot apron that said *Join the Bingo Bus*. She'd won it at the casino last year. "Busy morning?"

"Yes, we got a lot done. You know, my new client. Thanks for picking up the kids."

"Any time. You know that." Her mom gave her a hug. They were a hugging family. "Rebecca and Susan helped me make spice cake. No arguments."

"Thanks, Mom. My favorite."

"I know. Come back for dinner?"

"That sounds good. How about a trip to the beach?" she asked Rebecca and Susan.

"Yes, yes!" Susan jumped up, all ready to go.

"I want to watch the end of this show." Rebecca never turned her head and Lindsay had to count to ten.

"You're too young for *Friends*." Rebecca wouldn't even understand the problems presented on the popular show. Would she? "Rebecca."

Her oldest daughter must have heard the warning note in her voice. Unwinding herself from a bean bag chair, she grumbled but clicked the remote. "And my name's Becky."

How would Lindsay ever make it through their teen years if she couldn't even handle them now? "Scoot. Let's get in the car."

After they'd snapped on their seatbelts, the girls argued all the way home. If it wasn't about who got to sit on the sunny side, it was about who Mary Beth, the summer camp teacher, liked best.

"Want to take lunch to the beach?" Lindsay had learned long ago that diversion worked better than reasoning with them. Cheers went up. The beach was one thing they agreed on.

By the time she got them down there, it was two o'clock and they were cranky. She'd put them into their suits but a chilly wind blew from the lake. They kept their jeans and sweatshirts on.

"It's sandy," Rebecca complained, trying to brush off the blanket.

"It's the beach," Lindsay snapped, sorry that she'd brought them down here. Only June and the weather was too cool for the beach. Opening the quilted lunch pack, she doled out sandwiches, chips and pop. The napkins sailed away on a sudden gust and she had to go chasing them down the cool sand.

When she got back to the blanket, Susan was upset. "Mom, Rebecca is hogging all the chips."

"Am not," Rebecca shot back. "And I told you. My name's Becky now, Suzie."

"I am *not* Suzie. I hate that name. Mom, make her stop."

Lindsay's head pounded. Why not let them watch TV and be done with it?

"Finish your sandwiches and we'll take a walk to find stones. Whoever collects the prettiest stones will get a prize."

"Who's going to judge?" Rebecca asked.

Now that was a problem. If Lindsay said Grandpa, he might favor Rebecca. While Finn, no doubt about it, had a soft spot for Susan.

"We'll decide later."

By that time the sandwiches were gone. "Leave everything here," she told them. "Just bring your sandwich bag for the stones."

"It's not very big," Rebecca said, flapping the clear plastic bag in her hand.

"Fine. Use your pockets too." TV was looking better every minute.

As they strolled along the shore, the girls squealed every time the water splashed over their feet. "It's freezing," Rebecca complained with a sullen jut of her chin.

"Yeah, it's cold, Mommy." Susan arched up on her tiptoes.

"The prize will be a trip to Oink's. Winner gets a double dip."

Immediately their heads went down. Dipping and digging, they searched the shore for additions to the rock collection strewn across their book case. But the bickering didn't stop.

No wonder Tanner didn't like kids. His comments replayed in her mind. Children were a full time job. But the thought was quickly followed by guilt. She'd signed on for this job.

Cuddling on the sofa later, they watched *Dora the Explorer* together. Before long, their eyes grew heavy in the sunny front room until they all nodded off, arms and legs tangled.

That night she took the girls back over to her parents for her dad's grilled burgers. Rebecca and Susan filled Poppy John in about summer camp. Just when Lindsay thought she couldn't eat another sweet potato fry, her mother cut generous slices of moist spice cake.

"This kills my diet, Mom." She savored the spicy concoction with cream cheese frosting that stuck to her teeth.

"Nonsense. You're too thin as it is." Mom had always been good about pushing diets aside. Her father didn't mind Mom's gently sloping curves. The smell of cinnamon and cloves was enough to make any girl throw her diet out the window. While Lindsay helped her mother clean up, Rebecca and Susan spread out their rocks for Poppy John to admire.

"You've both done a great job," he finally said. "I just can't decide."

"We both win!" Both girls threw up their hands with delight. "Do we get to go to Oink's?"

"Maybe tomorrow night."

This was what life was about, Lindsay decided on the way home. Family and friendly arguments. Still, her mind wasn't on ice cream when she went to bed that night.

Chapter 5

The girls were still asleep. The next morning Lindsay took her time getting dressed, not that she had many decisions to make. Her wardrobe consisted of jeans, T-shirts and hoodies. The time alone this morning felt like a luxury. She wouldn't have to get them up to take them to her parents. Her dad was probably already downstairs. "No need to wake the little ones," he'd said. "When they get up, I'll take them back to our house. Everything in good time." Lindsay caught a warming whiff of coffee and smiled. Yep, Dad was here.

The weather had turned cool and she eased her bedroom window closed. Pulling on jeans with a blue and white striped T-shirt, she added a blue hoodie. The warm days couldn't come soon enough. Everyone in Gull Harbor seemed to be in a bad mood, especially the tourists renting cottages. Mercedes told her people were calling to complain. "As if we could do anything about the weather," she said with New York contempt.

Her parents were taking the girls into Michigan City to the outlet mall today. "For some summer clothes," Rebecca told her.

"Excellent." Usually when her mother did that, she brought home clothes for Lindsay too. Her wardrobe could use a little perking up. Maybe one of those tops with the cutout shoulders. Or a new pair of ripped cut-offs.

Peeking into the girls' room, Lindsay smiled to see Rebecca flung out on her bed, arms and legs wide. In the other twin bed Susan was coiled into a ball, one hand tucked beneath her cheek. Leaving the door ajar, she tiptoed downstairs.

"Good morning, Daddy." She found her father in the kitchen. He'd brought his morning paper with him and had it spread out on the table.

Slapping the newspaper with one hand, he said, "Will you just look at the season the Cubs are having?"

"Are you planning on going to some games this summer?"

"You bet." He gave her a cautious glance over the top of his glasses. "How about it? You coming with me?"

"Oh, Daddy." Baseball just wasn't her thing. "Ask Finn."

"Well, maybe the girls will want to go, although all they do is eat popcorn and ice-cream. I spend as much time at the concession stand as I do watching the game." But he was smiling. "Coffee?"

She checked her phone. "I'm starting early today. See you later?" Reaching down for a hug, Lindsay got a good whiff of Bay Rum cologne.

"Have a good day, sweetheart. No need to rush home. We know you have work to do."

"Okay. Make sure they behave." Things were so easy having her parents close.

Butterflies fluttered in her stomach on the short drive to Tanner's. Would he be totally cool and reserved with her now? She sure hoped not. The kiss? Lindsay still didn't know what to think but she didn't regret it.

When she got to Tanner's, the garage door was open and his black SUV was parked out on the road. She could hear him moving things around as she got out of the car. As a kind of peace offering, she'd stopped at The Full Cup and picked up some cheese crowns. Eyes twinkling, Sarah had been curious. "You're starting work early."

Lindsay almost dropped the box. "This is for one of my clients." She liked that word. Mercedes used it a lot and it sounded way better than "the people I clean for."

Now she felt a little foolish standing in front of the garage with her pastries. "Wow, you dragged all this furniture out here?"

Wiping a hand across his brow, Tanner was looking good in his low slung jeans and T-shirt that didn't hide the muscled arms. "Right. For the garage sale."

She couldn't believe it. Furniture filled the double garage. "What's this?"

"I'm doing a clean sweep."

"Did you drag this all out here by yourself?"

He shrugged. "I'm used to doing things for myself. Is that for me?"

"Cheese crowns. Six hundred calories and guaranteed to clog your arteries."

"Who could resist?" But his eyes were on her, not the box.

She went into overdrive. "They're a favorite around here. You can get them at the bakery in town. The Full Cup. Sarah. Sarah Pickard. She's a baker and a coffee maker." Following him into the kitchen, she kept babbling.

Setting the box on the island, he opened it. "Wow." He wore the expression of a little boy on Christmas morning.

"Do you have any milk?"

Tanner's face fell. "No. Do these need milk?"

Her laugh ended with a snort. Not very feminine. "Absolutely not, but my k-... I like them with milk." Now why didn't she want to mention her children? "How about juice?"

"That I have."

While she fussed with the napkins, he poured what looked like a tankard of juice for each of them. "Want to eat these on the porch?"

"Sure. Do you have any napkins?"

"Napkins." Glancing around, he snapped up a pack of Christmas napkins from one of the boxes. "Here we go."

Orange juice in hand, she followed him to the screened porch. Passing through the mostly empty rooms felt weird. Lindsay was glancing out the front bay window when she hit the coffee table with a thunk. Another bruise. "Darn it."

"You all right?" Turning, Tanner took her arm.

"I'm fine." Her shin throbbed but her elbow felt good cupped in his palm. "March on, soldier."

"How did you know I was a soldier?" He dropped his hand and they moved onto the porch.

"Some of the pictures on the walls, not that I was prying."

"Well, I'm not anymore."

That surprised her. "I thought once a soldier, always a soldier."

"I'm glad to be here. Home." He seemed to turn that word over in his mind.

Cardinals were calling in the trees. Morning mist rolled up from the lake over the twisted bushes and trees that led down to the shore. She caught glimpses of Lake Michigan. White caps rippled on the blue surface that stretched to Chicago. Still standing, Tanner wasn't looking at the lake. He was studying her. Dropping his eyes, he pulled out her chair.

"Such a gentleman." She sat down. "My dad does stuff like that all the time."

"Glad to hear it. Not all women appreciate it." His lips curved into a grin, as if she'd just made his day. Flipping open the top of the box, Tanner inhaled. "This was really nice of you."

"They're one of my favorites. Hope you like it." She wrestled with the stiff cellophane pack of napkins.

"Here, let me." Taking the napkins from her hands, he found a corner and ripped it with his teeth. Poinsettia napkins spilled out.

"You're an expert," she teased, reaching for the napkins before they fluttered to the floor.

"Not really. That's just the way you do it when you're...well, when you don't have a scissors or anything else handy."

She wouldn't press him about where he'd been. She knew.

Seconds later, they were both munching a little piece of heaven. A brilliant red cardinal hopped from one tree branch to other while his mate called to him. Tanner was eating with the gusto of a man tasting his first cheese crown.

"Did you sit out here a lot when you were growing up?"

"My mother loved to eat out here. Said it was like being in a tree house. But my stepmother thought it was too far from the kitchen."

Frowning, he took another bite. She didn't know what to say. Lindsay tried to picture him as a little boy. Her next bite filled her mouth so she couldn't talk. That was probably a good thing.

"You see, I've been gone a while," he said between mouthfuls. "In the service."

She merely nodded.

"But yeah, this porch reminds me of my mom."

"You must miss her."

"Sure. She liked to put puzzles together with me out here. Peter Pan and Captain Hook, that kind of stuff."

Her heart ached for that little boy. "I can't imagine losing a parent."

Tanner studied the bakery box. "Your folks live here?"

"Yes, just a couple blocks away from me. This town is all I know."

He smiled. "You're lucky. Sometimes I wish I'd never left Gull Harbor."

Questions rattled in her head but Lindsay pressed her lips tight. She was here to do a job. Pleased with her silence, she flinched when he said, "Look, I'm sorry about...well, you know."

"Don't worry about it." She licked the sugar from her lips.

"You aren't married, are you?"

"What? No. Would I have been at the Mangy Mutt alone if I had a husband?"

"You'd be surprised." His obvious relief made her ridiculously happy. "Any other questions?"

"Not right now. Gotta admit, I have an active imagination."

She pulled her hands back into her lap. "I'm not sorry about that kiss. Don't even think about it."

"But I do." Eyes twinkling, he leaned forward.

"You do?" Her heart fell into her tennies.

"Absolutely. But if you don't want to think about it...."

"You're a terrible tease." By this point, they were laughing. Thank goodness she didn't add her snort at the end. "Let's put it in the past," she finally said.

"Oh, I don't know. The past? That box in my head is already pretty full."

A loaded statement if ever she heard one. "You don't talk much about your father."

"Sometimes I think I hardly knew him." His eyes drifted down to the overgrown bushes and trees that obscured most of the lake. "Besides, after my mom died, he became another man."

Outside, the birds stopped chirping. The mist was burning off and the spring air carried a warm edge, as if it might just turn to summer.

"I'm so sorry."

He pushed himself up. "Life happens. Ready?" Swiping the box from the table, he led the way back into the house.

Of course, she babbled all the way. "You don't have to pay me for the time spent talking out there. I don't want you to think that. After all, I brought these pastries. Breakfast is on me. We have them around the office all the time."

He tucked the box into the refrigerator. "Office?"

"I work in the PR office in Gull Harbor." She didn't want him to think that she was only a cleaning lady. "And sometimes I pick up hours at the Mangy Mutt."

"Your brother's place?"

"Right. Finn owns it."

"Must be nice to have siblings."

"He's been a big help to me."

His brow wrinkled. "He seemed to remember me but I can't say the same. Of course, all I paid attention to was basketball."

"Finn said you were the freshman phenom." She wasn't going to tell him what else her brother had said.

"Maybe I was. That was before..."

"Before what?"

Opening a drawer, he grabbed an inhaler, took a breath and tucked it in his back pocket "Before I became a military man, not the freshman phenom."

"So you were sent to military school?" She couldn't even imagine.

"Right. I was sent to be a man. And by that time I wanted to go." He shrugged. "And now, let's get to work."

She looked around. All the boxes were filled. "But you've cleared everything away."

"I thought we'd work in the garage today."

"Okay." Good thing she kept rubber gloves and a bandana in her trunk. Garages usually meant dust. He was fingering his inhaler.

"Right, my folks kept stuff up in the garage. I mean, as long as we're having a garage sale, I might as well get rid of everything. Do a clean sweep."

"I suppose that depends on what everything is."

His brows peaked. "We'll find out when we get there."

Glancing over her shoulder, she gave the house one last look. "What are you going to put in here after people buy all your furniture?" She pictured these rooms totally empty. How would Beach Vacations ever rent this place to skiers or Notre Dame football fans?

He stopped suddenly and she just about ran right into him. "Good question."

Men. He hadn't thought about that little detail? Well, push on. It wasn't her place to tell this guy what to do.

"I'll be right back. Meet you in the garage." Dashing to her car, she popped the trunk and dug out her purple rubber gloves and a pink bandana. Feeling like a dork, she didn't want to get all dusty since she planned to stop at the office.

Back in the garage, Tanner had lowered a wooden stairway that led to a space over the garage. His eyes went to her hair. "Looks like you're serious."

When she reached up to straighten her bandana, her rubber fingers caught in her long bangs.

~•~

Lindsay looked so darned cute in a scarf that kept slipping over her eyes.

"Okay, I've got to fix this."

"I need fixing?" Her lips, the full lips he'd kissed, twisted into comical disappointment.

"Not really. Just this thing on your head." He adjusted the scarf, tucking some stray curls inside.

That one brush with softness made him want to touch more. *Control yourself, Phelps.* Clenching his hand into a fist, Tanner stepped back.

"Is everything okay?" Lindsay glanced up, her eyes gray suede, like a jacket Ursula had bought him one Christmas. He'd hated that jacket. But Lindsay's eyes were mesmerizing.

"Can you see all right?"

"Okay." Yes, just like a little girl. He wondered how far behind him she'd been in school. She was good at asking questions. Now it was his turn. "Were we in school together?"

"No." And she nudged him toward the stairway.

"I didn't think so." He would have remembered.

"I'm a few years younger than my brother, so I was just in grade school." They both began to climb.

An amazing number of boxes were stacked in the dim light. When he found a switch, the one bulb didn't help much. But each box was marked and that was a plus. Christmas Ornaments. Mantelpiece. Thanksgiving. He hadn't expected all this.

"Wow. Such organization." Lindsay looked around.

"My mom was like that." Her handwriting brought back the notes she used to put in his lunch. *Have a great day* or *You are my star!* Mom was always so cheery. She even loved rainy days because she said they gave her so much more energy.

Lindsay clapped her gloved hands together. "What's the game

plan here?"

"Honestly? I don't know where to start." He glanced around, suddenly sorry he'd started this. The air was hot and dry up here.

Jabbing at her bandana again with those purple gloves, Lindsay took stock. Her brows pulled into a delicate line. "Just because you're having a garage sale doesn't mean you have to give everything away at that sale."

"Really? Leaving the past behind sounds like a good plan to me."

"Don't you have a lot of happy memories here?" And the purple gloves motioned toward the boxes.

"Maybe." Then Tanner saw his father's real estate signs. He'd put them up here so the metal stands wouldn't scratch Ursula's Mercedes—one of his many gifts to her.

Lindsay edged past the decorations. "What's this?"

"Real estate signs. My father had a company here in town."

"What happened to it?"

His brows lifted. "I guess I own it."

Lindsay's gray eyes grew round. "You guess?"

"Yes, I own it," he repeated. "I finished my last tour of duty and came back to Gull Harbor to look things over." To settle the mess left behind.

"Oh, so you might live here now?" Lindsay seemed to be turning that over in her mind. Could she tell that he was just throwing spaghetti on the wall to see what would stick? He didn't have a clue what he was going to do.

That's when it hit. No matter how hard he tried to suck air in, it just wasn't happening. His chest tightened. Taking the inhaler from his back pocket, Tanner gave it a good squirt. He didn't have to wait long, thank God. The relief of breathing.

"Are you okay?" Eyes wide, Lindsay grabbed his arm.

"I'm fine. Maybe we should leave this for later." No way did he want to go through Christmas stuff from years ago. And from the look on her face, he was freaking Lindsay out. Starting down the stairs, he reached up for her hand. Instead he got the rubber glove. They both laughed. The air cleared.

For the rest of the morning, they went through rooms and took pictures off the walls. "I'm going to have the place painted," he explained when she looked horrified by all the holes left by the nails. "I mean, how many beach scenes can you have in one house, right?"

"Renters like beach scenes," she said in a small voice.

He cocked his head. "My stepmother sure liked them. But she moved here from Arizona. My mother was more into the impressionists."

They'd reached the master bedroom, one area where he agreed with his father. The huge addition added a lot to the house.

"Wow, I didn't get into this part of the house last week."

"Probably a good thing." He couldn't even imagine how horrified she would have been to find a naked man stretched out on the bed.

Standing in the center of the room, she turned around slowly. "This is really something."

"That's a polite way of putting it." Ursula had hung a chandelier over their king-size bed with a high tufted black headboard. A massive armoire and a triple dresser made the huge room look smaller.

"Walk-in closet?" She nodded to the one door now ajar.

"And double bath with Jacuzzi." He pointed to an open door. The double bath had been Ursula's idea. He couldn't even imagine what his mother would have thought of it. When his dad went out all out, he went big. Big and ridiculous.

"Do you mind?" Lindsay was already walking toward the bathroom door.

"Knock yourself out."

She pushed the door open. "Wow."

"I think the term is over-the-top. Way too much black marble."

"I love the shower door etched with seagulls though. People will like that. And double sinks?"

The wooden laminate silenced their footsteps. Opposite the sinks was a huge mirror. Ursula had been into mirrors. His dad? Not so much.

Lindsay turned. "Will you be renting this out?"

"Right now, my plans are uncertain."

Stepping back into the bedroom, Lindsay said, "I see." But it was clear that she really didn't.

Then her eyes traveled to two Monet prints he'd found high on a shelf in the guestroom closet, probably stuffed there by Ursula. Hanging up his mother's inexpensive prints brought some comfort to the room. They helped Tanner sleep better at night.

"Oh, I love those in here." Lindsay stepped closer. "That's the

Japanese bridge."

"If you say so." Peering over her shoulder, Tanner studied it with new eyes. "To me it's a green bridge over a very blotchy pond."

"It's really pretty," she said softly, in a tone so like his mother's it was creepy.

"Maybe that's it for today."

Lindsay was close. They were in the bedroom. Tanner had honed his instincts on night watch and he trusted them. This felt dangerous.

"Oh, all right. Sure." She stripped off the purple gloves.

But he hated to see her go. "I mean, unless you want to stay for lunch."

"I usually carry my lunch with me."

"Did you bring it today?" In his mind, they were traveling up Red Arrow Highway together, stopping at the Roadhouse or one of the other places that had been around forever. Maybe they weren't here anymore.

"No, I don't have my lunch. But I should get back. My k-." She seemed to lose her train of thought.

"So you're coming to clean Friday, right?"

"If you want me." She hesitated.

"Oh, I want you." The words came out too fast.

They both flushed at the same time. Blood was pulsing through his body and he wished it was going to his brain. "I mean, I'd appreciate it if you would come to clean."

"Okay, then. I will come... to clean."

When she let her eyes drop, her lashes feathered over her cheeks.

"You working on those cleaning products that aren't aerosol?"

Her cheeks reddened. "You bet."

"It's just that they're better for breathing." He wasn't going to go into it. It was embarrassing.

She stripped off her gloves and popped them into a tote she'd brought with her. "See you Friday?"

"Yep, tomorrow." As an after thought he added, "I probably won't be here Have tons of stuff to do." *Like look at my real estate signs and figure out what to do with my life.*

"That's fine." Lindsay looked relieved. She started for the door, her ponytail swaying behind her. When she turned, he was probably staring after her like a goon. Giving him a curious look, she walked out into the sunshine. He watched her get into her car and drive away.

"Hey, Tanner. What's up?" Red had arrived.

"Just saying goodbye to a friend." Tanner wasn't sure he liked this kid showing up like this.

Staring after the car, Red said, "The pretty girl?"

He smiled. "So you think Lindsay's pretty?"

"Tanner has a girlfriend. Tanner has a girlfriend…" Red began to chant. Then he caught sight of the garage. "Wowser. You've got a lot of stuff in your garage."

"Wowser?" Tanner hadn't heard that in a while.

"My dad says that all the time. Wowser." And Red made his lips extra round.

"Yep, I'm having a sale." Things were falling into place.

"Are you m-moving?" Red looked like he might cry.

"Heck, no. I just got here." The little guy would miss him? That felt good. "You coming to my garage sale?"

"You bet." Excitement sparked in his pale blue eyes.

"Red. Oh, Re-ed?" A young woman came around the lilac bushes between the properties. She was pushing a stroller with twins over the bumpy lawn. Tanner figured she was a bit older than he was. "There you are." Relief slowed her steps. One of the twins was sucking on some rubber thing in her mouth. Her sister was working on ripping the pink ribbon from tufts of blonde hair.

"Hey, Mom. I'm right here with my buddy."

Brushing blonde hair from her eyes, she smiled. "You must be our new neighbor?"

"Tanner Phelps." His hand shot out.

"I'm Leslie McGregor. So you're Jim's son?"

He nodded. "Yes."

"So sorry about your dad."

"Thank you." He'd been away so long. Neighbors had changed. He had no idea what they thought of his dad and his second wife.

Her eyes shifted to the jumble in his garage. "Wow."

"Mom, Mom! Tanner is having a garage sale. Can I come?" Red was more excited about the idea than Tanner was.

"Oh, I don't know, Red. Tanner will probably be very busy." Leslie looked to him, expecting agreement.

"I already told Red he's welcome."

"Yeah, Tanner wants me to come." Red looked so proud.

Leslie's gaze fell on her son. Tanner knew in that moment how much Leslie loved Red. She gently swept back his red curls, the hair he no doubt got from his dad. "Well, then. I guess I'll be stopping by too."

The twins began to whine. Leslie had quite a time turning the large stroller and Tanner tried to help. "Thanks, Tanner. Come on, Red. It's lunchtime, sweetheart. Your sisters are hungry."

"Okay." He lifted his shoulders as if to say, *what are we going to do about these women.* Tanner almost burst out laughing. "Can Tanner come for lunch, Mom?"

She hesitated. "Not this time, Red."

Another shrug. "Next time, Tanner, okay?"

"Sounds good. " He waved good-bye. Red was in good hands. Leslie reminded Tanner of his own mother.

Chapter 6

Lindsay's hands felt sweaty on the steering wheel and her head buzzed as she turned onto Red Arrow. Maybe it was all that dust in the attic. Or could it be the aerosol sprays and the sharp smell of chemicals? She tapped the brakes but when the guy behind her honked, she continued toward the PR office. The health food store in Michigan City might carry natural cleaning supplies, but that was half an hour away. Stress roiled in her stomach around the only thing she'd eaten that day—a cheese crown. For her, there was never enough time in the day. Ever.

When she reached the stoplight at Whittaker, she waited. Tanner had listened to her broken tale of Huck Finn as if he was really interested. For some reason that made her smile.

A horn blared behind her. She jerked forward and turned left. Mercedes was at the office. The champagne colored car that matched her name was probably all Mercedes had left of her high-powered New York job. Must have cost a bundle. Lindsay parked her hand-me-down Gran Marquis from her folks next to the Mercedes and got out.

She'd told Mercedes she'd have that poster to the printer this week and tomorrow was Friday. They had to be up in the local stores before July Fourth, the unofficial start of summer rentals.

Lindsay sprinted up the stairs and banged open the door.

"Hey?" Mercedes spun around in her chair. The noon sun fell through the front store window, making the jade green jacket draped over Mercedes' chair look lush and expensive. Well, it probably was. "What's up? You look like you've just been hit by a truck."

"Thanks." Grabbing for her office chair, Lindsay nearly missed. She had to keep steady or she'd have more bruises.

"Are you okay?" Mercedes peered at her.

"Of course I am." She scooted the chair into the desk. "Just stopped in to finish the poster and get it to Speedy Print."

Her partner sat back. "Uh, huh. The thing on your head? So cute."

Lindsay whisked off the pink bandana and tossed it on her cluttered desk.

"So you were at Tanner's?" Mercedes asked softly, lifting the end of Tanner's name.

"We're getting stuff ready for his garage sale on Fourth of July weekend." She couldn't look up. "I'm going back tomorrow to clean the place. Such a mess. All the packing."

Mercedes did this annoying tongue clucking thing. "You sure you have time for all this?"

"This will pay off in the end." Lindsay turned on the computer. "Time isn't the issue. Paying the rent is." But how could Mercedes know what it felt like to be a single mother, supporting herself and having other people depend on you?

"You know Finn or your folks would help if you asked."

"I can handle it, Mercedes." Did her sister-in-law know that Finn gave her a check once in a while? The screen went live and Lindsay clicked into her project folder. She was proud of this poster. The design had Jazz Age vibes with a woman in a bathing costume waving to a boat riding stylized waves out on the lake. Two little girls played in the sand at her feet.

Things were quiet at the next desk. No doubt Mercedes had told her staff what to do. No questions asked. But Lindsay didn't work for Mercedes, not really. The PR office was headed by Kate, Mercedes' younger sister. Kate hadn't been around much as her pregnancy advanced. After her miscarriage, she wasn't taking any chances.

"I know being a single mother is tough..." Mercedes began.

"No, you don't." Lindsay leveled a look at her sister-in-law. "How could you?"

Color drained from Mercedes' face.

What an idiot I am. Jumping from her chair, Lindsay rushed to give Mercedes a hug. "Look, I'm sorry. That wasn't fair at all. It's just that..."

But Mercedes wasn't a woman who soothed easily. She pushed Lindsay away and smoothed her white silk blouse. "What's the matter with you this summer?"

Opening her mouth, she closed it again. Maybe she *was* sick. The air in the office felt hot and dusty.

"Everything's fine." She walked over to the huge plate glass window that once displayed resort wear.

Outside, traffic had picked up on Whittaker Street. Folks were probably headed into Rosie's for a late breakfast or the Mangy Mutt for a burger. Across the street at Sun and Sail, Oscar Werner had hauled out his display of beach toys and summer merchandise. When a large pink beach ball escaped, Oscar scampered after it, hampered by a stomach that told of many meals at Rosie's.

"Girl, you need to start dating."

"What?" She brought her attention back to her sister-in-law.

Arms crossed, Mercedes wore a smug smile. "How long has it been since you've gone out with a guy?"

Lindsay pulled her ponytail tight. "Why?"

"You're a beautiful girl."

"Woman." Lindsay corrected her.

"Right. Woman." The shrug of Mercedes' shoulders said it really didn't matter. "Isn't it time to get out there? How long has it been?"

"Three years." She didn't like to think about it.

"Okay then. You loved Rich like crazy, but you have a life to live."

"What the heck do you think I've been doing?" This was getting irritating.

"Look, I didn't know Rich." Mercedes tone had softened. "But Finn's told me you were childhood sweethearts."

"Nothing wrong with that, Mercedes." Except that the two of them often acted like teenagers, although Lindsay would never admit that.

"But wouldn't he want you to be happy?"

"I am happy and the girls are fine too." This conversation was getting old.

But Mercedes was on a roll. "So where do you see yourself in ten years, Lindsay?"

"Here in Gull Harbor with my friends and family."

Glancing over at the wedding picture on her desk, Mercedes picked it up, her features softening. Finn and Mercedes had been married in the Inn at Gull Harbor on Valentine's Day. Then Mercedes set the photo down, angling it just right. "I know you have Rebecca and Susan. But don't you want someone to talk to in the evening? Plan your weekends with? Watch your favorite TV shows?"

"Now you're getting downright sappy." But that did sound nice. The air mellowed.

"You have it all planned out now," Mercedes continued. "But what about after your parents make retirement plans?"

"What do you mean?" Jumping up, she went to stand beside Mercedes' desk. "Dad *is* retired."

"Forget I said that." Mercedes shuffled some papers on her desk.

"Do you and Finn know something I don't know?"

Dropping her pile of work, Mercedes lifted her eyes. "Sorry, Lindsay. I had no business saying that."

The thought of her parents leaving gave Lindsay a hollow feeling. Can a girl be lonely with two kids to care for?

After that, they didn't say another word. Mercedes got back to work on press releases for the Fourth of July. Lindsay finished the poster and sent the file to Speedy Print. She had to get out of this office and said a quick good-bye.

When she got to her car, she texted her dad.

Have an errand to run. Is everything okay?

The reply zinged back.

We're fine. Having ice cream at the mall. Supper at our place?

Perfect. She had time to drive to Michigan City.

Sounds good.

Lindsay took off. Although she drove hard, no cop car came screaming after her. When she reached the outskirts of town, she slowed down and tried to catch her breath. Her mind was still racing. Would her parents leave Gull Harbor? It happened. The former owner of Michiana Thyme had relocated to be closer to her sister in Clearwater, Florida. Winters in Gull Harbor could be harsh, especially for older people.

Smelling of patchouli and lavender, the health food store had plenty of cleaning supplies made from vinegar, baking powder and ingredients she could pronounce. Sure, the bottles cost a bit more but if she were truthful, she sometimes had stinging eyes and a sore throat after cleaning all day. Maybe Tanner had a point.

Tanner. She turned him over in her mind all the way back to Gull Harbor. The way he walked, his back straight and shoulders level. The way he listened to every word. The way he'd kissed her. The memory wound through her like a satin ribbon.

After a quick lunch at the Whistle Stop deli, she drove to her parents' house. Their silver SUV was in the driveway when Lindsay pulled up. Getting out, she heard the girls' high voices coming from the yard. She walked back.

"It's my turn for the swing. You have to push me," Susan told her older sister.

Hands on her hips, Rebecca was in full attitude. "I don't have to do anything."

By that time, Susan had seen her mother round the corner. "Mommy, Mommy. Rebecca's being mean!" she said, racing for Lindsay and lifting her arms.

"Is that so?" Lindsay scooped up her daughter. At three years old, Susan was getting heavy to lift. Her baby days were gone and that brought a wave of sadness.

"My name is Becky." Rebecca set her chin at that stubborn angle.

"Now, girls! Look what Grandma Rose has." Her mother appeared at the back door with a tray of lemonade. "Oh hi, dear."

Setting Susan down, Lindsay ran to open the screen door. She took the heavy tray from her mother and carried it to the picnic table, the scent of the lemons tickling her nose.

Mom wiped her hands on her apron. "Girls, did you tell your mother about your new clothes?"

"Wait until you see!" Rebecca dashed for the door, a little girl of five again.

"Wait for me!" Susan was right on her tail. The screen door slapped shut twice behind them.

"Were they good?" Lindsay asked, settling at the table.

"Perfect angels." Pouring the lemonade, her mother offered her a glass. "They always are."

"Right." Lindsay laughed. "I think they behave better for you than they do for me. Don't know what I'd do without you and dad to help." There. She'd said it.

But her mother's expression told her nothing. Were her parents talking to Finn about decisions but not including her? The back door burst open and her daughters emerged, stumbling under the weight of heavy shopping bags. Wearing a bemused expression, her father followed. His cheeks were flushed. He must have been napping on the sofa until her hellions woke him up.

A breeze lifted the hank of hair her father combed over his bald spot. The glare of the afternoon sun accented the creases in his face. He'd aged since the accident in the warehouse had wrecked his back and ended his career.

The next fifteen minutes were filled with the girls dangling clothes in front of her. Tops and shorts, jeans and hoodies. The bags contained enough to carry them through the summer.

"You shouldn't have," she told her parents while the girls folded their new clothes back into the bags. Since her budget was sorely stretched every month, Lindsay was grateful. But her parents had a budget too.

"We like to do it," her father said.

"It's our fun," her mother added.

"This is for you, Mommy." Susan held out a bag and Lindsay peeked inside.

"Did you help pick this out?" Both girls nodded.

"Now what could this be?"

Susan held the bag open while Lindsay reached inside. Her mother watched when she pulled out a sundress. The top was banded with red, white and blue, held up by dainty straps. But the best part was the handkerchief hemmed skirt decorated with sparkly blue stars. The dress was magical. "I can't wait to try it on."

"I'm so tickled that you like it." Her mom nodded to Rebecca. "Rebecca's the one who found it on a rack."

"Aw, sweetheart." She kissed her oldest daughter and Rebecca wound her arms around Lindsay's waist.

"Love you, Mommy."

"Love you too, Rebecca. Becky," she added and her oldest beamed. Her five year-old could be such a prickly pear. Lindsay hoped this was just a phase.

"How did work go today?" her dad asked when the clothes had been taken inside.

"Fine, I'm working with a new client."

"That sounds interesting." Her dad had always supported any new venture.

"The rental business Mercedes and I started is going fine. This home owner might be a candidate." The comment held Tanner at a comfortable distance.

"I see. Sounds very promising."

"Promising. That's right, Dad." And then it hit her. "Did you ever know the man who owned Phelps Reality?"

"Jim Phelps?" Dad ran a hand over his thinning hair. "Yes, we knew him from church. A real go getter. His first wife Melanie was a lovely woman. Lovely."

But he didn't mention the second wife. Ursula. Lindsay's father never had a bad thing to say about anyone. "Will his son continue the business then?" her dad asked.

"I didn't ask. So busy working, you know."

The day had caught up with all of them. Ten minutes later she was bundling the girls into the car. "Put those seatbelts on, girls."

Her father had followed them outside. "You two curmudgeons behave now." They both giggled at his name for them and threw kisses.

Head down, Lindsay walked around the back of the car. Her father trailed behind her, checking the tires and poking his head in the open window to eye the gas gauge. He believed in keeping at least half a tank. "You working tomorrow and Saturday?"

"Yep, same as always."

Dad opened the car door for her and she slipped inside.

He threw kisses to the girls as darkness settled over the quiet street. Then his gaze circled back to her and stopped. "What is it?" Daddy knew her too well.

"Do you ever think about retirement?"

"I *am* retired. What are you talking about?" He stepped back. "Safe home, now. See you tomorrow, girls. And don't be giving your mother any grief tonight, you hear?"

He hadn't answered her question and they both knew it.

Chapter 7

Was the place messy enough? Tanner had scattered newspapers all over. Dishes were stacked in the sink. Wet crumpled towels lay on the floor of the master bathroom. Maybe he'd overdone it. Looked like fifty shades of hell. The Army would never tolerate a mess like this.

But he wasn't in the Army anymore.

Taking his coffee onto the screened porch, Tanner set the mug down on the glass table. Yeah, he'd leave it there, half empty. He wanted Lindsay to think the house needed cleaning.

The air smelled like early morning. He sucked in a deep breath and felt his shoulders relax. The night before he'd hauled more furniture out to the garage. More books, although he'd kept *Huckleberry Finn*. The work had left him sore but satisfied. Now the soothing sound of waves drifted up from the lake. He could almost feel the water splashing over his shoulders. Memories of this porch and lake glittering in the sunlight had gotten him through frigid nights in the desert. He'd close his eyes and be back here in Gull Harbor before his mother died. Before he had to lock his door at night. The ability to quickly come awake had served him well in the Army. Even when two of his buddies had night watch, he slept lightly, always on alert.

But why was he standing around? He checked his watch. No way did he want to be here when Lindsay arrived. Back in his bedroom, Tanner rumpled the bed, leaving the ugly gold comforter at the foot. He'd replace that later. At least the dark gray sheets were his. The room had to look as if it needed a woman's hand.

A woman's hand. When he'd kissed Lindsay in the study, her fingers had stroked his neck. Maybe she didn't even realize she was doing it. He'd never forget that gentle, mindless touch. Grabbing another section of an old newspaper, he let it fall open on the bed as if he'd just dropped it there. Maybe that was too much. Scooping it up, he folded it into a reader panel. Stepping back to admire his work, he stumbled smack against the box.

What would he do with the huge box of old pictures? He'd stripped the walls of prints and other crap Ursula had hung up during her occupation, as he called it. He'd also taken down personal photos and crammed them in this box. Now he didn't know what to do with it. Maybe he should keep the frames. Would he use them? Probably not. Lindsay would probably tell him that they could be sold at the garage sale. Some of the photos were keepers. But he didn't have time for this now.

Changing from his jeans to a bathing suit only took a minute. He wanted to be gone, like her other clients. The ones who weren't waking up at night from dreams about her. At least he hoped they weren't. Grabbing a towel from the linen closet, he jammed his feet into flip flops. She wasn't due until eleven or so. He was third on her list, or so she said.

As he left the house, Tanner knew he wanted to be first on her list. Strange how quickly that had happened. He'd been with the troops too long. Still, he liked her cute, sassy ways. He wouldn't return until quarter past twelve. Exiting through the porch door, he took the path that led through the trees, the route only he knew about that slid down through the dunes. A well worn public path was only a few doors down, but he liked the route his family had taken to the beach. Twigs snapped underfoot and bushes scratched him as he made his way to the sand. The hillside had gone wild. One more project for his list.

When he reached the sand, he dropped his towel and kicked his flip flops into the dune grass. Then he set out. Families had left their floats and sand toys in clusters on the beach in front of their cottage. Some kids were already down here. A cooling breeze hit him and gulls cawed overhead. Growing up, he'd always felt lucky to have the beach every day. But today he wanted to be alone so he turned north where there were fewer houses, not so many people. Along the shoreline the sand was hard-packed under his feet and the rippling water stretched to Chicago. Out on the lake, a motorboat was headed out for the day, its buzz resonating across the water. Maybe water skis or fishing poles were tucked in the boat. In the service when everything around him looked foreign and menacing, remembering this beach had brought comfort. But it never lasted that long. He kept walking.

~.~

"Hello!" Using her key, Lindsay stepped into the kitchen. This sunny room with the lacy white curtains was beginning to feel familiar. Picking up her bucket of supplies, she dragged her vacuum in after her. "Tanner?"

No answer. *Holy moly.* She glanced around. The place looked stripped. Every cheerful thing had been taken down. No sunflower calendar, no rack of seasonings and no beach prints. So, was he going to redecorate? Or was he going to leave?

The thought of Tanner leaving Gull Harbor didn't feel good.

"Anybody home?" There was no answer and the house felt empty. Lindsay didn't realize she'd been holding her breath until she released it. This was the first time she'd worn makeup to clean a house. She adjusted her bandana. Tanner's was the last on her list for a lot of reasons. The way his eyes crinkled in the corners. The way he studied her legs when he thought she wasn't looking.

But she was wasting time.

Lindsay had a system. First she'd strip the beds and grab the towels and start them in the washing machine. Last time she'd started in the front of the house with the guest rooms. After Tanner appeared, scaring her half to death, she never got to the master suite. Today she was starting back there.

Entering Tanner's bedroom, she felt like a burglar. "For heaven's sake, Lindsay. Get over it." Okay, now she was mumbling to herself. Tanner must have been reading in bed. A newspaper was left folded on the sheets. The fold was so crisp. So Tanner.

Snapping up the paper, she put it neatly on the side table. Pulling back the heavy gold brocade duvet, she tugged at the king-size sheets and shook the pillows from their cases. Scooping them into her arms, she turned. Jammed in a corner, a box caught her eye.

What was the harm in looking?

Dropping the sheets, she went to inspect. The edgess of silver frames were sticking up. Was Tanner planning to ditch these like the other stuff from the house? Coming closer, she saw the frames still held photos.

Her parents' family room was lined with framed photos, from baby shots to high school graduations. The latest additions were the wedding pictures of Finn and Mercedes, alongside Rebecca's graduation from pre-kindergarten. The Wheeler family photos would never end up crammed in a box like this.

For a second she stood there, sorely tempted to take a quick look. She was really only interested in the frames. That's all. But Tanner was a client. And Lindsay had rules. With some reluctance she pulled herself away from the box, stripped the towels from the bathroom, lumped them with the sheets and trotted out to the laundry room.

When the washing machine was filling, she snapped her Swiffer duster open, sprayed it with her new pump product and began to dust. Because most of the furniture was in the garage, she didn't have many surfaces that needed attention. But a quick swipe with one finger told her the doors and molding hadn't been touched. She went to work. Turning on her music, she popped in her earbuds. Wielding the Swiffer, she clicked on Taylor Swift and began to move with the music. Some time ago, she'd discovered that cleaning could be good exercise, since she didn't have time for the zumba class down at St. Mary's. When she reached the screened porch, a section of the newspaper was blowing around and she grabbed it.

The damp breeze sweeping up from the lake felt heavy, like rain was on the way. They needed it. If they didn't have rain, the blueberry picking would be sparse. Some cones shook loose from a pine tree and bounced off the roof of the porch. She craned her neck to see through the dense foliage that ran down to the beach. If the bushes were trimmed back, Tanner would have a spectacular view.

The screen door creaked when she stepped outside. The yard had gone wild too, with lilies, hollyhocks and black-eyed Susans springing up everywhere. Lindsay had always liked a natural look, but this was wild and crazy. Around the front of the house was a thick hedge of hydrangeas. Had Tanner's mother been a gardener? The yard looked untended and sad.

When the buzzer sounded on the washing machine, she ran back inside. After switching the sheets to the dryer, she stuck the towels in the washing machine. Just a little damp, the towels smelled like Tanner. Not any heavy perfume like the rose soap her own mother used, but clean. She buried her face in the towel. Now, this felt weird. But even after she lifted her head, his scent stayed with her.

With the washer and dryer whirring, Lindsay began to vacuum. Usually when she worked in these homes, sand crunched under her tennis shoes. Not here. Of course, she'd vacuumed just last week. Back in the kitchen, she arranged the plates and glasses in the dishwasher and then wiped down counters and the sink. She was surprised that Tanner would leave dirty dishes around.

When the dryer buzzed, Lindsay gathered an armful of clean sheets and carried them into the master bedroom. King size beds were unusual in cottages. Most bedrooms were too small. However, Tanner's dad had put on this addition and it was larger than the living room. A flower-covered chaise lounge sat in the corner along with a fancy desk with a leather top. The room even had a fireplace, although it didn't look as if anyone had ever used it. When she finally got the sheets on, plumped the pillows and spread out the duvet, everything looked nice and neat.

Lindsay couldn't help herself. The bed looked so inviting. Lying down for just a second, she was careful that her shoes dangled off the bed. Moving her arms, she pretended she was making snow angels. Closing her eyes, she wondered how it would feel to be in this bed. But when her imagination added Tanner, she jumped up.

Step away from the bed, Lindsay.

Who knew it would be this hard?

The master bedroom was the only room with carpeting. Hauling the vacuum from the kitchen, she plugged it in and clicked the switch. While she worked, she looked at the three doors. Those rooms might need vacuuming. She opened one door. Not much here. Just some boxes on the shelves. At one end hung a couple of long, slinky dresses. One was black with sparkles and shoulder pads. The plunging neckline of a red dress must be interesting. They hadn't been worn in a while. Vacuum roaring, she gave the room a swish it didn't need. Then on to the next door.

Well, she didn't need a map to know that this was Tanner's

closet. On the left, men's shirts were arranged by color on the higher rod with slacks down below. The closet had been inset with shelves and drawers, the whole she-bang as her dad would say. But Tanner didn't seem to have a lot of stuff. She quietly closed the door.

Was the third door a linen closet? Sure enough, this walk-in held shelves with sheets and towels. In the corner was medical equipment that brought her up sharp. She'd seen ads for this kind of stuff on TV. A raised toilet seat. A walker. Older people needed these when they got very sick. She tried to remember what Tanner had said about his dad. Who had nursed him?

She was breaking one of her own rules. Snooping.

Once you cross a line, it's easier to keep walking. The box was still on Lindsay's mind. She'd just take a peek at a couple of pictures. No harm in that. After all, she was in charge of Tanner's garage sale and he might want to sell these. Sinking to her knees in the deep carpet, she had to work with the frames and pulled out just a couple.

One was a wedding photo. Tanner resembled his father, a tall handsome man with his arm around a woman who had to be Ursula. Long blonde hair rippled to her shoulders, and her makeup was not subtle. If this was her wedding dress, it sure had a low neckline. Wondering what time it was, she set it aside. Other pictures were framed snap shots, but at the bottom were earlier pictures. She rifled through them, glancing at her phone. She should have plenty of time.

The shuffling stopped at the photo of Tanner with his parents.

All legs and arms, Tanner must have been eight or ten. A man in the making. Hand on her son's shoulder, his mother had blonde hair too, but unlike Ursula's it was fluffed around her shoulders and framed a sweet smile. Tanner's dad had a hand protectively around her waist. Squinting at the camera, Tanner looked as if he wanted to be anywhere but here.

They were the perfect happy family. Taking the shot from the pack, Lindsay set it on the dresser next to a lamp. She'd leave it while she checked the dryer.

After carefully folding the warm towels, she left them on the counter. Time to take a final spin through the house with the eyes of a renter. With three bedrooms and two full baths, she could book this house plenty once the walls had been painted. But Tanner didn't want children or pets. That might be a problem. The knot in her stomach felt more personal than business.

Time to leave. Her work was done here. She was packing up when the back door opened. Cripes.

"Lindsay?" In flip flops and trunks, Tanner had been at the beach. That shoulder tattoo made him look so badass. Badass and totally hot.

"Y-yes."

"Sorry, I thought you'd be gone."

"Oh, I am. Almost gone." *If I can stop staring at you.*

With a towel draped around his neck, Tanner was all lean muscle. And his skin was probably still warm from the sun. She swallowed. "How was the water?"

He grinned. "As cold as I remembered."

"Yeah, it never warms up until Fourth of July."

"Right. Still, it felt great." Tanner sniffed. "No chemical smell. I like it."

A hot flush worked its way up her neck. "I, ah, found special products."

"Thanks. So Clancy's carries them?"

"Um, no. I went to Michigan City." This felt like a confession.

He frowned but in a pleased way. "Sorry you had to drive that far."

"No problem."

They stood there, grinning at each other. Lindsay shouldn't ask about the breathing problem. After all, some things were private. "So do you have asthma?"

Tanner's smile faded. "Yeah. You could call it that."

The air felt edgy. More questions danced through her mind but Lindsay shut them down. If she asked more questions, then so would he. "Guess my time's up here."

He almost looked disappointed. But maybe that was her imagination. She turned to pick up the towels. "I'll just put these away."

"Oh, I'll take them." He held out his arms.

"But you're wet."

"Isn't that what towels are for?"

They stood there, breathing in each other's heat. Lindsay started to feel dizzy. Pretty soon she'd need his inhaler. Reluctantly, she handed over the towels. "Guess it's time to hit the road."

Too late, she remembered the picture she'd taken from the box.

She hadn't put it back. Tanner would knew she'd been nosing around. But she couldn't go back now.

Chapter 8

Standing there wet and dripping, Tanner didn't know what to say. Lindsay looked so huggable in her pink top and cut-offs. Fighting the urge to gather her into his arms, Tanner set the clean towels on the counter.

After all, he was soaking wet. And he'd made a promise. He wanted his word to mean something to her. "I-I..." He was stammering like an idiot. "Well, it sure smells good in here. But I don't want to become a high maintenance client."

Sliding the towel from his neck, he watched her eyes travel over his chest. He'd never been one to manscape. Goosebumps rose on his skin in the wake of those dancing gray eyes.

"I don't mind." Her cheeks blushed a pretty pink.

When she bent to pick up her bucket, he got a glimpse of cleavage. The soft tempting mounds rocked him, and Tanner jerked his attention back to the windows. Yep, the tree outside was safe. It had no soft curves, no shadowy depths. Man, he was hopeless and this was hard.

Meanwhile, Lindsay had sidled toward the door. "Guess I'll see you then."

"Right. See you."

While he stood there like a moron, she tried to open the door with her hands full. He jumped to help and grabbed the vacuum. For a second she didn't let go. They both stood there, breathing hard and gripping a plastic wand. What a weird turn-on. With his other hand, he reached around her. She let go of the door knob and he grabbed it.

Steeling himself, he let her pass as if this were a training objective. Vacuum in hand, he followed those shapely legs to her car. Really, he was so out of his league. Kick a door down and search for insurgents? Sure, no problem. Ask a girl out? A lot harder. That required finesse and he was sorely lacking in that department. A military school didn't teach guys subtle moves with women.

At the car she turned. "Hey, is something wrong?" Overhead a birch tree limb quivered in the breeze.

"Nothing. Just, uh." He looked around This wet suit was beginning to feel uncomfortable. He'd hated fording creeks or rivers in training and then staying in wet clothes all day.

Today he had a different mission. She was taking the vacuum from him when he blurted out, "Don't suppose you'd like to get a bite to eat tomorrow night." Not subtle. Not at all.

Eyes down, she crammed the vacuum into her trunk. "Oh, well, I'd like to. But I can't."

Of course. No doubt she had a date. But she wasn't married and he had a competitive streak a mile wide. "Some other time?"

"Sure, maybe. I'm sorry, but I have plans..."

"Of course you do."

Lindsay slammed the trunk and went around to the front. Her

frown didn't fill him with encouragement.

Tanner couldn't leave it like this. He liked things clear and understandable. "I guess I should ask...are you seeing someone? I don't want to be a pest." *But I sure as hell will be.*

"No. No, that's not it." She tugged on the car door, long lashes feathered over her cheeks.

Realizing he was blocking her, he opened it. Trying to slide inside, she stumbled, skinning her shin. "Darn it!"

Grabbing her leg, she leaned back against the seat. Great, so now she'd injured herself trying to get away from him.

"Let me look."

She was shaking and must be in pain. "It's nothing."

He peeled back her fingers. The abrasion was bleeding. "Don't suppose you have a first aid kit."

"As a matter of fact, I do." She reached for the glove box and popped it open. The emergency kit was right there and Lindsay handed it to him. "Really this isn't serious."

He opened the kit. "You come prepared. I'm impressed."

"My Girl Scout training."

"This will just take a second. You really shouldn't drive around like that. It's bleeding and could become infected." Tanner was used to opening antiseptic pads.

"That's okay. Maybe I like you fussing over me." She grinned.

"You do?" Dabbing at the superficial wound, he chuckled. "Guess I'll make a habit of it then."

"You don't know what you're in for. I'm a klutz."

"I think I know that." He glanced up. "Just kidding of course."

She was more a gazelle than a klutz. Just his opinion.

"It's just that I have plans, you know, tomorrow night."

The heat vibrating between them wasn't coming from the noonday sun. She took the pad from his hands. "I'll get rid of that."

Ripping open the square bandage, he placed it carefully over the cut. "Change this tonight. Keep it clean. Let me know if it gets red or oozy." Good God, he was rattling off commands.

"Oozy?" She wrinkled her nose with distaste.

Now it was his turn to blush. "Yeah, great pickup line."

"Works well, does it?" Her smile had turned impudent.

"Haven't used it much. Picking up women isn't my thing." Usually women hit on him in bars instead of vice versa, but he kept that to himself.

The bandage was on and he snapped the kit closed. She laid it on the seat. "Sounds like you know what you're doing."

"I've had a little experience." But the wounds he'd dressed in the fields weren't scratches like these.

"Guess I'll be leaving with my injury now." Her eyes drifted back to the closed garage doors. "How are you coming with the pricing?"

"Pricing?" Tanner was mesmerized by the way the shadows turned her gray eyes from silver to suede. "Oh, yeah. The garage sale."

"Remember? That thing we've been working on together?" Her eyes danced with mischief.

Sand had gotten in his hair. He'd have to shampoo. Raising his arm, he scratched his head. Her eyes dusted his chest again and coasted along his arm. Her scrutiny pleased him no end. "You must work out," she murmured.

"I do. Haul furniture. Fill boxes. Anything you want, ma'am. I'm your handyman." He was flirting and they both seemed to be enjoying it.

"Hey, wasn't that a song?" Lindsay wrinkled her nose.

He thought back. "I guess it was." The shared laughter felt good.

They stared at each other, their eyes doing the talking.

I want you.

You'll have to wait.

At least, he hoped that's what she was thinking. But he didn't want to rush things. Whatever Tanner had with Lindsay, it felt special. *She* was special. He wanted to tread carefully to have a successful outcome. He'd had field training in that. No way did he want to ruin things.

"Okay. See you next week." Lindsay started the engine.

He slammed the door closed and she rolled the window down. "You sure you're all right?"

"If I have to go to the ER, I'll call you." Wearing a saucy grin, she stepped on the gas. The car shot back and nearly took out Leslie's mailbox. Lindsay switched gears and pulled away, eyes facing forward and lips twitching.

Anxious to get out of this wet suit, he trekked inside. Passing the laundry room he spread his towel on the dryer. But on his way through the bedroom, he came to a halt. That picture.

The old color photo of him with his folks sat on the dresser just as it had in the past. The photo had been one of many he found in a closet, probably stored there by Ursula. On impulse this week, he'd taken down other photos and added them to the pack. Now he picked this one up.

Maybe he'd gone too far with his "clean sweep" approach. Maybe some things you need with you always. He set it down. Positioned it just right in front of the lamp.

So, Lindsay had searched through the box? Her interest flattered him. And she'd rescued this photo. He felt a personal tug and maybe he was blowing this way out of proportion. He went to shower, twisting the nozzles until the stream was ice cold.

~.~

She was a nut case. Gunning it, Lindsay took a right toward Red Arrow and left the leafy shadows of Tanner's street behind. Why did she always lose her cool with Tanner Phelps? And she'd left that picture out. Tanner would know she'd rifled through his personal belongings and that didn't sit right at all.

He'd asked her out. But that couldn't happen. For just a little while, she wanted to be fancy free and not a mother with two children. And that felt so disloyal. She loved Rebecca and Susan like crazy. But children complicated things. Now, if Tanner had kids that might be a different story. But he didn't, not from the pictures she'd seen.

She'd been doing some serious flirting with Tanner. And he was the wrong man. A man who hated messes.

A sugar craving seized her. Instead of traveling farther up the road, she took a left on Whittaker and pulled into diagonal spot on the left side of the street in front of The Full Cup.

The sunny cafe was empty when Lindsay arrived, but the tinkling of the bell over the door brought Sarah bustling from the back. Wiping her hands on the long apron, Sarah had obviously been working. How did she do it? Of course, she had her mother Lila. "Well, isn't this a nice surprise?" But one look at Lindsay and the smile twisted into concern. "What's wrong?"

"Everything. Got a minute?" Lindsay slumped into one of the soda chairs at the windows. "I could use some chocolate and coffee."

"Oh, my." Sarah eyed her with concern. Going to the door, she flipped the sign to Closed. That's how serious this must look.

Holding up a finger, Sarah said, "I'll be right back."

Lindsay got up to pour two mugs of coffee. Plain coffee was always free. The fancy types Sarah served from behind the counter. One look at the shiny glass cases told Lindsay the morning crowd had been brisk. The cheese crowns were crowded onto one of the trays with the leftover brownies.

Swirling back out of the kitchen area, Sarah held a plate. "I want you to try these. Fresh from the oven. Esper from Second Hand Rose gave me the recipe. Let me know what you think." The plate held four scrumptious looking chocolate cookies.

"Those look and smell wonderful." The welcoming smell of chocolate eased Lindsay back into the chair.

Sliding the plate onto the table, Sarah sat across from her. The sun streamed through the window, etched with the name The Full

Cup. Her parents had owned this shop for as long as Lindsay could remember. After her father died, Sarah and Jamie took over and had another baby. Then Jamie's reserve unit shipped out to Afghanistan.

Sarah's eyes held a twinkle as Lindsay took her first bite. "They're Mexican hot chocolate cookies and they have a little zing."

The chocolate exploded in Lindsay's mouth with a spicy zing. "Yum. What's in these?"

"Secrets of the kitchen." Sarah could be mysterious about her recipes. Reaching across the table, she squeezed Lindsay's hand. "Now what's going on?"

Where to begin? "Everything. In the last couple of weeks, my life is totally out of control." She kept nibbling.

Sarah gave a shrug. "Sounds exciting."

Taking another bite, Lindsay shook her head. "Trust me, it's not."

"Oh, I'm kidding. You and Mercedes can both be so serious sometimes."

Lindsay tried to make sense of this. "I love my children."

"Well, of course you do. Who says you don't?" Fists curled on the table, Sarah looked ready to take on the world.

"I'm not explaining this very well." Lindsay's orderly world tilted. "I'm cleaning the house for a new client..."

"Oh, that dreamy look." Sarah chuckled.

"No, no. That's not it. At all." But wasn't it?

"Uh huh." Taking a cookie, Sarah broke it in half.

The scent of something like cinnamon filled the air. Trying to find words for her relationship with Tanner, she took another bite. "Tangy and chocolate with a touch of something decadent," she whispered. Was that voice hers, so heated and husky?

"Are you still talking about the cookie or your...issue?" Sarah asked with the hint of a grin.

Lindsay slowed her chewing. "I'm not sure. I think I've done pretty well with my girls."

Nodding agreement, Sarah nibbled at her own cookie. "You're doing a wonderful job."

"And I can handle it. I mean, sure my folks and Finn help me. But mainly, it's on my plate." Plate, plate. Only two cookies left.

"Take another one." Sarah pushed them closer. "So what's the problem?"

"I don't want anything to —" Lindsay made a circle with her hand. "—disturb things. Dating takes time and with the kids? I just don't know."

Another head nod. "I totally understand. You also need an available man. Here in Gull Harbor we don't have many. So tell me about this new *client*." Sarah propped her chin on one hand.

Client. If only Lindsay could keep Tanner in that box. "Well, he's a vet. Tanner grew up here and then left for military school. And he's just back from a tour of duty. Sounds like he did more than one." She was not mentioning her brother's opinion of Tanner.

"A fine man. Sounds promising."

Lindsay rushed on. "His dad had a real estate business here.

Does Phelps sound familiar?"

"Oh, right. Phelps Realty." Sarah nodded and took another sip of coffee. "I think I remember that."

"Tanner contacted me when he saw our ad in *The Beacher*. He was there the first day I cleaned. The home is year round, not a cottage. But now he seems intent on emptying out that house. Bad memories. We're having a garage sale Fourth of July weekend."

"*We?*" Sarah dangled the word, provocative and teasing.

Lindsay shook her head. "There is no 'we,' Sarah. But I am helping him." She popped the last bite into her mouth.

Pushing frizzy bangs from her eyes, Sarah said, "I'm getting confused."

"He asked me out."

"A date? Oh, my." Sarah clapped her hands together, a plain gold wedding band still on her finger.

"No, no, no." Lindsay wasn't being clear. Taking one hand, she swept the crumbs from the table onto a napkin. Then she rolled it up tight. "I'm fine alone. My life is organized."

"But it can be lonely." Sarah reached for another cookie.

"Are you lonely? You always seem so self sufficient with your wonderful boys and Lila."

Giving a furtive glance to the swinging gates leading to the kitchen, Sarah leaned forward. "Of course my mother helps. But at night while I'm watching TV alone, or when I wake up in bed and reach out to that empty side, yes. I'm lonely."

"There is that." Nights when the TV felt like her only friend could feel empty.

"So back to your problem." Sarah leveled a look at her.

Trying to focus on Tanner's negative points was hard. "He's so organized."

"And that's a bad thing?"

"He likes things very tidy, and I haven't told him about my girls or..."

"Good heavens. Why not?" Shock drained Sarah's face.

"Because I don't like to mix my personal life with business." She had to believe that was the reason. "I'm hoping we can take him on full time in our new program, Beach Vacations. You know, rent out his house."

Sarah's shoulders lifted. "Yes, and so?"

Glancing out at the street, Lindsay watched the traffic. SUVs were packed with beach toys and kids, their faces pressed against the windows. It was Friday and some of the homes were turning over.

"He makes me feel..." She stumbled. How did those deep brown eyes make her feel? "Like I'm back in high school. You know, when everything was just fun."

"That sounds good." Sarah shrugged, her eyes growing distant. "High school was great, wasn't it? No real worries, although we didn't realize that then. Just football games and parties on the beach."

"But real life is messy, Sarah. A lot happens. You have no control over it and Tanner, well, I think for him everything has its proper slot."

"Have you talked to him about this?"

She shrank in embarrassment. "Heck no. He's just a client." The word became a lie on her lips.

After all, there was that kiss. And the crazy feeling when she pressed her face into his towels. Stretching out on his huge bed had felt amazing. She couldn't tell Sarah any of that.

The sun poured through the glass, heating the room. Shaking her head, Sarah said, "Oh sweetie. You're already gone on this man. You can't keep people in a box, Lindsay. Life isn't like that."

"I guess you're right."

Sarah craned her neck. "Here comes Cole. He'll want some cheese crowns for Kate."

Sure enough, shielding his eyes with a hand, Cole peered through the glass. Sarah scurried to the door and flipped the sign to Open.

"Looks like you're having a meeting." Cole ambled in— tall, dark and handsome.

"Not really. When's that baby coming, Cole?" Sarah asked, slipping behind the counter.

"Not until September. Right now that feels too far away." He ran a hand through his thick hair.

"Looks like you're ready now." Lindsay erupted into laughter.

"I sure am, Lindsay. And I guess you and Mercedes know that."

Rich had been like that with Rebecca. Eager and impatient. Fresh out of high school, they didn't even have a crib until a week before she was born. All they had was jittery excitement, unrealistic expectations and each other.

After Cole left with his box of pastries, Sarah came back to the table.

"I should be going." But Lindsay made no move to leave.

"So what are you going to do about Tanner?" Sarah asked.

Lindsay exhaled. "Clean his house. Help him with his garage sale. What else?" Pushing up from the chair, she started to leave.

"Take this last cookie for the road." After wrapping the cookie in a napkin, Sarah followed her to the door. "Leave your heart open. Right now your kids are keeping you busy. But what about later? What then?" A line of concern formed between Sarah's brows.

"Sarah. What about you?" Lindsay asked gently.

A sharp shake of Sarah's shoulders was her answer. "Oh, no. No, not for me."

"Sure. I understand." Jamie had only been gone a couple of months.

A group of teens came through the door with the bumbling haste of raging hormones. The boys were tall and awkward, and the girls wore too much makeup and giggled a lot.

Waving good-bye, Lindsay went back to her car. She needed a shower. She smelled like a salad, not that it bothered her. In fact, the vinegar scent was growing on her. Maybe she'd wear it as her signature scent from now on.

In the car, she decided not to wait to eat the cookie. She bit down.

Chapter 9

That weekend, Lindsay spent most of her time with Rebecca and Susan. Feeling as if she had to make it up to them, she even asked Cora and Ana, the two women who helped her and Mercedes, to take her three cottages on Saturday. Lindsay needed the money, but she felt guilty. She took the girls to a rerun of *Jungle Book* in Michigan City. It felt good to laugh at the silliness together, passing popcorn back and forth. Afterwards they stopped at the mall for an Orange Julius, which had always been their special treat. This was the life Lindsay knew and loved. Trips to the mall with Rebecca and Susan. Time with her parents.

But after the kids went to bed that night, her bungalow was sure quiet. She could even hear the tick of the flamingo clock her mother had given her. Sarah's words came back to her as Lindsay sat in front of TV with a bowl of cheese curls. *Sleepless in Seattle* played on the DVR but she forgot to laugh. That night she could not get to sleep. Somewhere in the woods, an owl cried, long and mournful. Maybe Sarah was right. She felt alone.

Her mother always cooked Sunday dinner, usually a roast with browned potatoes. But as she passed the green beans, Lindsay wondered if she depended on her parents too much. Did they want to move someplace warm? Sure summers were great. But winters in

Gull Harbor could last forever. After they'd finished her mother's chocolate oatmeal cake, Lindsay helped her mother with the dishes. Rebecca even stepped up to dry the pans that didn't fit in the dishwasher.

"Maybe next Sunday you'll come to our house for dinner," Rebecca said, handing Mom the roasting pan.

The suggestion caught them all by surprise. "Great idea, Rebecca," Lindsay said. Why hadn't she thought of this? Her oldest daughter beamed.

"We have lots of plates. Don't we, Mom?" Rebecca looked at Lindsay for confirmation.

They all laughed. A dinner was more than plates.

"You work so hard, Lindsay." Her mother patted her shoulder. "I like cooking for you and the kids. Don't even think about it."

But Lindsay wondered. Did she take her parents for granted? When her father bundled them into the car that night, she gave him a tight hug.

"Everything okay?" Head to one side, he studied her.

"Sure. You know I appreciate everything you do for us, right? It means a lot." She got in the car.

"What's going on with you lately?" he asked, closing the door.

"Nothing." She started the car and her father stepped back.

"Goodnight, Poppy John," Rebecca and Susan called into the still night air. "Good night, good night!"

"Sleep tight." Stepping back, he blew them a kiss.

Driving home, Lindsay reached for the familiar Sunday-night, full-tummy contentment. It wasn't there.

After the girls were in bed and their giggling had settled down, she checked her email.

Tanner.

Can you spare a couple of hours this week to help me price this stuff?

Of course she could.

Sure. Is Tuesday morning all right?"

Monday she'd be in the office with Mercedes. Besides, she didn't want to sound eager. And she was embarrassed about the photo she'd forgotten to stick back in the box. But maybe he hadn't noticed. After all, he was a guy.

But he was Tanner. Particular Tanner.

~.~

"Hey." That was all she could manage when Tanner opened his door that Tuesday morning.

"Hey." His voice was low and sleepy. Bringing a mug to his lips, he missed. Coffee splashed onto his blue T-shirt. They both laughed. But something else was there between them. Lindsay could feel it as she grabbed a towel and dabbed cold water on his shirt. His chest felt so warm and cozy. She resisted the urge to tunnel one hand under the soft fabric.

Instead she spread the dish towel out on the sink. "Time to get to work, right?"

"Right." He set his mug down.

They ended up in his garage. She'd brought over two tables left in a back storage room at the office. Mercedes had helped her wrestle them into the back seat—quite a site in her Louboutin heels and black suit. Tanner helped her set up the tables in the garage.

The dishes, pans and baking dishes just about covered one, along with the garden tools. The china and silver went on the other one. Tanner had organized the plastic containers by the color of the lids.

"What?" he asked when he caught her studying them.

"Nothing." But she swallowed a chuckle.

After all, the main selling point was the furniture.

"So, you haven't changed your mind?" She eyed the overstuffed chairs and the sofa and then shifted her attention to him. Tanner was way more interesting.

"Nope." Catching her slow study, he glanced down at a stomach she knew was rock hard. "What? Did I spill something else?"

"Ah, no." That was so not what was on her mind. "Now what about the office supplies?"

"In the corner." Tanner waved toward the back. The air felt dry and hot back here. Any breeze that wandered up from the lake didn't make it past that open double door. Tanner had bought stickers. He wanted to color code the stickers by price but that got complicated. "Too much?" he finally asked.

"I think so," she said with a smile.

Hands up, he backed away from the table. "Have at it."

Lindsay began labeling the boxes of clips and dividers.

"But what about all these signs?" She motioned to the real estate signs Tanner had dragged down from the attic.

"Those stay."

"You're keeping them?"

"Sure. You never know."

She didn't understand but this wasn't her business.

"I've been scouting Gull Harbor, talking to people. Everyone remembers my dad. He hasn't been gone that long."

When Tanner ran a hand over the back of his neck, her own neck tingled. Not too long ago, she'd had her arms around that neck. And she wanted to again. The realization rocked her. "Do y–you know anything about selling real estate?"

"Look, I grew up watching my dad sell properties. And when my mother was alive, she was part of the family business too." He moved toward the open garage door and she followed, straightening things as she went.

"What about your stepmother?"

"Hmm?" He turned.

She should stop right here. Keep a safe distance from her client. "Ursula, wasn't that her name? Did she help with the business too?"

He snorted. "Trust me, Ursula did not work. At anything. She just worked my dad."

"So the two of you didn't get along?"

"Not as much as she would have liked." When he stretched, his arms reminded her of a gull, ready to take flight.

Tanner gave her a curious look. Where was she? "Ursula didn't have any kids?"

"Nope. Didn't want any. That would have seriously screwed up her bridge club. My dad probably would have gone along with it. He was crazy about her. I have no idea why."

"So it was just the three of you?" She looked back at the house.

His face turned to stone. "Yep. Just us."

She had a million questions but this time Lindsay did zip her lips. "Do you mind if I use your bathroom?"

"Of course not. You know where to find it." He smiled. "You probably know this house better than I do."

Flushing, she seriously doubted that. Dashing through the back door, she paused to make sure Tanner hadn't followed her inside. When she heard the thump, thump of the basketball, she continued back to the master suite. The room felt dim and cool. And yes, she felt like she shouldn't be here.

The picture still stood under the lamp. A pleasing warmth coursed through her. Okay, maybe he hadn't seen it. But how could he miss it? Maybe he liked it. Her mind took a roller coaster ride.

But wait. She listened. Silence.

Hustling into the kitchen, she found it empty. Tanner was at the big bay window in the living room, looking down at the lake.

"Great view." She came up behind him.

"Well, it would be. The weeds have taken over."

He cast a glance at the guest room area. Any other woman would have used that bathroom, not the one in the master suite.

"Oh, I just wanted to make sure...you had enough towels." Now that sounded crazy. She wasn't his housekeeper.

"Really?" He didn't believe her. A laugh lifted the corner of his lips.

"I noticed some pictures in a box. Did you want to sell your frames or what? Just wanted to make sure we've touched on everything." She stubbed one toe into the floor, the way Rebecca did when she wasn't telling the truth.

"Oh, there are still some areas I'd like to touch on." Tanner breathed out the words in a wave of heat.

"There are?" They were way too close again. And he was looking at her the way she'd looked at Sarah's Mexican hot chocolate cookies.

Then he jerked his head back to the view. Sucked in a breath. "Maybe there are some lawn chairs or something else we can sell."

She jumped right in. "Great idea. People like lawn chairs They use them to sit on their lawns. Take them to the beach. Read in them and..." *Here I go again, rattling along about nothing.*

"The sale's what? Ten days away?" Arms crossed, he studied the tangle of weeds leading to the beach.

"The Fourth of July is next week and the sale, that Saturday."

"Right. I haven't decided about those pictures."

"The frames would sell fast."

"Maybe I should probably keep them."

"Your mom looked nice." Was that too personal?

"Nice?" He turned. Cops probably used that kind of expression during interrogation. Or maybe she'd been watching too many detective shows.

On Saturdays nights. Alone.

"Yeah. She looked nice."

"She was. Very nice." His smile softened, like he was remembering. "But then I was an only child."

"Would your mother have sent you to military school?" She was getting way too deep here.

The smile vanished. "Never. But there would have been no need to go."

Now she was totally confused. Backing away, she almost tripped. Tanner grabbed her. His thumbs flicked her skin softly. They were so close now. She could feel his warmth. Count the stubble on his chin. *Oh, mercy.* They did that panting thing together again. Raising a hand she rested it on one of his. She meant to brush it away. Really.

Finally, he dropped his hands but not his eyes.

"I'm going furniture shopping this Saturday. Want to come along and help me?"

Why in heaven's name would she do something as personal as look for furniture with a man? "Sure. What time?"

"I'll pick you up at ten."

"Oh, I'll come h-here," she stuttered. "You're going to Michigan City, right?"

"No, I'm going up Red Arrow. All you get in Michigan City might be big stores that smell of beaver board and formaldehyde."

The information rattled in her head. Her arms were still tingling. "I'll be here at ten."

~.~

After Lindsay left, Tanner had to do something. Pent-up energy made him jittery. Lindsay did that to him. He grabbed the basketball from the garage and started to dribble. Lindsay was a mystery. He'd mentioned the furniture trip on impulse and she'd almost said no. Refusal was in her body and in her eyes. But

Lindsay was full of surprises. Sure, he could have shopped for furniture himself. But it wouldn't have been fun. Lindsay was fun and he wanted to spend more time with her.

Pivoting, he tried his jump shot. The ball slammed off the backboard and hit the driveway. Snatching it up, he hammered it again. The movements felt familiar and strangely settling. When he practiced, he got results.

Lindsay? She kept him off balance.

"Nice shot, Tanner."

He went up for a layup. The hoop swished. Grabbing the ball, he turned to Red. "Wanna play?"

"Sure. I guess." Red gave a casual shrug.

Tanner handed him the ball. Dribbling wasn't easy for Red. It took a few tries to get the rhythm. Tanner didn't know much about children with Down syndrome, although he'd looked it up online. Bad break for the little guy although Red didn't seem to feel that way.

The look of concentration on Red's face made him smile. For a while they passed the ball back and forth. "Shoot! Shoot!" Tanner encouraged Red to try. But the hoop was impossibly high. Tanner had to think about that. He had to think about a lot of things.

Tanner had started studying online to get his real estate license. That shouldn't be too hard. The books he'd saved from the sale had been real estate books, probably outdated. Electronic materials were available on various websites and he could even take his exam online. He hadn't decided anything yet. But a real estate license might come in handy.

"Want a pop?" Tanner asked after they'd played a while. Summer was finally heating up.

"Sure. Okay." Red wiped his brow. "Boy, I'm hot."

"Stand in the shade. I'll be right back."

When he returned with two frosty cans of root beer, Tanner came through the garage. The look on Red's face when the garage door rattled up made Tanner smile.

"Wow. Look at all the furniture."

"Yeah." He handed Red a can. "I'm selling it all."

"You are?" Red's eyes grew round. "How come?"

"I don't like it anymore."

"Well, I like it." With a giggle Red sat in one of the chairs and bounced. Pop shot from his can and beaded on the cushion.

The kid looked horrified. "Oh, no! I'm sorry, Tanner." Scrambling from the chair, he tried to brush the pop off the surface.

"It's not a big deal. Hold on I'll be right back."

"My mom told me not to bother you. She'll be mad," Red said when Tanner brought out a dish towel.

"I think it's got that protective stuff on it, Red. The dish towel's sopping up the pop just fine. No need to tell your mom." He didn't like to see Red get upset.

The little boy gasped. "But I tell my mom everything!"

How should he handle this? Tanner had no experience with children. But he didn't want to teach Red anything his mother would object to. "If it's something that isn't going to hurt your mom, then sometimes it's best not to mention it. At least, that's what I always figured. Only tell on a need-to-know basis. Now drink your soda."

"Need to know." The little guy's chest expanded. "Then that's what I'll do too. Because I don't want to hurt my mom. I love her."

They both sat on the sofa in the shade of the garage. "I can tell your mother loves you very much."

Red's entire face lit up. "Yeah. She says that all the time."

"She does, huh?" Tanner liked to hear that.

Red nodded his head so hard, Tanner was afraid he'd spill the pop again. "Easy, buddy." He pointed to the can and Red settled.

"Yeah, my mom feels bad that she can't take me to the parade."

"What parade is that?" Tanner tipped his can back. He was probably sweating into the sofa and he didn't care. This red and gold sofa was history.

"The Fourth of July parade, silly. They have a band and everything. And they throw candy to the kids." Red's smile fell. "But my dad's out of town and she says we're too much to handle. You know, my twin sisters and me."

Leslie McGregor clearly had her hands full. Why did her husband leave her alone with two babies and Red? "Tell you what. How about I take you to the parade."

Red blinked. "Really?"

"You bet. I haven't seen a parade in a long time." Tanner remembered decorating his dad's big white Oldsmobile convertible for the event. Taking Red might be fun.

"I'll have to ask her if it's all right," Red said, his pop forgotten. "She told me not to bother you all the time."

"Hey look, we can ask her now." Leslie McGregor had come out for her mail. Shutting the mailbox, she kept walking toward them and she was smiling.

"I knew he was over here." Leslie didn't wear much makeup and her blondish brown hair was pushed back by a pink plastic headband. But she looked at Red with such love and ruffled his curly hair. "I hope you're not becoming a pest."

"Mom, Tanner is going to take me to the parade. Is that all right?"

Leslie hesitated. Seeming to evaluate the situation, she looked over at Tanner.

"He's going to show me how Gull Harbor celebrates the Fourth. I've forgotten." Tanner didn't want her to think Red had pressured him into this.

"Thank you, Tanner. That would be great." Had he ever seen such gratitude? Taking a tissue from her apron packet, she dabbed at her eyes. The emotion caught him by surprise.

"Sleep deprivation," she explained, tucking the tissue back in the pocket. "The girls still wake up a lot."

"Yeah," Red said, as if he were the man of the house. "They can cause a racket."

"I'm looking forward to it. After all, you gotta have a parade on the Fourth of July, right?" Tanner kept talking until she got ahold of herself again.

"Just send Red home if he gets to be a bother." She gave Red a warning look, but the little boy smiled back at her. "There are no kids in this neighborhood and Red, well..."

"He's not a bother."

"Not unless his girlfriend's here," Red broke in with an impish smile. "Then I stay away." The kid really was a kick.

Taking out his phone Tanner handed it to Leslie. "Tell you what. Put your contact info in here. I'll let you know when he's with me. We have a good time together."

"Tanner's teaching me to play basketball."

Working with the phone, Leslie smiled. "That's real nice."

"That's about all I have to teach him."

Glancing up, she handed back the phone. "I don't believe that for a minute. Working with children? That takes a lot of talent."

Tanner felt nine feet tall watching Red and Leslie walk back to their cottage.

Chapter 10

A shopping trip for furniture. With Tanner Phelps. Lindsay could hardly get her mascara on Saturday morning. She wasn't used to using the wand. Stepping back from the bathroom mirror, she checked it out. Not bad. In a makeup bag she found pink lip gloss and swiped it on her bottom lip. Even better. Her hair was clipped high in a ponytail, falling over one shoulder.

Sometimes she'd catch Tanner studying her hair with a secret smile on his lips. Lips. Tanner's lips. That thought didn't help her jitters at all.

Glancing around the pristine bathroom she'd cleaned this morning, Lindsay stuffed her work clothes in a tote. Then she added the towel and washcloth she'd brought with her. Shell shaped soaps filled the soap dish. The washcloths and towels were fresh and fluffy, and the sink and tub sparkled. Edna Willoughby would never know she'd used the bathroom of her rental to freshen up. Besides, she wouldn't care.

This was the third summer Lindsay had cleaned for Edna, who lived in Chicago. She also did periodic house checks for her. The widow had already signed on for the winter program. "I hardly ever use the place, dear," she'd told Lindsay over the phone. "Just don't have time to sell it. Besides, I like feeling it's there if I need it.

Might be more reliable than the stock market." They'd laughed together. Lindsay loved clients like Edna, who felt more like a friend than a client.

Grabbing her tote, she did a final check before locking up. Crickets were singing in the grass when she left. Edna had a gardening service so her clumps of daisies and black eyed Susans formed a neat hedge around the white cottage.

Her car felt warm from sitting in the sun. The air conditioning was broken. Her dad had made an appointment for her. She rolled down the window and let the morning breeze cool her flushed face. No way did she want to reach Tanner's looking all hot and bothered.

These last couple weeks, she felt as if she were playing a role. Carefree, single woman. A lot of women were still single at twenty-six. But that wasn't her situation. She was a widow with two children and she hadn't felt the attention of a man in a long time.

Although she told herself she was just helping Tanner out, she caught his sidelong glances, felt the brush of his body when they were marking prices together. She'd read *Sleeping Beauty* to her girls so many times. Was this how it felt like to be awakened from a deep sleep? When she was with Tanner, she felt as if she was back in high school again.

When she reached his place, she parked on the road. The back door flew open as she walked across the yard that smelled as if it had just been cut.

"Good morning." Tanner stood in the doorway, a mug of coffee in his hands. From his wet hair to the bare feet, he looked freshly showered and oh, so handsome. She grabbed the door frame.

"How about some coffee?"

"I had mine already. Did you just get up?"

A sheepish grin was the answer. "It *is* the weekend."

He was so close. She inhaled that fresh soapy scent, the same smell that clung to his towels and sheets. "Some of us work on the weekends."

"Good to know." One more gulp from the mug and he jammed his feet into sandals and scooped keys from the counter. "Ready?"

"You bet." She followed him out of the almost empty home.

"How many cottages did you clean this morning?" he asked as when they were barreling north on Red Arrow.

"Three. The women who work for me each do three too."

"Busy business."

"Yes, in the summer. So what's the plan?"

They had left Gull Harbor behind. Soon they were passing Gulistan's Cafe, the Harbert Swedish Bakery and the antique mall.

"I'm going to stop at a place up ahead that sells wooden furniture."

"Sounds nice." And expensive. For a change she kept her opinions to herself.

"I hope you'll like it."

"Does that matter?" She almost laughed.

"Yes. It does." He'd pulled into a gravel parking lot of Naturally Wood. Killing the engine, he pivoted toward her. "You've become a friend in the last couple of weeks. Do you mind that?"

"No. Not at all." But she did mind. *Friend?* Lindsay wasn't sure she liked that.

Getting out of the SUV, they stood in the sunlight.

The stones crunched beneath her sandals as they walked across the lot. He opened the main door and they stepped into the air-conditioned shop.

The place was packed with furniture that smelled of wood and oil. Overhead lighting brought out the rich grain of the pieces. Many were made by hand, according to a sign.

"Take a deep breath," he murmured, whisking his hands lightly over a tabletop. "Smells great, right?"

"It does smell good." Heck with the smell. Looking at his hands caress the wood made her woozy.

"Sometimes I think I should have been a carpenter. What do you think?"

You have great hands. "You would have been a natural."

He burst into a surprised chuckle and took her elbow. "What have I done to inspire such confidence in me?"

"Nothing." *Everything.* One touch and her body turned to warm taffy, the kind they sold at Silver Beach.

"Let's try these out." Dropping his hand, Tanner motioned to two sturdy chairs with leathers cushions and armrests.

Although the wood was beautiful, they looked so plain. "So you don't have a color scheme?" When she sat down, the soft leather closed around her. Not bad.

Tanner took the other chair. "Nope. No reds, no golds. Just wood. Natural colors."

"What about blues or greens? The colors of the sky and the woods." Those were her personal favorites.

Eyes closed with contentment, Tanner tipped his head back onto the cushion. "I like this just fine."

"Don't you two look comfortable" The saleswoman stood there beaming. "Can you picture these in your living room?"

"Oh, I'm not..." Startled, Lindsay sat up.

"Yes, I can." Tanner took over and Lindsay fell back into the leather. While Tanner asked questions, Lindsay let her mind drift back. She'd never really shopped for furniture with Rich. Newlyweds, they didn't have any money. Their parents pitched in with some pieces they no longer wanted. A sofa, one chair and a kitchen table. At the time, Rich's folks were moving back to Chicago. They'd had enough of small town living, or so they said. For awhile Lindsay worried that Rich would want to go too. But time passed and he didn't. Gradually it had dawned on her. Moving would have required a plan. Her husband lived minute to minute. Tanner was more of a planner.

"Look, we're just starting out. Could I have your card?" he asked the saleswoman.

"Oh, newlyweds, huh? Sure. I'm Dorothy." With a knowing smile the woman handed Tanner her card while Lindsay stood there, choking. Tanner told Dorothy he'd call. He wore an impish smile as they left.

Zipping her lip was so hard.

"I want to stop at a couple more stores but I liked those two pieces a lot," Tanner said as they crossed the lawn.

Her parents had looked for their new sofa for a full two months. Of course, her mother limited their choices to pink cabbage rose prints, whether it was drapes or a sofa. At least the pink went with the flamingo accents. "You've only been to one place."

Tanner opened the door on the passenger side. "I usually know what I want. " His eyes caught hers. Electricity crackled in the air.

Somehow she climbed inside. Whistling, Tanner went around the front.

"I wish I could do that," she said when they were on the road again.

"What, whistle?"

She nodded. "Finn caught on early but I never got the hang of it."

"We'll work on it."

And so for the next ten minutes he taught her how to whistle as they drove on up the road. Tanner got her giggling because she couldn't get the hang of it. "My lips just can't handle it."

"Oh, I think they'll do just fine," he murmured with an unnerving grin. "It just takes practice."

They came to another store but Tanner didn't see anything he liked. "What are you looking for besides chairs?" she asked. "You're selling just about everything."

"I need something for the dining room. Eating at the kitchen counter works fine. But I'd rather be out front where I can hear the lake. The screened porch can be too cold some mornings."

"I have a swing outside on my porch and after I..." But Lindsay stopped. She'd almost said *after I put the kids to bed.* "At night I like to sit on my swing and listen to the night sounds. There's an owl deep in the woods behind my house."

Her rambling stopped there. Lindsay was running into roadblocks. Life roadblocks. She'd been keeping Tanner in a nice, safe compartment. This was getting complicated.

"A penny for your thoughts." Tanner gave her a curious side look.

"Nothing, nothing." Rubbing her forehead, she stared out the window.

Tanner didn't say anything. They came to another shop. Tanner pulled in but they didn't stay long. "This might be trickier than I thought," he said as they drove away from the store that sold household items, like stoves and refrigerators, but no furnishings.

She laughed. "You can't expect to buy everything for your house in two hours."

"Why not?" He looked perplexed. "I don't want to make a career out of this."

"Such a guy. What about the bedroom furniture?" *What am I saying?* She choked.

"I'm not crazy about that set. It's a place holder." He glanced at his watch. "Are you hungry?"

"Starving." Her phone read almost one thirty.

"I know just the place. Do you like burgers and ice cream?"

"Culver's?" Lindsay often drove Rebecca and Susan up to Culver's. They loved the sundaes.

"You bet."

He gave her a high five. She cradled that hand in her lap.

Fifteen minutes later, Lindsay and Tanner were in a booth, munching on burgers and fries. "Thanks for coming with me," Tanner said. He ate the way he lived, wiping every bit of ketchup from the corners of his lips. Neat and tidy. If an onion string fell to his plate, he scooped it up. She wished Rebecca and Susan were this careful. Sure would save her some cleanup time.

"So, are we all set for the garage sale?" Tanner asked when he was finished.

"Everything's marked. I put an ad in *The Beacher*. We have road signs and balloons for the mailbox. If that doesn't pull people in, I don't know what will."

"Your smile would draw people. You'll be there, right?" For a second he looked panicked.

"Of course I'll be there. One person can't handle an estate sale."

"Just wanted to check." All his tough masculinity could turn vulnerable in unguarded moments. The switch surprised Lindsay.

"Have you made any progress on getting a real estate license?"

"Thank God for the internet. I can do everything online."

"How long will all that take?"

"I'm not in any hurry. Kind of looking forward to summer."

Summer and Culver's. Lindsay had a sudden flashback. Rich used to bring her here. They'd order sundaes and hang out. How young they'd been back then. Young and awkward with each other.

"Lindsay?'

"Sorry, what are you looking forward to?" She pulled herself from the past.

"Summer. It's been a long time."

"Oh right, the lake and the beach. Toes in the sand, all that."

But his happy expectation disappeared.

"What did I say?"

He shifted uncomfortably. "The sand is different for me now. Stupid but true."

She tried to process that. "You don't like the sand?"

He gave her a level look. "Heat and sand? Been there, done that."

Tanner's past darkened his troubled eyes. He'd been fighting in a desert for years. How could she have forgotten that? "I'm sorry I'm so stupid."

"No need to apologize." Reaching out, he took her hand. Lindsay didn't pull away.

"Is that where you developed the asthma?"

He nodded. "The doctors think the burn pits caused it. In Afghanistan there were no incinerators. A lot of plastic went into those huge pits, and my body didn't take to it. They didn't want a guy my size passing out during a maneuver. It could get dangerous for everybody else."

His fingers stopped stroking. This time it was Lindsay who gripped his fingers tighter. "Thanks for telling me."

"Yeah well, guess this is a time for sharing secrets, right?"

"I was married." It was time to come clean. "My husband died in the war."

"Oh, my God. I'm so sorry." His eyes darkened.

"Rich died doing what he wanted to do. The service meant a lot to him."

This was when she should mention Rebecca and Susan. Instead, she let the silence lengthen while she choked on words she couldn't say. Tanner squeezed her hand. Like the coward that she was, she said nothing.

"How about a sundae?"

"Sure." Anything that would distract her from telling the truth that would make him pull his hand away. A man who would only order wooden furniture knew nothing about kids who needed soft edges when they stumbled.

Caramel cashew sundaes had always been her favorite. Tanner ordered the standard hot fudge and he ate every bit. When they finished, she took out her phone and checked the time. "I should get home."

"Sure, right. I don't want to take up all of your Saturday."

Was he fishing? She said nothing.

The return trip seemed a lot longer. Tanner took his time and that was fine. When he pulled into his driveway, she almost felt sorry. It had been a nice day.

She turned. "I hope you got what you wanted."

His lips twitched. "Almost."

Tanner pulled the card from a shirt pocket. "Guess I'll call Dorothy and order the furniture. Thanks for coming with me. But I didn't get what I wanted." Mischief sparkled in his brown eyes.

"Well, it's too late to go to Michigan City."

"Trust me. What I want isn't in Michigan City." His voice had dropped to a low register that sent shivers down her spine.

"It isn't?" A girl could be mesmerized by those eyes. He pulled her closer and her heart kicked up.

When Tanner's lips closed over hers, she trembled at the gentleness, sank into the softness. They took their time, tilting their heads to find just the right angle. Each kiss made her want more until she was breathless with need. Was that his moan or hers? When his tongue flicked the seam of her lips, they opened. The delicious tangle of their tongues trickled through her body.

Shaken, she finally pulled away. "I should go." Cripes, she was on overload.

"Yeah. I guess." He ran his hands down her shoulders. Heaving a deep sigh, he got out.

Her lips would never be the same. Maybe her life would never be the same either. When he opened the door, she stumbled out.

"Be careful now," he said after she somehow managed to get into her car.

Careful? She snorted. It was way too late for that.

Chapter 11

When Tanner arrived to pick up Red on the Fourth of July, Leslie was fussing over him. Their kitchen door was open, but he could hear through the screen. "Now, keep this cap on your head."

"Knock, knock," he called out.

"Come on in, Tanner." Leslie waved him inside.

Red lifted his eyes to Tanner and sighed. "My mom worries about me all the time."

"You have very sensitive skin, Red." She'd slathered him with sunblock. The kid might glow in the dark. But the red fisherman's cap looked cute. Turning to Tanner, Leslie began ticking off points. "Watch out for the sun. He burns easily. Not too much sugar. Don't let him get too close to the floats."

Obviously, Red was used to his mother worrying. He didn't move a muscle. Sitting in their high chairs, Red's twin sisters looked pleased to be wearing scrambled eggs in their hair.

Sometimes you had to fake it 'til you make it. Tanner told himself he could handle this. He'd been a kid once. "Don't worry. I'll keep him out of the sun."

But his self confidence eroded when Leslie hauled out a booster seat. "I'll show you how to put this in your car. Red, watch the girls now."

Tanner reached out. "I'll take that." But the clunky seat felt weird as he followed Leslie outside to his SUV. He watched carefully while she strapped it into his back seat. Finally, she tested the straps, nodded and stepped back. You'd think they were going to Mars.

Back inside, Red patiently stood guard over the twins, a zip-lock bag in his hand. The girls were still man-handling their food.

"What's that bag for, Red?" Tanner asked

"The candy!" Red threw him an amazed look.

"Oh, right. Of course." This was a whole new experience, although he was trying to hide that. How Leslie handled all this was beyond him. "Well, see you later, Leslie."

Red gave his mom a smack on the cheek when she bent to hug her little boy. Simple things like this always got Tanner right in the gut. He opened the screen door.

"You're all set. Off you go." Leslie followed them outside and watched Red climb into the booster seat. Tanner strapped him in. Red didn't even have to help him and Tanner felt a certain satisfaction. Okay, he wasn't leading his men through a field of IEDs, but he hadn't goofed up. Yet.

Fourth of July and the day was warm and sunny, but not blistering hot as they drove to town. From what Tanner could see in the rearview mirror, Red was a happy camper. "This is the most happiest day of my life." Then his forehead wrinkled. "Well, so far."

Tanner chuckled. "I think you're going to have a lot of happy days. You have great parents." Tanner knew he'd approve of Red's dad, even though he hadn't met him yet. For Red, everything was new and exciting. Maybe all children who were born with Down syndrome were like that. Tanner had been studying up on the internet. How lucky to always live in the present.

Red might never wrack his brain about a woman who kissed him like it meant something and then pushed him away as if he were her brother. What was he missing here? They parked on a side street. Red unsnapped the safety belt himself and Tanner helped him out. Together they walked up to the main street, where the noise level was rising. Tanner guided Red to the shady side of the street.

Flags fluttered in the cool breeze that swept up from Lake Michigan. Decked out in red, white and blue, families jammed the sidewalks. This all felt familiar but strange, a scene from long ago. Here Tanner was, twenty years older but feeling like a little boy again. When he'd come with his parents, he was a part of the parade. The three of them would wave to the crowd from his dad's white Oldsmobile convertible. He could almost feel that warm red upholstery.

Next to him, Red fidgeted, shifting in his navy tennis shoes. "Is it time, Tanner? Is the parade coming?"

"Not yet, buddy. Soon, though." They were a little early. Tanner believed in being punctual—a holdover from his military days. The smell of coffee from a place behind them made him wish he had a cup. He'd stopped in there once or twice. The woman behind the counter seemed to own it and had a name badge with Sarah on it. She was very friendly.

Finally, a band blared in the distance. Red clapped his hands and the spectators craned their necks. Swinging down the street came the high school band. The brass section dominated a march that got everyone stamping their feet. He could feel the drums deep in his stomach. Red dropped his plastic bag twice before Tanner took it. "Just for safe keeping."

"Okay, Tanner. Oh, wow! Here they come!" Red peeked out and looked down the street. Tanner kept one hand on his shoulder. Red fell back. "I'll be good. I promised my mom."

Tanner gave him a gentle squeeze. "You're always good, Red. No problem there."

Lifting his head, Red shot him a smile that stunned Tanner with its sweetness.

Tanner had never thought much about having kids. In the service a lot of the guys were married. He could hear them talking to their wives and kids, a laptop often propped open for Facetime.

Although Tanner had dated casually, no one made him want to go the distance. And he was cautious. His father's situation, the result of loneliness, sometimes gave him nightmares.

A float from one of the hardware stores rolled slowly past. Smiling employees dressed in red aprons tossed handfuls of candy. Kids scrambled into the road. Tanner handed Red the bag. "Be careful."

When Red bolted out, Tanner was right behind him. The wheels on the float were huge, like a tank. Scrambling after a few pieces of wrapped candy, Red shot him a look. "You okay, Tanner?"

"Yeah, sure. Only three feet out, okay?"

"Sure. Got it." Red retreated to the curb.

The floats weren't Rose Bowl level but the crowd loved them. Crepe paper streamers floated from the flatbeds and balloons were everywhere. Trained to shut out distractions, Tanner kept a sharp eye on Red. The boy had no fear. Anytime Red made a dash for it, Tanner felt his own heart beat in his throat. Was this how parents felt all the time?

In addition to his preoccupation with Red, any swish of honey-colored hair caught his eye. More than once, Tanner jerked to study a woman whose head tipped a certain way or whose laugh hit a familiar note. But it wasn't Lindsay. He'd texted with her about the garage sale Saturday but that was it. She hadn't mentioned the parade and they might not be her thing.

What was Lindsay's thing?

Tanner didn't know much about her, while she'd been in his closets, for Pete's sake. She'd even rummaged through his family photos. He knew she was a widow but that was about all.

So he'd gone on a reconnaissance mission and looked her up. Last night he'd driven past her little bungalow, sliding down in his seat. This felt stupid and adolescent. The drapes had been open and a faint glow suggested a TV. That hadn't been much to go on and he slowly drove home. What was the point? How embarrassing for a grown man to act like this. But he wanted to know everything about her, and he liked her little, old-fashioned place with a porch. So much of Gull Harbor had been converted into slick new condos. Tanner hated them. They ruined the whole feeling of the town.

The politicians were marching past now, handing out flyers. But paper wasn't what the crowd wanted. They waited for the candy and the bands. Behind the civil servants came the float for the PR department in Gull Harbor. His hopes lifted since Lindsay did some part time work for them. The blonde on the float was attractive but she wasn't Lindsay. In fact she looked like Finn Wheeler's wife. He'd seen her in the Mangy Mutt more than once.

Behind him the door of the coffee shop burst open, releasing a wave of coffee. The owner bustled out and gently elbowed her way through. She smelled like pastries as she searched the crowd. "Lindsay!" she called out.

He followed the direction of her eyes. When Lindsay turned, his heart stopped. Tanner was used to seeing her in cut-offs or long jeans. But today? He forgot to breathe. Held up by tiny straps, the top of the dress was red and blue like a flag. Her shoulders looked smooth and tan and probably so soft that his hands ached to touch that skin. When she spun around, the skirt swirled with her. More than one child pointed to the blue stars that sparkled in the sun. Standing next to her were some children, along with an older couple.

"Mommy," the smallest boy called out, waving at Sarah, who seemed to know everyone.

"Can I eat some of the candy, Tanner?" Red touched his arm. "Can I? Would that be all right?"

Tanner gave himself a shake. He was on duty. "Sure. Just unwrap it first." When Red had trouble untwisting the cellophane,

Tanner did it for him.

"Thanks, pal." Red popped a root beer barrel into his mouth and grinned. Craning his neck, Tanner tried to keep Lindsay in sight. Right now she was hugging the other woman. Was she babysitting for all these kids?

The parade had ended. The air echoed with brass and holiday excitement. But the feeling in his chest had nothing to do with the Fourth of July. "Let's a take a walk, Red. Okay, buddy?"

"Sure. I don't get to come to town much." He leaned closer. "My mom's so busy with the kids."

"I know." Tanner imagined Leslie hardly ever brought all three into town, if she could help it. Still, he knew what it felt like to get sidelined in a family. Backing out of the crowd, he led the little boy along the shop windows. There was more room here. Tanner lifted his head to keep Lindsay in sight.

"Look at all the stuff, Tanner." Red came to a halt in front of a store that sold beach toys. His eyes filled with longing and he pressed both palms against the glass. "Wow, an inner tube that looks like the Batmobile."

Not wanting to lose Lindsay, Tanner quickly glanced at the toy. "Is that what it is?"

Cheek bulging with the root beer ball, Red nodded. "Heck, Tanner, everybody knows Batman."

He felt old as the hills. Glancing ahead, he watched Lindsay turn into the Swirly Top, along with about thirty other people. Tanner felt torn. "Come on, Red. We have to be quick."

Tanner towed Red into the store and bought the inner tube.

Red was elated but had trouble carrying the toy. Tanner ended up with it looped around one shoulder. Hand in hand, they headed for the Swirly Top. But all Tanner could think about was Lindsay in that little sundress. And all those children.

The holiday crowd was dispersing, filtering down the side streets. Some folks strolled toward the harbor. Boaters would probably spend the day on the water and gather along the shore for the fireworks that night.

Tanner and Red approached the crowded ice cream stand. This had to look casual. The huge twirly cone sign had marked this place for as long as he could recall. Gazing up at the cone, Red just about turned inside out.

"That sign was there when I was your age," he said. The paint was worn through in spots. When Tanner was growing up, he'd spent plenty of time at the Swirly Top. A chocolate and vanilla twirl cone had been their treat after Sunday dinner. Of course, that ended when Ursula hit the scene. His stepmother had always been on a diet.

"Wow. That long?"

Great. Now he felt like Red's grandfather. But Tanner cut any memories short. Lindsay was sitting at a picnic table with a group. Laughing and chattering, they were all busy with their ice cream. Surrounded by kids, Lindsay looked up as he approached. The color drained from her cheeks. "Tanner."

Not the welcome he'd hoped for.

~.~

Lindsay tried to catch her breath. "What are you doing here?" Was that the little boy she'd seen at the mailboxes?

"Watching the parade."

Great. As if that explained everything. Sarah and her parents were staring at her, waiting for an explanation.

"Hi." The little boy waved at everyone, a few red curls escaping from his hat. Then he glanced up at Tanner with adoring eyes.

Ice cream dripped over her hand while Lindsay fumbled through introductions. "Tanner, I want you to meet my parents, Rose and John Wheeler. My friend Sarah and her boys, Justin and Nathan." Tanner was nodding and shaking hands. She took a deep breath. "And my two girls, Rebecca and Susan."

"*Your* girls." He looked dumbfounded.

She'd messed this up in a major way. "What are you doing here?"

"Ah, I'm here with Red."

"Tanner lives next door to me," Red announced proudly. "We're buddies, right, Tanner?"

"Yep, we are." But Tanner's eyes were on her and they held a question. Dropping her eyes, Lindsay fingered the grain of table so hard that she picked up a splinter.

Of course her mother jumped right in. "So you're one of Lindsay's customers?"

Tanner grinned. "Yes, I guess I am. She's been a big help to me."

"Oh, I'll just bet," her mother said, batting her eyelashes.

"Lindsay takes her job very seriously," her dad added.

Sarah seemed especially pleased. "I'll bet Red would like some ice cream, wouldn't you, Red?"

"Yep. I sure would." And then he giggled.

Tanner's head snapped as if shaking himself from a deep sleep. Shock was probably more like it. "I'll be right back. Can I get anyone anything?" He looked to the group.

"Nope. I think we're doing just fine." Sarah's eyes circled from Tanner to Lindsay and back again.

Inching over toward her daughters, Lindsay patted the seat next to her. "Right here, Red." Her parents sat quietly at the end of the long table. Eating their cones, Rebecca and Susan eyed the newcomer.

Tanner turned to go into the Swirly Top. Laughing, Lindsay called to him. "Tanner?"

"Yep." He wheeled around.

She motioned to him with the hand not holding the cone. "I'll take the inner tube."

Slipping it from his shoulder, Tanner handed it over. His face was probably the color of Red's hat.

"Don't take that in there, Tanner," Red scolded. "You won't be able to carry the ice cream, silly."

Lindsay tucked the inner tube at Red's feet. She owed Tanner an explanation and it was long overdue. What had she been thinking? For those few wonderful days she'd been fancy free. She'd enjoyed that feeling but it hadn't been real. Looking around the table and the people she loved, she knew this was real and right.

While Lindsay thought about her next step, Red talked a mile a minute about the garage sale. He knew more than she did. Lindsay and Sarah exchanged glances over the heads of the children, her friend's eyebrows raised in amusement. Lindsay's parents just listened.

Before long, Tanner returned with two cones. Red's eyes lit up. "Gee thanks, Tanner."

"You are so polite," Lindsay said, hoping that Rebecca was listening. Red beamed. The boy was the cutest kid ever. But what was he doing with Tanner, the man who hated pets and children?

"Red's been telling us about the garage sale," Sarah told Tanner. "What are you selling?"

"Not much."

"That's not true," Lindsay broke in. "He has some very nice furniture, including a dining room set. Lots of dishes. Kitchen accessories. Something for everyone." After all, she'd written the ad for *The Beacher*.

"Lindsay's my marketer," Tanner said between licks of his cone. "This was all her doing."

"I can see that." Sarah was looking very smug.

"Mom, can we go?" Rebecca asked. "I have money saved. And we can help." She looked to her sister for support. Lindsay should have expected this.

"Can we, pretty please?" Susan added, squeezing her cone so hard it cracked.

"Of course, you can come." Tanner nodded in her direction. "Right?"

And just like that Lindsay was outnumbered. Having the girls at the sale might distract her from her work. But she didn't have a good excuse.

"I'll have popsicles for everyone that day," Tanner said.

Who is this man? Astonished, Lindsay could only stare at him.

"Will they be banana popsicles?" Susan asked. Lindsay almost howled. Rebecca and Susan were boxing Tanner into a corner.

"You never know." But when Susan frowned, Tanner folded fast. "Sure. Banana it is." If Tanner had just landed in a spaceship, Lindsay would not have been more amazed.

The kids erupted. "Hooray, hooray!"

"Lindsay's been telling me about you," Sarah told Tanner after the commotion had calmed down.

"She has?" Lindsay's mom threw her an injured look. "We haven't heard a word."

Oh boy. Now Lindsay was really in trouble.

Sarah gave Tanner a charming smile. "You're from Gull Harbor?"

"Yes. But I went away to school. A lot of folks don't remember me." He glanced over at Lindsay. "You didn't like the ice cream?"

She glanced down. Her hand was a mess, chocolate and vanilla dripping onto the table. Rebecca grabbed a napkin. "Here, Mommy. I'll help you."

While the girls cleaned her up, Sarah and Tanner kept sharing information, her parents chiming in. They covered anyone their families might have in common. Turned out that Lindsay's father had known Jim Phelps. "But not personally. Just church events."

"I think I met your stepmother once," her mother added.

Tanner fell silent, suddenly very busy wiping off Red's hands. Sarah picked up the slack, talking about changes on Whittaker Street in the past ten years.

Jiggling one knee, Lindsay was ready to leave. Tanner had retreated into his safety zone, his face revealing nothing. The children had finished their cones. Rebecca and Susan began to pick at each other. Perfect just perfect.

She was tossing napkins in the trash when her mother turned to Tanner. "You'll have to come for dinner." Lindsay jerked and caught her hand in the flap of the trash can. Her gasp could probably be heard in Chicago.

"Sometime. Dinner *sometime*," her father added. Lindsay saw him squeeze Mom's hand under the table. "We can talk about a time."

"Sometime soon." Shaking off Daddy's hand, her mother gave Tanner one of her coquettish smiles. Usually Lindsay found that cute, but not today. Things had gotten out of control.

Tanner had finished his ice cream and was helping Red. Once Lindsay caught him staring at her but she could not read his eyes. She felt relieved when Tanner got up and shook out his long legs. "Well, Red, I think we've bothered these folks long enough."

Scrambling from the table, Red said, "I've tried to be good, Tanner."

"Oh, no." They all spoke at once. "You're fine."

"We just have to get home," Tanner told him, straightening Red's hat. "Your mom will be wondering where we are."

"You're a perfect little gentleman." Her dad winked at Red, who puffed out his chest. The boy was seriously cute.

"So, maybe I'll see you Saturday?" Tanner looked toward Rebecca and Susan as he backed away.

"You bet," Rebecca said.

Susan stood up. "Don't forget ..."

"...the popsicles," Tanner finished for her with a grin. Everyone laughed.

Tanner and Red were ambling up Whittaker Street when Lindsay came to her senses, the black plastic warm against her bare leg. "Tanner!" she called out, scooping up the inner tube. He turned.

"You forgot something." Lindsay waved it in the air.

Galloping back, Red grabbed it. "Thanks." When Tanner slung the inner tube over one shoulder, Lindsay wanted to hug him.

Her eyes followed him down the street, with Red talking away at his elbow. "Seems like a nice young man," Lindsay's father said. The table had fallen silent and all eyes were on her.

"He's very...nice."

"I wonder if he likes pot roast or grilled steaks," her mother mused.

"Mom." But Lindsay's mother was already drawing up a menu.

Chapter 12

She should have gotten out of this. Told him the kids couldn't come to the garage sale. Lindsay was a total mess as they approached Tanner's house that Saturday. Getting the girls dressed had been an ordeal. She couldn't imagine what proms would be like with these two. Susan wanted to wear the same outfit she'd worn on the Fourth so Tanner would recognize her. Even Rebecca had taken time with herself, braiding pink ribbons into her hair. What was going on here?

The girls chattered with excitement all the way up Red Arrow while Lindsay's stomach did cartwheels. She should have insisted that the girls stay with Poppy John and Grandma Rose. But here they were. She would never forget the look in Tanner's eyes at the Swirly Top when she'd introduced him to her children.

The children she'd never mentioned. What had she been thinking?

When she reached the house on Sleepy Hollow Lane, Tanner was dragging the long tables out into the sunlight. Dressed in a gray T-shirt and shorts, he was an eyeful. But this wasn't the time for gawking. Red was trying to help. The rising sun beamed through the trees, where birds chirped. The forecast called for fair weather, which was a relief. The sale began at eight and the ad she'd put in

The Beacher clearly stated *No Early Birds*. But she spotted two cars parked down the road.

"Look!" Rebecca pointed. "There's Red!"

"Looks like he's going to help us today." Lindsay pulled down the road a bit so customers could park closer, but not as far as the gawkers. When Lindsay opened the back door, the girls spilled from the car and streaked toward the house. "Red! Tanner! We're here."

Yes, they sure were. And this was real life. Her life. She'd hardly slept last night. After today, maybe he'd tell her he didn't need her services anymore. She'd been so stupid.

Red greeted the girls with a big smile. The little boy was such a wild card. She didn't know what to think.

As Lindsay approached, Susan ran toward Tanner. "Tanner, did you get the popsicles?"

He arched a brow. "You'll just have to wait and see."

Wait? Her daughters? Impatience was their middle name and, sadly, they'd gotten that from their mother.

"Yeah, he did," Red burst out. "I tried one. Yum." He rubbed his tummy with a teasing smile. Lindsay burst out laughing.

"You'll get one too," Tanner told the dismayed girls. Pacified for now, Rebecca and Susan checked out the tables.

"Don't touch anything!" Lindsay warned them as she handed Tanner a sack of plastic grocery bags. She'd also brought some newspapers for packing.

Abandoning the tables, Rebecca and Sarah hopped onto the red velour sofa. "We should buy this, Mom," Rebecca announced.

"Yeah. I like it." Susan gave the sofa a little bounce.

"Off, off." Lindsay ran a hand over her forehead. "You have sand on your shoes." The last thing she needed was a red sofa. Rebecca and Sarah headed for the gold chairs.

This might be the longest day of her life.

"They can't hurt anything, Lindsay. I'm selling it as is, anyway." Tanner drew closer. One hand fell onto her shoulder. "Relax," he whispered.

His words warm on her neck, she knew relaxation wasn't possible. "Sure. Right."

He nodded to the garage. "Can you help me carry out the table of office supplies?"

"Absolutely." Anything to keep busy. Together they lifted the table, bringing it out into the sunlight. She looked around. The girls had already started to pick up the kitchen items while Red followed behind them.

"We don't have one of these." Rebecca held up a glass juicer.

"That's because I buy orange juice in a container," Lindsay said. "Put it back, please."

Tanner was trying to lug out the dining room table and she ran to help. "You're pretty strong," he said with appreciation once they had the chairs lined up behind the table.

"So I've been told."

He disappeared inside.

Lindsay took advantage of the time he was gone to go over the ground rules. "Now I know this all looks fascinating," she said. "But Tanner is selling everything. Hands off."

"But why is he selling it?" Rebecca's asked. "Is he moving?"

"Oh, no he's not." Red looked upset by the very thought.

"He's just...clearing things out."

When Tanner emerged from inside, he held a bag and looked uncomfortable. "For the kids." To her amazement, he pulled three activity booklets from the bag along with sets of markers. Who was this man?

"Did you pick these out yourself?"

He scratched his head. "The lady at the drugstore said kids liked these books. Was she right?"

"Oh, wow," Susan said, sitting right down at the table.

"Wow is right," Red agreed.

Leafing through the three books, Rebecca said, "I want Frozen."

"And I want Batman." Red held the book tight against his chest.

"But *I* want Batman," Susan said in a tiny voice. She wasn't used to getting what she wanted. Not unless Lindsay stepped in.

Fine. Now let Tanner see that this is what it was like. All the time. Every day.

"Oh, okay." To Lindsay's amazement, Red handed the Batman book to Susan. "I like the Avengers too. Can we use this table, Tanner?"

"You got it." The relief on Tanner's face almost made her laugh. Within minutes, they'd transferred the cashbox and stickers to the dining room table. The children pulled folding lawn chairs up to the card table. Contentment reigned.

"He sure is a happy little guy," she whispered to Tanner as they set small appliances on one of the long tables.

"Always. It's amazing."

"And Red lives next door?"

"Yep. Really nice mom, but she has twin baby girls. Her husband travels a lot."

"She must have her hands full." Lindsay knew how that felt.

She glanced over at the cottage next door. The back door was open and so were the curtains, as if Red's mom might be watching.

"I guess she does," Tanner said, carefully winding a cord around the bottom of a clock. Then he did the same to a hand mixer. "I don't mind Red coming over when I'm outside. She keeps an eye on him."

Ten minutes to eight. One of the cars on the road edged closer. The second car did the same. More people pulled up. "Early birds," she muttered.

"What?" Tanner wheeled around. Had he ever been to a garage sale?

"Might as well start. They're only ten minutes early. Game on." After tucking her phone in her back pocket, she pointed at the kids. "Listen up. No one wanders away and don't go inside."

The three of them nodded and went back to coloring. Lindsay waved to the cars and their doors flew open.

The early birds bought a coffee grinder and six wine glasses. Red left the Avenger book to take on wrapping and packing, with Rebecca helping. Susan was still happy coloring. Lindsay became the cashier. Tanner knew the merchandise and circulated, answering any questions. A poster taped on the garage frame pictured the armoire and breakfront inside. There was no way they could haul those two pieces into the garage. Tanner and Lindsay took turns escorting interested shoppers inside. It didn't take long before a man and his wife bought the breakfront, promising to return in two hours with their son and a pickup truck.

"Piece of cake." Tanner gave her a thumbs up, and glanced around. "I can't believe this."

"Better than carting everything to Goodwill or Salvation army, right?"

"You are a very smart lady." When he smiled, his gaze settled on her lips.

She could feel her face flush. "Sometimes."

Then his attention shifted to the kids and he frowned. As if he didn't quite know what to make of them.

Lindsay stayed on high alert. It wasn't easy to keep both the shoppers and the kids in sight. When she heard glass shatter on the garage floor, she turned. An elderly man in blue-striped seersucker pants stood there while his wife gave him an earful. "Walt, I told you not to touch anything."

"No problem, really. Don't worry about it." Lindsay turned to go inside just as Tanner appeared with a whisk broom and dustpan. The glass was soon cleaned up.

"Am I doing a good job, Tanner?" Red asked when the numbers thinned.

"Don't know what I'd do without you."

This was a totally amazing day.

~•~

Tanner felt relieved as the kitchen items sold. The fussy throw pillows and stacks of red and gold dishes were carted away by smiling folks who seemed happy to have them. He was starting over. When he thought about those dinners with Ursula, his stomach knotted painfully tight. But stuff was selling. What the heck. He went inside and snapped polaroid pictures of the bedroom set.

"What are you doing?" Lindsay asked, her eyes widening as Tanner taped the shots to the For Sale poster at the garage entrance.

"Getting rid of my past," he said.

"Oh." That was all she said. But how could Lindsay understand? Any good memories he'd had about that room belonged to his mother. After Ursula got finished redecorating the master suite, it looked nothing like the sunny, happy place it had been when his mother was alive. All the Monet prints disappeared and the heavy gold drapes shut out the natural sunlight.

When lunchtime came, Lindsay produced a hamper from her trunk. The woman was amazing. Ham sandwiches, pop and chips were passed around. They took turns eating in the kitchen, so they could keep on eye on the sale scavengers. "Can we have the popsicles now?" Susan asked when they were finished. When she gave Tanner a beguiling smile, he melted. Now he knew where Lindsay's smile had come from.

As he doled out banana popsicles, Tanner didn't mention his trip to Stevensville, thirty miles farther up the road, to get the right flavor. Clancy's was sold out. No way was he failing in this mission. Who knew a banana popsicle could make a kid so happy? The children took them over to the big oak tree and sat in the shade.

Lindsay was cashing out some plastic storage containers when her smile froze. Following the direction of her eyes, he spun around. Lindsay's mother and father were picking their way through the crowd. Dressed in a purple outfit, her blonde hair shining in the bright sun, Lindsay's mom wore clear plastic heels, painted with pink flamingos. John Wheeler looked uncomfortable. Tanner would bet this had not been his idea. Throwing her arms wide, Susan ran toward them, a popsicle dripping from one hand. "Poppy John! Grandma Rose! You came!"

"Had to check up on you." Lindsay's father smoothed his granddaughter's long blonde curls. "Have you been behaving?"

"Oh, yes," she said in such a serious voice. "We're helping. Tanner bought us popsicles."

"Just don't drip it on me, okay sweetheart?"

Tanner had to smile. That is until he saw Finn advancing across the lawn. This was starting to feel like an ambush. Her mother had disappeared toward the tables, where Rebecca was showing her a set of dishes. But Poppy John and Finn stopped with Tanner. Clearly, they were checking him out.

"How's it going?" Finn asked, glancing around. "Looks busy."

"Yep, it's been a crowd scene since about eight this morning, thanks to your sister."

"Selling a lot of stuff?"

"Looks like it. Big ticket items, like juice squeezers and old dishes." No need to say anything about getting rid of the past.

Leaving Red in charge of the cash box, Lindsay approached. "Hey, Finn. Are you looking for something special? You and Merc doing some redecorating?"

Now it was Finn's turn to look uncomfortable. "Mercedes mentioned you were involved in some kind of sale today. Just thought I'd stop by."

"Sure. Right." Lindsay gave her brother a suspicious look. But she was smiling. "Like I believe that."

This was getting interesting. Lindsay had kept a lot about her family to herself—like the fact that she had children. Tanner didn't like that one bit. Didn't she trust him with things that really mattered?

Rebecca and Susan lost no time in latching onto their grandmother. Picking up a gravy boat, Rose waved it in his direction. Looked like it belonged to Ursula's red set of china. "Will you sell this separately?"

"I don't see why not."

"John, sweetheart." Rose turned to her husband. "Do you have a spare five dollars?"

Before they knew it, Red was wrapping up the gravy boat. As the day moved on, he had puffed with importance, even though the customers often had to help him make change.

Lindsay hovered on the edge of the crowd, looking like she had pulled riot duty. But her folks weren't budging. Rose turned to Tanner, mischief sparkling in her eyes. "I was hoping you might come to Sunday dinner."

Closing in on them, Lindsay overheard the comment. Her skin turned the color of the white china. "Mom, I'm sure Tanner's very busy."

"That depends." Tanner ignored the panicked look in Lindsay's eyes. This was just too good to miss.

"On what?" Rose waited, her head tilted.

"I'd be delighted to come to Sunday dinner sometime, if you babysit for Lindsay tonight."

Lindsay's dad muffled a chuckle with one hand.

"I'm sure they have plans." Lindsay looked to her parents for confirmation.

Tanner waited.

"Oh, I don't believe we do," Rose finally said, her eyes sparkling with mischief. "Will it be terribly late, though? I do like to get my beauty sleep."

Was she really asking if this should be a sleepover? Tanner wanted to laugh, but he caught John Wheeler's eye. "I'll have your daughter home by ten."

"Ten?" The number hung in the air.

"Well, maybe eleven." They needed to talk. And the garage sale would not be the topic of their conversation.

Swinging her ponytail over one shoulder, Lindsay crossed her arms. "Do I have any say in this?"

"No sweetheart," her dad said with a somber look. "It looks as if you don't."

"Do you like pot roast?" Rose Wheeler asked, leaning toward Tanner in a conspiratorial way. Her flamingo earrings quivered in her ears.

"Love it." Then he turned to Lindsay, whose face had paled. "Six?"

"Six. Sure" Reaching up, she yanked her ponytail tighter. How would she look with all that hair falling around her shoulders? Tanner's knees weakened.

"Pardon me." A man holding his dad's humidor nudged Tanner. "Could you come down a little on this?"

The pretentious thing had been a gift to his dad from Ursula. She thought cigars were so "manly." His father had sat out on the porch and smoked maybe half of one before storing the humidor away. Taking the man's elbow, Tanner steered him toward the cashbox, where Red sat smiling. "Sir, this is your lucky day. I'll give you fifty percent off."

The buyer nodded and Tanner set the humidor in front of Red. Together, they figured out what the man owed.

By the time they finished the transaction, Lindsay's family had left. "That was pretty underhanded," Lindsay muttered, waving to them as they drove away.

"Let's just call it strategic." Checking his phone, Tanner saw that they only had half an hour left. The sale ended at four. Most of the stuff was gone, except for some books and a few of the household items. As promised, the man had returned for the breakfront with an adult son and a friend. They'd wrestled it into the back of a pickup truck. After that, there wasn't much traffic.

"What do we do with the rest of it?" He looked to Lindsay for an answer.

"You want me to drop it off on my way home?"

"Absolutely not. I'll take care of it."

Snugging his arms around her waist. "I want you to go home and take a bubble bath."

"A bubble bath?" She giggled.

"Get prettied up. We'll go some place special." Then he totally blanked out. "But where? Not the Mangy Mutt."

She drew back. "What? You don't like my brother?"

"Let's just say I don't want to be under his eagle eye tonight."

Lindsay seemed to understand. "Brewster's might take us," she suggested.

"That place is still there?"

"Yep. Outdoor garden." Her eyes got dreamy. "Little white lights. Or we could eat inside."

"The garden will be fine. I'll call." If little white lights gave her that soft smile, then that's where they'd go.

"Mom!" Red's voice brought Tanner back to earth. Leslie was trundling the twins down the road. The sandy surface made the going tough. Red ran to meet them. "Mom, I counted out money today."

"You did?" She turned to Tanner. "I hope he wasn't a pest. I'm sorry to leave him here all day. I saw him at the table and everything looked fine."

"Don't know what I would have done without him."

"You're a kind man." She swept the hair from her eyes and took Red's hand. "I think you've been here long enough, honey."

"So many people came." Red was quick to fill in his mom.

As his mother lead him away, Red turned to wave good-bye.

"Bye, Red!" Rebecca and Susan both shouted.

Lindsay clapped her hands as if she were a drill sergeant. "Girls? Time to go."

"You can keep the coloring books and markers if you help me out. This will only take a minute." Tanner set a couple of boxes on the long table. "Can you fill these boxes with everything left on the tables?"

The four of them got to work and then he lugged each box to the SUV. When he saw Lindsay reach for a box, he took it from her. "Too heavy for you."

"Says who?" She lifted that stubborn chin.

"Says me." Hoisting the box up, he said, "Why don't you go home and get prettied up. Wear that dress you wore to the parade.

Her cheeks flushed red. "You liked it?"

"Oh, yeah." Tanner wanted to see more of that soft skin. But her daughters were giggling. So he zipped his lips and watched them drive away. Then he whistled all the way to Goodwill.

Tonight would be special. Just how special depended on Lindsay.

Chapter 13

How had Lindsay ended up in this romantic garden, staring soulfully into Tanner's eyes? Tiny white lights were looped through the trees and night was falling, soft and seductive. Tables were arranged for privacy in Brewster's outdoor garden. She fingered one of her shoulder length curls. How had this happened?

Her family had railroaded her into this date. Hilarious.

"What's with the smile?" Tanner's lazy grin sent shivers down her bare back. Good thing she'd brought a shawl.

"Oh, nothing." She dropped her eyes to the menu. "Want to share a pizza?"

"Sounds good."

"What do you like?"

"Surprise me."

Their eyes locked and sparked. Thoughts of food left her mind.

The waiter approached with her Cosmo and Tanner's beer. Still rattled, she threw out some pizza toppings, and then they were alone again. Around them, the friendly chatter faded away. They seemed to be the only two people in the world.

Raising his mug, Tanner said, "To our successful garage sale."

Our? Lindsay clinked her glass against his. "It was great, wasn't it? You didn't even have to take much to Goodwill." She felt pretty proud of suggesting it.

"The sale was good in lots of ways." His voice had that clipped, no-nonsense tone that was becoming familiar. Sometimes it was as if he switched into military mode. Taking a sip of beer, Tanner swiped the foam from his upper lip with a thumb. Her own lips prickled.

Sipping her Cosmo, she tugged on her curl again.

"I like your hair like that." The drill sergeant tone was gone.

Self conscious, she dropped her hands.

"The pigtails are cute, but this?" His eyes brushed over her hair and a chill rippled through her. Her dad had picked up Rebecca and Susan at five, so Lindsay had time to get ready. The hairdo had been worth the effort.

The breeze had turned cooler and she tugged on her shawl, which had caught on something. "This sundress probably isn't very practical for evening."

Jumping up, Tanner came around to release the snag. "Who cares about practical? You look beautiful." His hands squeezed her shoulders, and her heart rate kicked up a notch.

But back to the garage sale. "I didn't expect so many people," she said as Tanner settled in his seat again, stretching his long legs out to the side.

"I didn't expect to meet your whole family." His eyes pinned her.

"Oh. Well." Lifting her martini glass, she took a hearty gulp.

"When were you going to tell me, Lindsay?"

"About what?"

"That you're a mother." He leaned forward, hurt glimmering in his brown eyes. Or maybe it was anger.

"I was just doing work at your house. It didn't seem appropriate for me to bring my family into it." Words came tumbling out in her usual erratic fashion. They all sounded lame, and she stopped, ashamed. Twirling the stem of the glass, she wondered. Had she been protecting her children or protecting him?

"I don't get it." Shoving back, Tanner looked wounded. "I thought we were hitting it off."

"We were. We are." How she wanted to smooth that confusion from his face.

"So why? You have two daughters and never mentioned them?" He really looked lost. "And I didn't ask questions, even after you helped yourself to my family photos."

"I'm so sorry." Her cheeks felt brick red. "So you noticed."

He leaned closer. The tea light in the center of the table created mysterious shadows on his face. "Lindsay Wheeler. I notice everything about you. Every breath you take. And that's the problem."

"Swanson," she supplied.

"What?" He looked confused.

"My married name is Swanson. It was on that card."

"Right." Tanner looked around. "I suppose you came here with your husband."

"Sometimes. We were townies, Tanner. A young couple with a baby and a tight budget. Rich and I weren't like these families from the yachts or expensive homes in Chicago."

"What did your husband do? I mean, before he joined up."

Lindsay thought back. "A lot of things. Woodworking. Construction. Even waiting tables. We were high school sweethearts and got married right after graduation." The phrase that had once sounded romantic now felt foolish and naive. "We probably should have waited, but Rebecca came along."

"Sounds tough." No judgment in the words. "Good thing you have a family."

"They've been very supportive. And in Gull Harbor, you can pick up part time gigs. I started a business cleaning houses. And I waited tables at Finn's after he bought the place and fixed it up."

"You're a strong woman."

"I like to think I am." Sometimes the kids wore her down but she wasn't about to admit that to Tanner.

"At least now I know more about you."

"Yes, you do. And I know a little bit about you."

A little bit? Cripes, she'd gone through his closets. What had she been thinking? At least, she'd held the line at the drawers. Not that she hadn't been tempted. It was so wrong that she wondered if he wore boxer shorts or briefs. "Look, I'm so sorry. I shouldn't have gone through your things."

"Maybe I was flattered."

"Really?" Tanner could be so intriguing.

"Sure. Beautiful, mysterious woman handles my shirts. That is kind of hot."

Definitely good that she hadn't explored his drawers. "How did you know?"

"I had to take my shirts to the cleaner. They smelled like, you know, cleaning stuff." He wrinkled his nose.

"Boy, you should have been a hunting dog."

"Yes, I would have been excellent." His lips did a downward turn.

"I bought all those new products. They weren't supposed to smell. That's the whole point." And they'd been expensive.

"They still have an odor. Vinegar or something. It was kind of kinky standing there in my closet." The boyish grin invited her to smile too.

But she didn't. "It's just that you're so tidy."

"You say that like it's a disease. 'Tidiness, second only to cholera or the plague.' " Tanner delivered the line in a newscaster's voice.

She had to laugh. Their chuckles cleared the air a little. But she still owed him an explanation. The waiter brought fresh bread and olive oil with parmesan. Breaking off a chunk, she swirled it though the oil. "That first day, you said you didn't have pets or children. Didn't allow them or want them."

Tanner exhaled. She was ruining this beautiful evening. "I didn't mean anything by that. As I recall, you caught me unaware."

"Oh, Tanner. I'm making such a mess of this." She crumbled a crust of bread in her fingers. Maybe this gulf between them was too wide.

"I'm trying to understand. We're talking things through." When Tanner took her hand, she didn't pull away. He dusted the bread crumbs from her hand with his fingertips. Lindsay felt his soft touch clear to her toes.

"I wanted some time." How could a man without children understand the responsibility? Still, there was Red. That little boy adored him. But from what she could see, they were playmates. An everyday responsibility? That was something else entirely.

Raising kids was all about the grind and the glory of daily living. Laughing together watching *Sheldon* and then telling them to clean their room.

Their waiter arrived with a pizza that smelled fabulous. Nudging the tea light aside, he set the pizza on the table, asked if they needed anything else and then disappeared.

"What's on it?" Puzzled, Tanner stared at the bubbling surface.

"I have no idea."

That cracked him up.

"Give me your plate." He grabbed the knife and served slices. "Let's guess."

"Marinara sauce and cheese," she said around her first mouthful.

"What kind of cheese?" He bit down and chewed.

"Mozzarella?"

"Maybe a little gorgonzola?"

"If you say so." She took another bite. "Kalamata olives."

"Bacon?" His brows lifted.

"If you say so." She felt as if she hadn't eaten in years.

"Spinach." He nodded with appreciation "Very healthy."

"How do you know that?"

"Read it somewhere. Or maybe this is kale. I get them

confused."

"You know the difference?" He really was amazing.

"No. Are you kidding?"

For a while they ate mindlessly. When a drop of sauce ended up on his chin, she swiped it off with a finger. His stubbled chin grazed her skin. Kissing him would probably leave her cheeks pink. She had to remind herself to chew.

Only one piece remained. "Take it," he said.

"I can't." She was glad this sundress had a full skirt. "You eat it for me."

"Happy to oblige."

By that time she had no idea what they were talking about. But those lips closing around the final piece? She wanted them in the worst way. The touch of them, the feel of them against her own lips. She wanted *him*.

Maybe the drink had gone to her head.

Lindsay knotted her hands in her lap.

Except for a few crumbs, the pizza tray was empty. She was full, but other parts of her body felt as if they'd been on a hunger strike. Lindsay squeezed her eyes tight, thankful for the darkness.

"You know what I think?" When Tanner took her hand, her eyes flew open. "You're thinking too much."

"Can anyone think too much?"

"Absolutely. Those wrinkles in your forehead might freeze. Right here." When Tanner touched his forehead, she imagined those fingers on her own skin. "Are you cold? I like seeing those shoulders but you could wrap your shawl tighter."

The waiter came to clear the table. "Dessert? We've got some fresh chocolate chip cookies." Brewster's sold homemade baked goods, displayed in the front case.

"Sound good?" Tanner looked to her.

"None for me, thanks."

"Just the check." Tanner's attention never left her. But she felt he was waiting for something. "So, I'm trying to understand why you didn't remarry. I mean, you're attractive and it's been a while, right?"

That felt like a trick question she didn't want to answer. "Maybe I haven't had time. The girls keep me busy. So what about you? You've never married?"

Tanner's lips tightened. "Haven't had the time or the inclination."

"So you're fancy free. Looks as if you could live anywhere."

He gave her a wry smile. "Anywhere sounds like nowhere to me."

"Really? You wouldn't like to live in Paris, Toronto or London?"

"Have you visited those cities?"

"Oh no, just read about them. I like living here in a small town where we know everyone. Sure, a lot of kids move away after school. But they often come back. Look at Kate or Mercedes Kennedy."

"There's a lot to like about Gull Harbor."

So did he intend to stay? But she couldn't ask.

He glanced through the tall bushes toward the line queued up at the front door to the restaurant. "Maybe it's time to leave."

Lindsay hated for the evening to end. The chair scraped against the stones when she pushed back.

Walking out, Tanner took her elbow. The stores along Whittaker Street had darkened windows. "Summer's here." She breathed in the lake air wafting from the beach a couple blocks away.

"Yep, the kind of summer people pay to experience. Look at the license plates."

Many were from out of state. They'd reached the SUV and he opened the door. "Want to drive to the beach?"

"Sure, but we could walk."

"I didn't mean this beach."

Another adventure. She smiled. Closing the car door, he came around. In his crisp blue oxford shirt rolled at the elbows, he looked so handsome. The khaki shorts were standard wear but not a lot of guys had his long, muscled legs. Tanner climbed in the driver's side, closed the door and turned. "There's something I've wanted all evening."

"And you didn't order it?" She swiveled in her bucket seat. Smelling of leather, the front seat felt small and intimate.

A soft smile on his lips, Tanner reached to twine a strand of her hair around his finger. "This wasn't on the menu."

"My hair?"

"I want more than your hair." He leaned toward her.

Tanner's kiss blossomed inside her like a summer flower. Her hands swept up to his cheeks. The scratch of stubble teased her palms. The kiss felt new. Exciting. Like she'd never been kissed before. She wasn't a high school junior anymore kissing Rich under the football stadium bleachers.

Tanner's lips teased her. Made her breathless. She wanted more. He pulled back, eyes deep and mysterious.

"So, beach?"

"Yep. Beach." She needed something cold to douse this heat. Splashing through the cold shallows of Lake Michigan would do just fine.

"I like your parents," he said, turning onto Red Arrow highway.

"They're pretty great. Rebecca and Susan are crazy about them."

Tanner chuckled. "I'd say the feeling's mutual."

"Oh, it is. Where are we headed?" They were driving up the highway away from town.

"A private beach."

"Such mystery." She sat back. His profile revealed nothing. He was good at that.

"I don't like to explain too much. You always say no."

"Wow, that hurts. I do not."

"Yes, you do. Look at what it took to get this date." He laughed. "And just to be clear, this *is* a date. But your mother had to finagle it."

"She's good at that. This is new to me, Tanner." She leaned her head against the cool window as they passed the Harbert Antique Mall, now darkened for the night. "Parenting? That I know and it's a full time job. And from what I've seen, so is dating. My brother became a different man once Mercedes hit town and they started seeing each other."

"That's a good thing though, right? You get along with Finn's wife?"

Lindsay had to think about that. "It took a while. I was protective of Finn, just the way Finn would be with me."

When Tanner turned off the highway, she tried to read a street sign. "We're not going to your house, are we?"

"No. Why? Would that be so terrible?" He squeezed her hand. "Relax. I said we were going to the beach and that's all."

"Good." She wasn't ready for anything more.

"For tonight."

Okay, that made her stomach tighten. Lindsay turned to study the landscape or what she could see of it. Didn't take long to leave the blacktop behind. The side streets outside town were not lit so it was totally dark. The dirt road became bumpy, but Tanner seemed to know his way, maneuvering his SUV to avoid the pockets.

Finally, he pulled up under a pine tree at the front of someone's driveway. At the end of that road, a large home loomed dark against the night sky. Although there were other homes along this road, most were dark. Either the owners weren't at home yet this season or they'd gone to bed.

When Tanner opened her door, night sounds rushed to meet her. A breeze high in the trees. The shush of waves brushing the shore. An owl deep in the woods.

"Where are we?"

He helped her out. "An old friend of mine, Gip McGuire, used to live here. I don't know if his family still owns the place but it looks deserted right now."

"Why didn't we just go to the beach near your house?"

Tanner laced his fingers tighter with hers. "With my luck Leslie or Red would show up." They both laughed, slipping down a sandy path that led to a landing. Their steps echoed on the wooden stairway that took them down to the beach.

Her eyes skimmed the shore to either side. "I never get tired of this. Will you just look at that moon? And all the stars?"

Kicking off his sandals, he left them in the sand. "Let's walk."

She shed her sandals and took his hand. Tanner led her down to the shoreline. The breeze pressed her skirt against her body and sent her hair whirling around her. At the edge of the sand, water lapped with a sleepy rhythm. Tiny, flat pebbles were cool against her feet.

Tanner sucked in a deep breath. "I thought a lot about this beach when I was in Afghanistan."

"I'll bet." But now that she thought about it, Rich had never mentioned the beach,

"Plenty of sand over there," he said. "But no lakes like this. Not for everyone."

"Are you glad to be back in Gull Harbor?" She wondered what his plans were? And hated the fact that she cared.

Dropping her hand, he put an arm around her shoulders. "I am now." Stopping, he tilted her chin up. Her heart throbbed in her throat with expectation. Tanner kissed her.

Oh, yeah. Tanner ignited a fire that had never been lit before.

With the moon and the stars the only observers, they explored. She gave herself to a delicious awakening.

"You taste like pizza," she whispered.

"Mozzarella? Gorgonzola?"

She felt his smile beneath her lips. "I have no idea." Cupping his head in her hands, she kissed him, letting the feelings wash over her.

He traced her chin with a finger. "God, I've thought of this so often."

"You have?" She threw her head back and caught his grin.

"Yep, you bet. The beach, I mean. And now you." He took her hand. "Let's walk."

Her heartbeat settled. "Did you take your leave here in Gull Harbor?" she asked.

"I did. But it wasn't relaxing. By that time Ursula had shown her claws and my dad had health issues." The air grew heavier under the weight of those words.

"I'm sorry." His stepmother sounded like a piece of work.

"Finally my father saw her for what she was. But I wanted him to be happy. With my mother, he had always seemed content. They were in sync with each other —private jokes, favorite dinners...and me. Ursula was never in sync with my father. Not really."

"That sounds sad."

"Sometimes you don't know what you have until you've lost it."

Thinking of her own parents, Lindsay totally understood. "What my parents have is special. They finish each other's sentences. My mother laughs when my dad tells the same joke again and again. Rose can be a bit of an airhead and my dad is very patient. He thinks it's cute."

"Yeah, that is special. Lucky people." There it was—that longing.

The lake kept serving up waves, lapping the shores like soft serve ice cream. If it were daytime, she would see the faint line left in the sand by each wave, overlapping in a beautiful pattern.

"So what about you? What are your plans?" She hated to ask. It always came back to this.

"What do you mean?"

"Do you think you'll be staying in Gull Harbor?"

His forehead wrinkled. "Wish I had an answer. I have to be able to support myself. My father left me the house and a modest inheritance but I need to find..."

"Your groove?" she offered.

He nodded. "Exactly. The service was one thing. I fit there. At least for a few years. But I didn't want to be a career soldier."

She felt a tiny sense of loss. The guy who always seemed to know what he was doing. The man who could throw out all his furniture. "You surprise me, Tanner."

"Really?" He lifted a brow. "And you're the woman who sprang two kids on me."

That hit her the wrong way and her steps dragged in the wet sand.

"Look, I'm sorry." Turning, he hugged her to him, resting his chin on top of her head. She felt secure with those strong arms wrapped around her. "I meant that to be funny. I like what I've seen of your daughters."

That didn't feel like enough. But she wasn't about to drill him about kids. It would really be rude. She should just let that go. It was bad enough that she'd rifled through his family pictures. No need to probe here. "So, have you ever thought of having a family?"

Sometimes her mouth had a mind of its own.

He took her hand again. They began walking. "I don't know. Guys don't think about that stuff the way women do."

"I suppose not." She'd pressed him too far. Darn it all. Lindsay slipped her hand from his.

"Hey, I didn't mean anything by that." Lifting her hand, he kissed it. She fought the feelings awakened by that brush of his lips. "Why don't we just see where this goes? Can we do that?"

The moon shone across the water, a wavering uncertain path.

"Sure." Her voice was a mere whisper. After all, who was she to press him about plans? She'd only just met him. The summer had just begun. But the uncertainty took her back to Rich and the frustrations that had shredded their marriage a little bit at a time.

They didn't say much more. When they turned and walked back to the car, Tanner seemed lost in his own thoughts.

A fragile contentment settled over her.

That lasted until they reached her house.

"Good night, Lindsay Wheeler Swanson," he whispered, with a kiss gentle as a spring breeze.

But summer heat was pressing down. That kiss unleashed a raging torrent of feelings that kept her tossing all night.

Chapter 14

He'd come up short. All day Sunday Tanner fought the feeling that he'd missed something with Lindsay. And it didn't sit right. Sure, he finally scored a date with Lindsay but she was holding back. And he wasn't thinking about sex. After retrieving the Sunday paper from the driveway, he couldn't even read it. The words didn't mean anything. He kept searching for what had gone wrong.

Dinner went well. The walk on the beach ended with kisses that were cosmic. But just when things were heating up, she'd thrown up a blockade.

Tanner told himself that was fine. He was satisfied for now. But his body didn't agree.

Early Sunday morning he got a text from her saying that she wasn't feeling well. They'd have to schedule the dinner with her family for another time. She was holding him off. Tanner didn't call her Sunday and he didn't call her on Monday either. Instead he worked on his studies. He didn't talk about his classes. How many times had he listened to guys who talked a good game but never produced? No, he wanted to have the license in hand before he told her about it.

By Tuesday he was going nuts. He needed to think about this, so he pulled on some shorts and a ripped T-shirt, laced up his tennies and went outside to shoot hoops. The garage was pretty much emptied out now and so was the house. The asthma attacks had faded. No more feeling like his lungs had turned to iron. He had breathing room.

"Hi Tanner."

Tanner turned. "Hey, Red. You're up early."

"I always get up early, just like my sisters." When Red did an eye roll, Tanner swallowed a laugh.

"Does your mom know you're here?" Tanner had left his phone inside.

"Yeah. I told her I was going to check things out."

Sometimes he seemed so adult. "How old are you, Red?"

"Six." He said it with surprise, as if Tanner should know his age. Red wandered into the garage. "Wow. So you sold a lot of stuff, right?"

"A ton." Basketball balanced against one hip, Tanner turned. "And you helped with it."

Red's grinned with pride. He was dressed in khaki shorts and a green shirt. Leslie always had him looking squeaky clean. Even his shoelaces were tied. Then he noticed that they closed with Velcro. That made sense. Making change at the garage sale hadn't been easy for Red, but he had plenty of help. Tanner didn't care if he never made one dime on the stuff.

Squinting up at Tanner as the early morning sun rose over the trees, Red said, "I like your friends."

Tanner began to tap the ball again. "Do you mean the little girls?"

Red's face colored. "Yeah. I really liked Rebecca. Well, Susan too but especially Rebecca."

Looked like this might be serious crush time for Red. "They're nice girls." But Lindsay's older daughter had an attitude. Being an only child, he had no clue how siblings interacted.

"I'm in second grade. Rebecca will be in first grade this year." Red had jammed his hands into the pockets of his shorts.

"So maybe you'll see her in school."

"Maybe. I have some special classes."

"How do you feel about that?"

"Different." As if he was about to share a top secret, Red leaned closer. "I have Down syndrome."

"Yes. I know."

"You do?" He gave his shoulders a little bounce. "No big deal." And that was Red.

Time for some ball. "Here you go," Tanner said, dribbling the ball closer to the little boy. "Grab it when I pass it off to you, okay?"

Red held his hands up. "I'm ready."

The boy was so intense. It was all Tanner could do to keep from chuckling. Bouncing the ball took a lot of concentration. Tanner gave him room and purposely made errors. When Red got close to the hoop, Tanner lifted him to dunk the ball.

After the third time, Tanner dashed inside, grabbed his phone and made a call to Leslie. "I have to go into town for something and I wonder if Red could go with me."

"Fine. You'll need his booster seat," Leslie said.

"I'll be right over." In the background, Tanner could hear the twins fussing.

Twenty minutes later, Tanner and Red were walking the aisles of Toys and Trinkets. The place sold everything from can openers to baby dolls. Families never seemed to come on vacation with enough toys. But the store had what Tanner was looking for. When they got back to the house, Tanner sat on the back stoop with Red, putting it together. The pieces of the hoop slid together pretty easily. Then they threaded the rim through the netting. Red wanted to help so Tanner took it slow.

"Just the right size." Red stood back with satisfaction when they were finished.

"Exactly. Where should we put it?" Tanner had a spot in mind but the hoop belonged to Red.

"Right there. Under yours." Red pointed.

Tanner felt touched. "But what if I hit it, backing out of the garage?"

Red was swinging his arms, like he wanted to get started. "Just be careful."

Tanner would bet that Red heard that all the time from Leslie. "Let's leave it here now and then I'll push it to the side of the driveway when we're not playing." With Red giving directions, he positioned the hoop.

But they couldn't play basketball all day. For one thing, the sun was rising. What had been a soft glow rolling over the treetops became a brilliant hot ball of fire.

Pulling at the collar of his T-shirt, Red said, "I'm getting hot."

"Come on into the house. Want something to drink?"

"You bet." Every freckle on his flushed face stood out.

Stowing the ball in a corner of the garage, they went inside.

After chugging down water, Red went home. He couldn't wait to tell his mom about the basketball hoop. Going inside, Tanner sat down at the computer to knock off more of his class work. With any luck, he'd be in the market when the summer people were still here. From what he could remember, the summer months had been good for his dad. So was football season. Lindsay had that right. Notre Dame fans came for football games and enjoyed seeing the leaves change along Red Arrow. It was a time for making memories. Seeds were planted during those golden autumn days. Families decided they wanted their own home with more frequent stays.

After a quick lunch of peanut butter and jelly, he took his laptop out onto the porch. But the setting was a distraction. The breeze blew enticingly, reminding him of Saturday night with Lindsay. The sound of kids playing drifted up to the porch along with gulls screeching. He closed his laptop. Enough for today.

After slipping into a pair of navy trunks and his flip flops, Tanner grabbed a towel and took the trail down to the lake. Tuesday was usually a quiet day at the beach. Taking a deep breath, he felt the damp air soothe his lungs and worked at internalizing that feeling, just as his therapist had said.

But it was hard to clear his mind. He couldn't make Lindsay a mission that he had to accomplish. There was no denying that he was attracted to her. He loved her outspoken ways. But he'd felt her back away when he was vague about the future. Tanner wanted his plan in place.

The lake brought relief when he waded in, did a shallow dive and swam out to the sandbar. Bobbing in the water and looking up to the house, now barely visible, brought back so many memories. The first day he swam from the sandbar to the shore, his mother had cheered him on. Toward the end, she'd sit down in the shade of a tent his dad had made for her, watching him in the water and smiling. Always smiling, no matter how rotten she felt from the treatment.

Tanner submerged himself in the water. After holding his breath as long as he could, he shot up, shaking off the droplets and brushing back his hair.

Swimming back, he loved the slide of the water over his shoulders. But he still felt restless so he set off down the beach. The sun felt warm on his wet shoulders. The heat in Afghanistan had been crushing. Even the shade didn't offer relief. There was no escaping memories of the hot stretches and barren hills. That took a lot of effort. When he felt his lungs constrict, Tanner slowed down. But the tightness in his chest didn't ease so he turned back toward the house.

Trying to suck in air, he struck a measured pace, just as he'd been taught to do. Finally he reached the house. Scooping up his flip flops and towel, he climbed up, the bushes scratching his legs. He had to spend some time out here, cleaning this out. When he reached the upper level, his cell phone was ringing on the screen porch. Yanking open the door, he scooped his phone off the table.

Lindsay.

"Yes?"

"Tanner, can you come over? My dad is in the hospital." Her voice broke. "Can you watch the girls for me? I don't want them to be stuck in a hospital waiting room."

~.~

Lindsay faced her daughters. Rebecca and Sarah had heard everything. Her mother's panicked call. The call that came from Finn right after that.

"I want to go with you." Rebecca's stubborn bottom lip came out.

"Tanner's coming over." Dashing the tears from her eyes, Lindsay wondered what she should write down for him. How long would Dad be in the hospital? She had no clue. Her invincible father had collapsed in the kitchen. That's all Mom or Finn told her. And it wasn't enough.

"I want to be with Grandma Rose and Poppy John." As usual Rebecca wouldn't give up. The mother-daughter struggle could be exhausting.

Wrapping her arms around Lindsay's leg, Susan said, "I want to come too."

Dressed in the new summer clothes, they looked so cute. Ready for summer. And now this. "Do you want to help Poppy John?" They both nodded solemnly. She hugged them tight. "Then let me go help Grandma Rose. That will help Poppy John. I will call you, okay?"

Another nod. Scenarios surged through Lindsay's head like a

blinking yellow stoplight. "Okay then. Rebecca, will you make sure to tell Tanner where everything is? I need you to do this." For once, her oldest daughter didn't correct her about her name.

Instead, she heaved a miserable sigh. "Okay."

Grabbing a pen, Lindsay jotted down Finn's number. She was still in cutoffs and an oversized shirt that had been her brother's. There was no time to change. The sound of a vehicle pulling up made her run to the door. Getting out of his SUV, Tanner looked so serious, so solid in his gray T-shirt and navy shorts. She pushed open the door. "Thanks for coming. I didn't know what to do. Who to call. My parents usually take care of the girls."

"No problem." His eyes went to Rebecca and Susan. She sensed his trepidation. The three of them would have to work it out. Lindsay wished she didn't have to involve Tanner. But she didn't know who else to call. She just could not picture Mercedes with the kids. Besides, her sister-in-law might be with Finn.

"Look, I'm glad you called." Taking her upper arms in gentle hands, Tanner studied her. "You okay? What's going on?"

She looked away. "We don't really know yet. I don't know how long I'll be there. Rebecca will be able to answer any questions you might have." She could hardly keep back the tears and she hated that. Hated the girls to see their mother so weak.

Opening his arms, Tanner enfolded her. Comfort. He was offering comfort and this felt way too good. A tear squeezed out and dribbled down her cheek. He whisked it away. "None of that, now," he whispered. "I've got you."

As she stood there being a wimp, Susan's hold on her leg

tightened. To Lindsay's amazement, Rebecca joined in the group hug. Then Tanner stepped back and so did the girls. Sniffling, Lindsay ran fingers under each eye.

"Call and let us know what's happening, okay?" His deep brown eyes became pools of reassurance. "We'll be waiting."

"Yeah, Mom. We'll be waiting," Rebecca added.

Nodding, she gulped. Her mind had quieted. Grabbing her keys, she headed for the kitchen door. "I'll talk to you."

The three of them followed her out the door. "And don't drive too fast," Tanner yelled behind her as she climbed into the car.

"I won't." Lindsay's fingers trembled. It took two tries to get the car started.

That drive to Memorial Hospital in Michigan City was the longest twenty minutes of her life. When she barreled through the door of the ER, she saw her mother right away. With a glittery flamingo on her T-shirt, she was slumped in a beige vinyl chair beside Finn. Her brother was leaning forward, elbows on his knees, as if he were waiting to be called into the game. He stood up as she approached. "We don't know much, Lindsay."

Dabbing her eyes with a tissue, Mom raised her red-rimmed eyes. "We were just having coffee. He was reading the paper. Suddenly he was talking gibberish." Finn rubbed his mother's shoulders.

"I kept saying, 'John, are you all right?' But he couldn't answer."

"They're running some tests right now." Finn seemed to be struggling. If her big brother was worried, Lindsay was too. Her heartbeat kicked up. "They'll come out and get us when they bring Dad down. We could sit in the imaging area, but I thought we'd wait for you."

Stepping up to the desk, Finn talked briefly with a receptionist. Lindsay had always hated the smell of a hospital. The sharp antiseptic smell, the funeral home silence of the halls – she hated it all.

Her father's doctor had been called but he was busy with office hours. The hospital staff here were keeping him apprised of the situation. In a corner of the waiting room sat a coffee pot. They drank cup after cup until her stomach burned. Rifling through some magazines, Lindsay couldn't concentrate. Even Finn seemed nervous, tapping messages into his phone.

"Who's with the children?" her mother asked.

"I called Tanner."

Her brother's eyebrows rose.

"I didn't know what to do."

"You could've called Mercedes," Finn said with that big brother tone that made her crazy in their teens. "She's on her way here, but she could have gone to your place."

"What's wrong with calling Tanner?"

Finn ran a hand through his hair. "Nothing. It was nice of him to step in." Her brother was looking tired and stressed.

When a nurse came to the waiting room, they all stood. "You can come back now. He's asking for you."

"He is?" Relief flooded her mother's voice. Finn took her arm. Their footsteps rang on the white tile floors. Inside a cubicle, her father was lying in a bed, covered with a white sheet. Everything in the area was white and silver. The overhead lights bounced off shiny instruments and impressive equipment. Stuff she hoped they never had to use on her dad. Her father gave them a weak wave. "The doctor will be right in," the nurse told them.

"John, honey." Her mother looked like she might collapse onto the bed right with Daddy. "What happened?"

Her dad managed a sheepish smile. "You tell me. One minute I was reading about the Cubs and the next thing I knew, the paper didn't make sense. I couldn't say the words that were in my head. Everything felt strange." She'd never seen her dad look so uncertain.

Thank goodness a doctor arrived. He looked official in blue scrubs with a stethoscope looped around his neck and a clipboard in his hand. After introductions, he told them that that Daddy had a mini stroke. The very word *stroke* made Lindsay's legs feel rubbery. The actual kind of stroke had a much longer name that sifted through her mind like sand. She'd look it up later.

"I tell most patients that is a warning sign that something has to change. Your diet, stress level and maybe your medication. I know it's troubling but a TIA can be a positive thing. I see that Dr. Mercer is your physician and he'll want to see you tomorrow in his office. Call when you get home."

Her mom was busy with Daddy as the doctor talked. Mercedes arrived and Finn introduced her to the doctor who continued his explanation. "The MRI didn't show any brain damage so that's a good thing. I've given your father medication to dissolve any clot.

He can be discharged when he's ready."

Forty-five minutes later, Lindsay was relieved to be out of the hospital. Mercedes went back to the office while Finn drove their parents home. Lindsay followed behind. The drive back gave her time to think of what she wanted to say to the girls. Her brother intended to stay with Dad for a while.

When she pulled into the driveway, the screen door flew open. Rebecca and Susan tumbled out, faces smeared with chocolate.

"How is Poppy John?"

"Is he still at the hospital?"

"Can we see him?"

The two peppered her with questions and she held up a hand. "Poppy John is fine. We can probably go over later. He's resting now, or he should be. You know your Poppy John. He might be out cutting the lawn."

Being children, they accepted that. Tanner was quiet.

"Tanner took us to Oinks," Rebecca announced.

"They have a new flavor called peanut butter and jelly," Susan said, licking her fingers.

"Is that what's on your face?" she asked, studying Susan's chin.

"You were going to call," Tanner reminded her.

"I'm so sorry. I completely forgot." Relief had left her legs wobbly. When she sat down on the blue sofa, the girls flopped next to her. Tanner dug his car keys from his shorts. "Guess I'll hit the road."

"You probably have things to do." But she still wondered what he did all day.

"Oh, I don't want you to leave." To Lindsay's amazement, Susan pulled on Tanner hand.

Tanner tugged one of her braids. "Suzy Q, I think this is a family thing."

Suzy Q?

Lindsay looked from Tanner to Susan, who once hated to be called Suzy. A lot had changed since she left.

Susan's smile was as wide as Lake Michigan "Tanner gave me a nickname."

Chapter 15

When Lindsay showed up at the PR office the next morning, Mercedes threw her a cautious look. "How are you?"

Lindsay snorted, collapsing into her chair. "That's a good question and I don't have an answer. My dad has an appointment with his doctor today. He thinks he's going to drive."

"Finn wants to take them." Mercedes' forehead puckered.

"Good luck with that. My dad's acting like this never happened. I felt guilty dropping the kids off there today." When did her desk get so messy? Pulling out some file folders, she began to sort through the piles. Anything to keep busy.

"And they really don't know what caused it?"

"No. Apparently these mini strokes just happen." The word *stroke* still gave her shivers. She kept filing.

"Finn thinks John should take it easy."

Pushing back, Lindsay studied her sister-in-law. "Wait. Are you talking about the babysitting?"

The look on Mercedes' face gave her the answer. Lindsay slumped in her chair, the filing project forgotten. "When are you going to stop wearing suits?" she asked, feeling super grouchy now. "This isn't New York. And those expensive shoes?"

Staring down at her peep-toe pumps with the red soles that

screamed expensive, Mercedes frowned. "You really are in a bad mood this morning."

"My dad could have died."

"But I thought this was a warning."

"Right. To take it easy. The ER doctor called it 'an opportunity to look at some things.' But my girls aren't stressful. Are they?"

Her sister-in-law gave her an *Are you kidding me* look. Opening her desk drawer, Mercedes took out a nail file. "So how's Tanner?"

Nausea sloshed in Lindsay's stomach. "Fine. The girls got along with him okay, I guess."

"Ah huh." Dropping the file back in her drawer, Mercedes got back to work.

But Lindsay couldn't concentrate. She'd hardly gotten any sleep last night. Her parents had always been there for her. Especially her dad.

The back door opened and Sarah swirled through, the undeniable smell of bakery followed her.

"What's this? Delivery services?" Lindsay teased.

"Calories coming right to our door. Excellent." Mercedes didn't look up.

Bustling over to Kate's empty desk, Sarah set the white box down and opened it, as if she were dispensing medications. "I just thought you girls might like a little something this morning."

News traveled fast in Gull Harbor.

Bakery tissue rustled. The smell of cinnamon blanketed the room. "I'm trying a new recipe. You're my taste testers."

"You are wicked." Glad for the distraction, Lindsay ambled

over and peered down. Frosting had melted over the warm buns, collecting in the cinnamon creases. "Darn. My cutoffs are getting tight."

Sarah nudged the box closer. "Oh, I know a certain someone who won't mind that one bit."

Ignoring the comment, Lindsay lifted out a warm bun. "Who's taking care of the shop?" she asked, taking a bite.

"My mother. I left Nathan and Justin at one of the front tables with some crayons. But I don't intend to stay long." Her eyes settled on Lindsay. "I certainly liked Tanner."

"Ah huh." Lindsay took a bigger bite. Sarah obviously wanted details about the man whose very name made Lindsay's lips swell. "He's just a new client." But putting Tanner in that box felt disloyal. And dishonest.

"Don't believe that, Sarah." Mercedes dug into the box. The moaning she managed with her first bite was almost orgasmic. "He babysat for Rebecca and Susan yesterday. Lindsay actually called for help."

Sarah's smile turned serious. "How is your dad doing, Lindsay?"

"Okay, I guess." She hated the uncertainty. "They're going to dad's doctor, so I'll know more later."

"Finn thinks John should take it easy. Golf. Hang out with the guys," Mercedes said, now deep into the cinnamon buns.

"My father hates golf." Lindsay crinkled up the paper.

Sarah knitted her hands together. "Well, they have that nice Florida week to look forward to every winter."

Mercedes chewed with deliberation. "Maybe they need more

time away. Didn't your mom once live in Florida, Lindsay?"

"Yes, but like your own mother, Mercedes, my mom isn't leaving Gull Harbor."

"Sure but your folks might need more down time." Mercedes just wouldn't stop. Lindsay clenched her jaw. This was like having a tooth drilled.

Eyes circling between the two of them, Sarah looked caught in the middle. "Well now, back to Tanner. What do the children think about him?"

"They can't stop talking about him. It's Tanner this and Tanner that."

Both Sarah and Mercedes smiled. Lindsay wanted to be very careful about the kids. Tanner definitely didn't seem to have any use for children when she first met him. But now with Red around, had his feelings changed? Children weren't a toy to be taken off the shelf when you felt like playing.

Perching on the edge of a desk, Sarah said, "I'd say that's a good sign, right?"

"It's too early for anything."

She'd been telling herself that a lot lately. It was way too early for her to have these crazy feelings about a man she barely knew. But Tanner made it easy to dream. Every slanted look. Every casual touch that set her skin on fire. The way he'd played with her hair on their first date? It felt weird and strangely dangerous. He'd been letting his own hair grow. She longed to run her fingers through it. Lindsay curled her sticky hands tight.

"Good to keep your heart open. You know, in case anything

comes along." Dusting her hands as if she were back in the bakery, Sarah made tracks for the door. "Have a good day, ladies."

The door closed behind her.

Wiping her fingers on a tissue, Mercedes swiveled back to her screen. Together they went over their rising sales figures. A quick call to her mother assured Lindsay that everything had gone well at the doctor's. But as for details, Lindsay would check with Finn.

As she was working in Photoshop on a new ad for *The Beacher*, a text pinged on her phone. Tanner. A chill slithered down her spine. This man had awakened so many feelings. Lindsay felt so alive again. Clicking, she opened the message.

How about supper on the beach tonight? Kids included.

Kids? But she really wanted to go. And so would the girls, especially after their time with Tanner. This felt weird though.

Fine. I'll bring the picnic. What time?

She pressed send. *Fine?* Did that sound abrupt and unappreciative? Would *wonderful* or *terrific* been better? More enthusiastic? While Lindsay sat there and stewed, a reply came zinging back.

Sounds good. I'll pick you up at six.

Her concentration fragmented. What would she bring? Lindsay managed to complete the ad and sent it off. For the rest of the afternoon Lindsay devoted herself to advertising, passing the final copy over to Mercedes. Then it was off to Clancy's to pick up supper.

The small grocery store was crowded with summer people, shopping carts jammed every which way. Standing at the deli, she missed seeing Carolyn Knight behind the counter. A high school teacher at Gull Harbor, Carolyn usually worked the deli during the summer vacation. But this summer she was in Santa Fe, where her grandmother was getting married this month. The wedding wasn't the real draw. Carolyn had met Brody during her last trip. Hopefully, she'd be bringing him back to meet everyone later this summer. Stacking her deli containers of chicken and seafood salad in her cart, she wheeled off to pick up potato chips and pop.

Fifteen minutes later, she was walking through her parents' kitchen door. The air was filled with the spicy scent of chili, her dad's favorite. It didn't matter if it was ninety outside, her mother cooked crockpot chili for her dad once a week. "So, is Dad okay? Did the doctor say everything was fine?"

"Of course." Dressed in her bingo bus apron, her mother looked up from the crockpot and smiled. "Why wouldn't it be, dear?"

So that's the way it was going to be. Mom didn't want to talk about Dad's medical issue. Lindsay walked through to the TV room, where the girls were watching *Dora the Explorer.* "I have a surprise."

"What is it? What is it?" the girls clamored.

"How about having a picnic tonight on the beach?"

"Oh, I love picnics!" Susan clapped her hands with excitement.

"Yuk. I don't want to go." Rebecca stared at the screen.

"Too bad, Rebecca. Tanner is taking us." She dangled that last bit of news.

"What's this about a picnic?" Daddy arrived from the

bedroom, hair rumpled. Had he been napping?

"We're going on a beach picnic. Everything go okay at the doctor today?"

Daddy gave her a hug. "Nothing to worry about. Just some new rules."

Uneasiness plagued her all the way home. She'd talk to Finn. Her brother would give her a straight answer.

When they got home, the girls ran to get dressed while Lindsay filled a cooler with the picnic supplies. A glance at the clock told her she didn't have much time. Pulling her hair into a ponytail, she pulled on clean jeans and a pale pink sweater. They were all good to go when Tanner pulled up. Dressed in a blue V-neck sweater and khaki shorts, Tanner looked boyishly handsome as he strolled up the walk.

"You're a brave man," she said, opening the door.

"Don't scare me." And he leaned in to brush a kiss on her cheek. "You look wonderful, as always."

From the corner of her eye, Lindsay saw Susan nudge Rebecca. This was beginning to feel like a date for four, but she remembered what Sarah had told her today. They were off to the beach.

This time Tanner pulled into the sandy space that led to Chickaming County Beach. So they weren't going to his house. Somehow that made her feel better. Gave her more distance. Lindsay helped the girls from the backseat while Tanner hoisted the cooler to one shoulder. They followed him down the sandy stairs and everyone kicked off their shoes off at the bottom.

Long evening shadows stretched across the sand. Two families were packing up their beach toys. A flock of gulls flitted overhead while others settled in clusters for the night. Sunsets in Michigan were long and lazy. She loved them. Usually the beach brought her a deep sense of peace.

But not tonight.

Rebecca and Susan had brought their beach towels and they were arguing about which way to lay them out.

"Girls! Enough." Everyone was crabby. She felt Tanner's eyes on her as he flapped out a blanket.

"Everything okay?" Coming up behind her Tanner massaged her shoulders.

Rebecca snickered, and Lindsay turned slightly out of Tanner's reach. "We're good." Kneeling on the blanket, she opened the cooler. "Who's hungry?"

Keeping her mind on her task, she doled out the food. The girls wanted chicken salad while Lindsay and Tanner went for the seafood mixture. Legs folded beneath him, he looked comfortable. Sucking in a deep breath, she studied Tanner from the safety of her sunglasses. His hands on her shoulders had felt so nice.

"Aren't you going to eat?" he asked.

"Oh sure, sure." She took her first bite. Lindsay caught the girls glancing at each other and giggling. This probably felt strange to them. After they'd polished off the salad and slices of watermelon, Rebecca and Susan started on the brownies. For a few moments, all was peaceful.

As the horizon turned pink with the setting sun, Tanner placed his hand over hers on the blanket. Heat shot up her arm. Lindsay gently slipped her hand away, pretending to brush sand from her hands. The wind kicked up, sending longer waves onto the sand. She sipped her pop.

"Do you have kids, Tanner?" Rebecca asked.

Lindsay choked and root beer shot up her nose. Tanner handed her a napkin as if he did this every day. "No, I don't have children because I've never been married."

"Do you ever want to have children?" Rebecca asked.

That did it. Jumping up, Lindsay brushed the sand from her jeans. "Why don't we go for a walk? Let's collect rocks." She whisked the empty sandwich bags from the cooler. "You coming, Tanner?" she threw over her shoulder as the girls ran to the shoreline.

"You bet. Just enjoying the view." Coming up behind her, Tanner gave her a soft shoulder bump. "And I like what I'm seeing."

"You're nuts."

Hands in his pockets, he smiled sideways at her.

With the girls in the lead, they walked along the wet edge, studying the tiny pebbles tossed up by waves. Out over the lake, the sun set clouds afire as it passed through them. A comfortable hush lay over the beach. Distracted, Rebecca and Susan scooped up handfuls of stones, made their selection, rinsed them in the water and then plopped them into the bag.

Lindsay fell back to walk with Tanner, who seemed to be enjoying himself. "I love this time of day. We get so busy up at the house that I don't get to come here anymore."

"Why not?" Tanner glanced over with amazement. "Sometimes we take things for granted. Then they're gone."

"Is that how you felt in the service?"

He ducked his head. "Yep. The service and, well, other things in my life."

Lindsay had struck a nerve. She should let it go right there. Before her question, he'd seemed so relaxed. But she wanted to know about that time. "What was it like over there?"

His silhouette stiffened against the evening sky. "It was like being a rubber band, stretched to its limit. You never really slept. You didn't eat the food you wanted. I would have given anything for a chili dog."

"So it's good to be back." He'd turned pensive, remembering. Why had she asked this question?

"Yep." His smile returning, Tanner studied the lake and the shoreline that stretched forever. "Don't get me wrong. Serving my country was what I'd been trained to do. But nothing really prepares you. Enough about that."

Tanner laced his fingers through hers and they walked, their bare feet leaving footprints in the wet sand. Ahead of them, Rebecca and Susan were exclaiming over the stones and filling their bags. Reaching down, Tanner grabbed a flat gray rock. "Do you two know how to skip a stone?"

"Show us!" They were on him in a minute. With Tanner's encouragement, they gathered flat stones. Lindsay wished she could capture their attention the way he did. With the flick of his wrist, Tanner sent a stone winging over the waves. The stone made three splashy skips before sinking and the girls cheered. Then it was their turn. Settling into a slight rise in the sand, Lindsay watched, gathering her knees to her chest. Would this be how it would have been with Rich? Somehow she didn't think so.

A chill settled over Lindsay. What if Rebecca and Susan grew to like Tanner? What if suddenly he wasn't in the picture anymore? The night had darkened, the blue waves turning gray. Susan came to sit beside her, while Rebecca wandered ahead with Tanner. "Will you help me sort my stones, Mommy?"

"You bet." They bent their heads together.

~.~

Rebecca marched ahead of Tanner, but Susan had stayed behind with Lindsay. He twisted to study them. The two made quite a picture, the glow of the setting sun outlining their features as they sat on the sand. It was hard to pull his gaze away.

"These rocks are heavy." Rebecca let her bag fall to the sand.

He didn't know how to take Lindsay's oldest girl. "Then let's have a contest. Skip them over the waves. Get rid of them."

Rebecca perked up. "Great." She nudged the bag between them.

They both grabbed a handful. "I'll count to three," he said.

Things got crazy fast. Even the gulls nearby screeched and flew away. For a little girl, Rebecca had a pretty strong arm. Susan's stones usually sank after one skip, but Rebecca threw them level. "You know how to move your wrist," he said.

"Yeah. You taught me." Rebecca threw him a shy smile.

"Game on." He was enjoying this. The competition got tougher when they both started to laugh.

In the end Tanner did more watching than pitching. Rebecca counted out loud.

"You beat me," he finally announced, collapsing to the sand. She'd skipped thirteen stones and he'd only managed nine.

"I did!" Rebecca looked amazed. She dropped down beside him. "I beat you."

She turned and they grinned at each other.

This was like playing with Red. Maybe Tanner needed more fun times. Kids seemed to have that down pat. "How old are you, Rebecca?"

"Five. I'll be in first grade this year."

"Happy about that?"

"I guess." She wrinkled her nose. "I won't have Susan tagging behind me all the time."

"Does that get to you?"

"Sometimes. My little sister gets all the attention." Obviously this was a sore spot.

Tanner rested back on his elbows. "I always thought it would be nice to have a little brother or a sister."

"You don't have one?" Her chin lifted in amazement.

"Nope, I'm an only child. Trust me, it can get lonely."

"I bet. No one to read stories with at night."

"And no one to teach stuff to. You know, like skipping stones."

"Yeah right." Rebecca seemed to turn that over in her mind. "I guess so."

"It's pretty important, being the oldest one." Okay, he was

laying it on pretty thick but Rebecca seemed pleased. Tanner glanced down the beach. "Maybe we should head back. Your mom's waving to us."

Jumping up, they brushed off and raced each other to the towels.

"Save your old bread," Tanner told the girls, pointing to the gulls that had settled farther down the beach. "Next time we'll feed the birds."

"Okay. All right." They looked excited by the possibility.

Maybe he did know things to teach a child. But Lindsay didn't look convinced. "What?" Tanner looped an arm around Lindsay's shoulder. Glancing up with those smoky gray eyes, she caught her lower lip between her teeth. He could almost taste her lips. "You know I want to kiss you."

"And you know you can't," she whispered. "Not now."

But the girls were busy pulling on their sandals at the stairs. He went for it. Her lips softened under his. She tasted like sunblock and summer.

The breeze teased strands of hair from her ponytail. Brushing her hair back with one hand, he cupped her cheek and gave her a coaxing smile. "Relax, Lindsay."

She chuckled. "It's not easy."

Tanner helped her fold the towels. She was probably worried about her dad. "Everything will be all right." He lifted the cooler onto his shoulder.

"Will it?" She didn't look convinced.

Chapter 16

For the next few days Tanner lived on coffee and junk food. The caffeine kept him revved up for his online courses. Terms like *titles*, *easements* and *fiduciary responsibility* took his mind off Lindsay's lips. Her warm gray eyes. Her legs that ran forever. Usually he was good at focusing. Military school had taught him that. If you had a mission, you blocked everything else out. Otherwise you'd be a dead man.

He was a dead man.

How could he concentrate on fluctuating mortgage rates? All he could think about was Lindsay. He'd texted her about her father but the response came quick and short. John was fine. Everyone was fine.

Well, no. Tanner was not fine.

His hormones were raging as if he were sixteen again.

When he needed a break, he turned to basketball. Usually Red appeared. Together, they positioned the new hoop. The idea was to match each other's shots. But in the end, Tanner followed Red's lead. "You're sure missing a lot, Tanner," Red said with an amazed shake of his head. "You feeling okay?"

"Cut me some slack, Red." And he'd take another shot, aiming right of the rim. The ball bounced off. Red ribbed him some more.

It was great.

Leslie had come over to thank him for the hoop. "I don't know why I didn't think of this," she said. She had a way of standing in between her back door and his driveway, calling out her comments with an ear cocked to the twins inside.

"You probably never play basketball." *And you have three kids to mind.* But of course he didn't say that out loud.

Head tilted to one side, she gave him a quiet smile. "You know, I think you're right."

Blowing a kiss to Red, she'd walked back into the shadows of the birch that stood at their back door. Tanner kept coaching Red. The kid was getting pretty good now that the hoop was the right height.

Coffee sloshed in his stomach. The acidity made him feel nauseous. Or maybe it was Lindsay's silence. Tanner took out his phone to call her at least three times. But what would he say? He wanted to have a plan in place before he took this relationship any further. Right now, he had no prospects and no plans, just a modest inheritance and this house. That wasn't enough. Not in his eyes.

He'd been walking the beach a lot. The lake stretched to the horizon—endless, mysterious and soothing. He liked to come down early before the damp sand was full of footprints. As he walked, Tanner scooped up rocks to wing out over the lake. Smiling, he'd think back to how hard Rebecca and Susan had tried until they succeeded. They were competitive. He didn't know that about girls, and he filed it away.

Sometimes he'd come upon a fire pit. The charred remains took him back. High school kids probably came down here. He could almost hear the music and feel the campfire singe his skin. But he'd missed all that. Maybe he'd play catch-up with Lindsay some night.

One day the wild brush out front bothered him bad. The place looked rundown. He'd noticed all the houses on his morning walks looked well tended. His wasn't measuring up. Pulling on his work boots, Tanner started to work clipping, cutting and pulling. Buzzing around his face and neck, the mosquitoes drove him crazy but he kept going. By the end of the day, he had a pile of trash at the curb for next Monday's pickup. Best, of all, he could see the lake from the house. After he showered and put hydrocortisone cream on all his bites, Tanner chilled out on porch with a peanut butter and jelly sandwich and a beer. The lake unrolled before him. The drone of boat motors drifted up from the water. It had been a good day's work.

Toward the end of the week the furniture arrived. Beefy guys brought in the chairs and angled them toward each other in the living room. Tanner drank in the rich smell of leather. The furniture reminded him of that special day with Lindsay. He couldn't wait to show her.

The coffee table made a nice addition. Like the dining room table, the surface had a rich grain. He ran his fingers over the smooth finish while the men brought in the six spindled chairs.

After watching the truck leave, he went back inside and tried out an armchair. The leather squeaked a bit as he settled. The armrests were the perfect height. The pieces changed the room completely. What a relief to have that awful red and gold gone. One piece after another, he was eliminating his stepmother. That night he picked up a sandwich at Whistle Stop and took it onto the screened porch. He breathed in the clear night air. Set among the tall trees, the porch helped him forget the house and everything that had happened there.

~.~

"I thought I'd invite your boyfriend for Sunday dinner," Lindsay's mother mentioned on Thursday, flamingo earrings dangling from her ears.

Lindsay had just arrived to pick up the kids. They were both standing in the kitchen. Rebecca and Susan had run to stow away their puzzles and coloring books.

Have Tanner here for dinner? No way. "He's not my boyfriend. But he did send me a text asking about Daddy." That's all it had been—a polite inquiry. Sometimes she couldn't understand him.

"That's sweet." Her mother lifted the cover of the slow cooker. The smell of her father's favorite pork roast wafted out.

"But we're not dating. Nothing like that."

"Oh, I think he's very interested in you." Her mother's eyes sparkled. Smelling the roast brought on a crazy craving. Maybe it was for pork. But maybe her hunger involved something else entirely.

Lindsay pulled her focus back to the food. It would be so easy to eat here every night. But lately, she'd been pulling out her own recipes and experimenting – not that the girls appreciated it. They could eat hot dogs and be happy.

"Isn't Tanner your boyfriend, Mom?" Susan asked, coming back into the room with Rebecca. "I told Grandma he was."

"No, he's not." She recoiled from the word.

"But he taught us how to skip stones," Rebecca said, as if that settled everything.

"That doesn't mean he's my boyfriend." Lindsay worked to keep her voice steady. Her mother was humming what sounded like "Here Comes the Bride."

"He taught me too." The defensive tone Susan often used with her older sister made Lindsay crazy.

"But mine went farther."

"That's enough." Lindsay slammed the drawer shut. The humming stopped.

Susan's eyes brimmed. "I know. You have longer arms."

"Doesn't matter. I even beat Tanner."

"You did?" Susan drew back in amazement.

Rebecca shrugged. "Well, he taught us. But yeah, I beat him." She gave her sister a high five.

Tanner seemed to have won Rebecca over. "See you later, Mom."

"You go home and put your feet up, sweetheart."

Sure, like she could do that. Her mom gave her a hug and Lindsay led the kids out to her car. But as the girls climbed into their booster seats, her mother stuck her head out the door. "What about Sunday dinner?"

Lindsay was tempted to pretend she hadn't heard. But her mother had enough stress in her life right now with dad. "Let's just see."

Her mother didn't look happy. Waving good-bye, Lindsay backed out of the driveway.

"Are we having hot dogs for supper again?" Rebecca asked on the way home.

"I thought you liked hot dogs."

"I'm sick of hot dogs."

Susan caught Lindsay's eye in the rearview mirror. "I like hot dogs, Mommy. I could eat them all."

"I want peanut butter and jelly," Rebecca said.

It was only July. How would Lindsay make it through the next six weeks? "We're having beans too."

"Yuck." Both girls spat out the word that made them friends again.

While Lindsay fixed supper, her mind circled Tanner. Why hadn't he called? She thought that evening on the beach with the girls went pretty well. But she couldn't blame him. After all, she wasn't a single woman. She was a package. That made things different for any man. She understood that. Cole Campbell had one daughter Natalie when Kate came back to town. Sparks flew and they dated. But one child was simple. Two sisters who competed for attention? Whole different ball game.

Sitting on the sofa after the girls went to bed, she opened her laptop. Nothing from Tanner. She wished hot dogs and beans weren't churning in her stomach. He'd kissed her on the beach as if it meant something. Lindsay hadn't dreamed this up. Or had she? She tapped her fingers on the keyboard. Her resolve melted under the heat of her memories. But she wasn't a woman who waited around.

She began to type. *My mother wants to know if you'd like to come for dinner Sunday night.*

Lindsay stared at the words. Subtext was *I miss you. Miss the way you look at me as if you have something on your mind. Like making love in that big bed. I can almost feel those gray sheets against my back because, oh Tanner, it's been so long. And you're the sweetest man ever, even though you don't know where you're going.*

Whoa. Where had that come from?

For at least five minutes she sat staring at a water stain on the ceiling. She had to have the roof patched. Her fingers drummed the keys. Where was she? Right, she was inviting Tanner to Sunday dinner.

She pressed Send.

Getting up, she tossed a bag of popcorn into the microwave. Then she crept down the hallway and peeked into the girls' room. Rebecca and Susan were both sound asleep. The day with grandma and grandpa must have exhausted them. While she melted some butter, Lindsay wondered if she should hire a babysitter this summer. So far, she'd avoided that. Sitters were expensive. Her parents might be offended.

Or would they be relieved?

Maybe they wanted to move to Florida. A nervous shimmer swirled in her stomach at the thought. But things were changing. Always so vibrant and active, they were getting older. Her mother's most exciting activity was the bingo bus on Wednesday and Friday nights. In the winter they were stuck inside a lot.

Fingers buttery, she was watching a rerun of *Jeopardy* when she heard the ping. Lindsay swallowed carefully. Setting the bowl of popcorn aside, she picked up her laptop.

The message was from Tanner.

Although that sounds great, I was hoping you might come over here. I'd like to show you the new furniture and cook for you. The last part of your message? Don't know what to say, except I need mouth-to-mouth.

What? Clicking into her Sent box, Lindsay felt a wave of nausea scuttle the popcorn in her stomach. There it was, the whole message. Her meandering, passion-filled thoughts, all there for him to see.

Oh, crap, crap, crap. What had she been thinking? Why wasn't she more careful? No wonder he wanted her to come over. First she felt embarrassed. Then she got mad.

What kind of woman did he think she was?

She'd show him. *The girls would love that. What time?*

No hesitation on his part. His answer came right back.

Well, fine. Six o'clock? Want me to pick you up?

A nice gesture but no.

Not necessary. I can drive myself.

He didn't hesitate a bit.

Do the girls eat hot dogs?

She chuckled.

Sure. And chips. Nothing fancy.

The guy did not seem at all put off.

Done.

Lindsay stared at the one word a long time. The front windows were open. A cool breeze filtered through the sheers. She needed it. Lindsay felt feverish.

Done? Oh, she was so done.

Done in was more like it.

What was happening? When had she ever felt this disoriented?

And it hit her like one of the trucks out on the highway. Was she falling in love?

~.~

All the way over to Tanner's, Lindsay rattled off directions. "Watch your mouth. Don't be grumpy. No arguing. And whatever you do, don't touch anything."

"Okay, Mom." In the back seat, Susan clapped her new pink tennis shoes together. She'd worn them especially for Tanner. The soles lit up when she walked.

"But what if I wanted to touch something?"

"Rebecca?" Glancing in the rearview mirror, Lindsay sent a stern look at her oldest daughter. "Why would you want to touch anything?"

Lips pressed together, Rebecca looked out the window. The stores and restaurants along Red Arrow Highway were whizzing by. "Well, if I sit down, I'll be touching something, right?"

The Roadhouse was coming up. Lindsay was tempted to pull into the parking lot and send Rebecca inside with twenty dollars for dinner.

I am a terrible mother.

Lindsay pressed the accelerator and they shot past the popular restaurant.

"Geez. Slow down, Mom," fretted the child she'd almost abandoned.

Lindsay should be sent to jail for even having such a thought. She would appeal to Rebecca's common sense. "I meant touching glass windows and table tops with your hands. None of that. Hands to yourself."

Why hadn't she turned down this invitation?

Turning onto Sleepy Hollow Lane, she slowed down. Her heart was pounding like Lake Michigan on a stormy day. She should have insisted that he come to her parents' house. At least there the adults would outnumber the children.

Pulling into the driveway, she parked. How she hoped she didn't make a fool of herself. On Friday she'd cleaned the Morgans' kitchen floor with dish soap. Swishing her mop from side to side, she noticed bubbles rising. What was happening to her?

Tanner Phelps was happening.

The garage doors were shut. Although she had a key, using it for a social occasion didn't seem right.

Opening the back passenger door, she straightened her new blue top with the chilly shoulder cut-outs and hoped her white shorts weren't too short. She'd been told many times that her legs were her best assets. But tonight? After that totally sexy text, she didn't want him thinking the wrong thing.

No, she had that covered. "Come on, girls." She herded them from the car.

They didn't need to ring the bell. Tanner opened the kitchen door when they reached the top step. "Come on in."

"You've been in the sun." His dark tan set off the white T-shirt. Inside the kitchen hot dogs were laid out on the island, along with ketchup, mustard and bags of chips. Opening her arms, Susan went up on her tiptoes for a hug. Surprise widened his eyes, but Tanner bent and gathered her into his arms. "Suzie Q!"

Then he turned. "And the girl who beat me at stone skipping." He gave Rebecca a high five. She was all smiles.

Lindsay could smell his fresh cotton shirt. Hands on the counter, she made a great show of studying the bags of chips. "Barbecue flavor?"

"Yeah. Are those okay? You like barbecue?"

"Love it. I mean, it's fine."

When his eyes lifted, she saw a kiss in those eyes. Did he make a slight kissing bow with his lips? Maybe she'd imagined it. But he was grinning.

She had an overactive imagination.

Tanner turned toward the dining room. "Want to see the new furniture? Your mom helped me pick out this set."

The wood glowed in the late afternoon sun. "Oh my gosh. This table looks better in your dining room that it did at the shop."

"I thought the same thing." Tanner ran his hand over the top of the table. She did a quick cut to Susan and Rebecca because of course they wanted to touch the table.

"No touching," she mouthed to her daughters while Tanner swept a hand over the surface. Oh, how she wanted to be that wood. Feel his fingertips on her skin.

I am losing my mind.

Then it was on to the living room where the new chairs looked, well, stiff.

"Wow, these are big. Can I sit in one?" Susan asked.

"Of course." Tanner shrugged. "They're chairs."

Susan scrambled into it and Rebecca took the other chair.

"Can you feel how the seat fits your body?" Tanner asked.

"I can." Susan said.

"Of course *I* can." Taller than her younger sister, Rebecca lifted her elbows to rest them on the arms. "Where's all the rest of your stuff?"

"We sold it at the garage sale, remember?" Tanner looked to Lindsay for confirmation.

"I think it looks wonderful. Can I try, Susan, er, Suzie Q?" The leather squeaked as Susan slid from it. When Lindsay sank into the chair, the leather was buttery soft and so were the armrests. But alone in this living room the chairs resembled two awkward guests, the coffee table stretched in front of them.

"There's something for both of you out on the porch." Tanner motioned to the door.

Sure enough he had coloring books and crayons. She had to smile at his thoughtfulness.

"What do you say, girls?"

"Thank you, Tanner." At least they'd have something to do. The coloring books were both from a popular new kids' movie. Tanner was learning and she smiled softly at him. He winked back.

When Tanner went to start the grill, she followed. "Hey, I can see the lake. The view is beautiful from up here."

"I thought it was time to clean things up."

Lindsay wasn't sure what that meant. Was he getting the house ready to sell or ready to rent? The air felt cooler and she wished she'd brought a sweater.

"I like the top," he said, stirring the coals.

"Thanks." Suddenly she wasn't sorry about leaving the sweater behind.

Although she couldn't see the girls sitting on the porch around the corner, she could hear them.

"What do you know? They aren't arguing," she said.

"I think you handle them beautifully." The franks sizzled when he dropped them on the grill.

"So you're tossing compliments around? Just like that?" But she felt pleased.

"Come here," Tanner said, setting his fork to the side.

"But the girls..." She hesitated.

He opened his arms. "They're still busy. And I haven't seen you in a long time."

"Just a week"

"Forever." He kissed her.

She could feel her skin sizzle, as if she'd been dropped on that grill. *Forever.* The word echoed in her mind and heart. Was Tanner forever?

Dinner went fine. They ate on the porch. After they'd cleared the table, Rebecca and Susan played tic, tac, toe. He asked questions about Lindsay's work, and she told him about the insert planned for the paper. Tanner seemed genuinely interested in the progress their PR department was making. The girls were sleepy, even after eating Dove bars with the dark chocolate that breaks off in huge chunks. The sun set and a hush fell over the lake. Fireflies flickered over the lawn, disappearing into the trees. A natural sense of peace seemed to come with the darkness.

Then it was time to go. No arguments. Her girls had droopy eyes. Tanner walked them to the car. After settling the girls in the back, Lindsay closed the door and turned. Crafty man that he was, Tanner edged her into the space between the back window and the trunk—the car's "blind spot."

His kiss was barbecue and chocolate, everything that she liked. Every bone in her body melted against him. How she wished they weren't out here, leaning against the car. Finally she pushed back. "Thanks for tonight."

For a long moment, he gazed at her. Then Tanner frowned.

"What is it?"

He chuckled. "Just thinking about your text."

"Oh, that." Her cheeks stung with embarrassment.

"Did you mean it?" He gave her a little shake, as if to dislodge the truth.

"Yes and no."

"His frown deepened. "Yes to what...and no to what?"

"You figure it out," she said kissing his cheek and sliding into the driver's seat.

Chapter 17

"Look at these numbers," Mercedes crowed the next time Lindsay stopped in the office. "Your insert was a big success."

"Lindsay peered over Mercedes shoulder. "Wow. Have you told Kate?"

"She's coming in today. Let's surprise her. She's been grumpy. The pregnancy's getting to her."

Adrenaline surged through Lindsay. She had to share the good news. Only one person came to mind. Grabbing her bag, she said, "See you later, okay Mercedes? I've got errands to run. Um, more inserts to drop off."

"Sure. Later." Mercedes went back to studying the screen. "Kate will be so excited to see this."

Lindsay nearly tripped on her way down the stairs. Bursting into the fresh air, she felt the world had never looked brighter. She would not be cleaning cottages all her life. This business venture with Mercedes could change everything. Hope soared.

Taking out her phone, she called Tanner. He picked up on the first ring.

"We're celebrating."

Tanner laughed. "Great. What are we celebrating?"

"My insert was a big success. Our numbers are on the rise

and…" Excitement knotted the words in her throat. She sounded like a fourth grader with a good report card.

"That's wonderful. I think I should take you out for lunch."

How could she refuse? "Brunch at Blue Plate Cafe?"

"Is that place still there?" He sounded nostalgic.

"It is. You can take a trip down memory lane."

"Great. I'll pick you up. Where are you?

"The PR office. I'm parked on the side."

"I'll be right there."

Of course after she hung up, Lindsay wondered if she'd been too bold, calling him like this. But he was the man she wanted to call. Leaving her car door open, she sat in the shade of the oak, enjoying the breeze. From here she could see Whittaker. Families with shopping bags strolled past. Most of the stores opened at eleven. What they were doing would benefit those shops. Satisfaction filled her. Together with Mercedes they could build Beach Vacations.

The black SUV rounded the corner and Tanner pulled in, looking mysterious in his aviator sunglasses. He pushed opened the door and she climbed in. "It's warm in here."

"And it could get warmer." Reaching across, he brought her close. The kiss was long, thorough and reminded her of what she'd been missing.

A couple walked past, Lindsay backed away. "What was that?"

"A congratulatory kiss." Tanner turned the air up higher.

"I like it." That must be obvious.

"Me too." He looked as dazed as she felt. "You look pretty."

"Just my jeans and a white shirt.

He put the SUV in gear. "Now tell me about the insert. I'm not getting the local paper yet. Just the *Wall Street Journal.*"

As they traveled up Red Arrow, she outlined the insert. "I added shots of various houses, with their permission of course."

"Hey, I feel hurt. You never asked me." He was cute when he pouted.

How could she tell him that his house, as it was now, wasn't exactly welcoming? And then there was the occupancy issue. Would he even be renting it out? "I focused on clients whose homes have been with us for a while."

"Hmm. That sounds as if I have to prove myself."

You just have to be around. "Sort of."

Gravel crunched under their tires as they pulled into the lot in front of Blue Plate Cafe.

"This is amazing." His eyes scanned the few shops strung together with the restaurant at the end. "Some things don't change."

"Are you happy about that?"

"Sure. But I welcome new experiences." Arching a brow, he opened the door. She jumped out, her stomach doing somersaults.

Two minutes later they were seated at a window. The place smelled of cinnamon coffee cake and bacon. They both ordered coffee. He decided on bacon and eggs with hash browns and she defaulted to the chocolate chip pancakes. "My usual," she said.

"Tell me all about the insert." Leaning across the table, Tanner looked interested. So she launched into some details.

The moment felt special, the sun falling through the window. "This feels great. So normal, as we were..." She clamped down on her lip. If only she could learn not to say everything that popped into her head.

"Not sure I follow you." He looked puzzled.

How could she explain? Sitting here, they felt like a couple. But Tanner might be leaving. His plans weren't clear, at least not to her.

"Earth to Lindsay." His low, husky voice called her back. "What are you thinking?"

"Oh, nothing." She took a sip of coffee, although she sure didn't need any caffeine.

Tanner's twisted smile said he didn't believe her. The waitress slid two plates onto the table. Tanner dug into his eggs. Lindsay spent time spreading butter on her chocolate chip pancakes before drizzling syrup on top.

She glanced up to find Tanner watching her. "Is this some sort of a ritual?" he asked.

"Sort of. I love chocolate chip pancakes. And I like them a certain way."

"I guess. Maybe I ordered the wrong thing."

Lifting her first forkful, she savored the warm chips exploding in her mouth. Tanner was still studying her and she closed her eyes.

"You're a lot of fun, you know that?"

Her eyes flew open and she swallowed. "In what way?"

"You take on projects like a trooper. Manage to be a mom to two girls while you work. But you also know how to have fun."

"Doesn't feel that I've been having much fun lately."

"It doesn't?" He looked stricken.

"I don't mean us." She waved a sticky fork between the two of them.

He caught her hand. "Damn, I sure hope so."

They were dancing on the edge of something. Easing her hand from his, she went back to her pancakes. "We have more than fun."

His expression shifted. "Glad to hear it. So what's the problem. I hear a *but* in your voice."

For once in her life, she considered her words. Kept her mouth stuffed with chocolate so she wouldn't say something she'd regret. "Hard to explain," she finally said. "But I really like you."

His brown eyes got that warm syrup look. Only halfway through the hash browns, Tanner set down his fork.

"What, you're not hungry?"

"Yes. I'm very hungry." He pushed his plate aside. "But not for breakfast."

"Then I guess it's a good thing we're almost finished."

Although she'd downed a glass of orange juice, Lindsay felt parched.

Thirsty. Hungry. Wanting him. "Well?"

He threaded the fingers of one hand through hers.

"My hands are sticky."

"I don't care." He waved for the check.

They escaped into the July heat. Swirls of dust billowed when a truck roared past. Her heart was pounding. By the time the two of them piled into the SUV, her eyes were watering.

"What's wrong? Are you crying?" Tanner turned up the air.

"No, I've got something in my eye."

"Hang on." Clicking open the console, he whipped out a small bottle.

"You're amazing."

Hands gentle, he tilted her head back. "Glad you think so. Look up."

He was being so sweet. So close. Eager to help, he squeezed out drops and she blinked. "Lindsay?" The bottle slipped from his fingers.

Her name was a whisper, a soft breath on her cheek. Gathering her into his arms, Tanner kissed her. Teased her first with a soft brush of his lips and then really kissed her. He tasted of coffee and bacon, a lethal combination.

She'd never wanted anything more than she wanted Tanner right now. This dear man had walked into her life totally by accident just at a time when she thought her life was arranged and running smoothly. But it wasn't. She knew that now.

"Hey, you okay?" Tanner drew back. She laid one palm on his thudding heart.

"Yes, yes." She shut her eyes tight against the sunny day and everything rational. All she wanted right now was Tanner.

"Then we're off. My place?"

"Yes. Definitely."

Hammering down on the accelerator, Tanner roared onto the road. While he drove, Lindsay threaded her fingers through the back of his hair. "You're letting your hair grow out."

"That buzz cut was marking me. People kept asking me if I was in the service."

"What, you didn't like that? You should be proud." When she lifted her hand, he brought it right back with his own.

"I don't like to be thanked. I did what any man would."

The garage door rose as they drove down Tanner's driveway. Nerves zigzagged through her body, like electrical wires trying to connect. She wasn't going to overanalyze it. Lindsay wanted to stay in the moment.

But what am I doing? Shutting down any questions, she just felt.

The wide door open, Tanner drove into the cool shade of the garage. She thought he might drive right through the back. When he slammed on the brakes, her seatbelt caught her. She tumbled out of the SUV and he was there, pulling her into his arms. He smelled of sunshine and hope when he kissed her. His hands were landing in spots he'd never explored before and that felt good too. "Oh, Tanner."

"Hold that thought." Leading her up the stairs, he fumbled with the back door key. Then they spilled into the kitchen. Heated kisses led them to the master suite. A lot of moaning was going on and she couldn't tell if that was her or Tanner.

Lindsay opened her eyes. "Wow." She'd forgotten that they'd sold all the bedroom furniture. Only the mattress lay on the floor, covered by the gray sheet and that ugly gold comforter. "This looks like camping."

"Sorry. Guess I should order a new bed frame."

"It doesn't matter."

Cupping her face in his hands, he whispered, "Good. We have all we need."

Her worries were dissolved by his kisses, swept away like footprints in damp sand.

Sliding her T-shirt up and off, he kissed her neck. The soft spot under her chin tickled and she crunched her chin down. Her hands reached out. He was so tempting. When she pulled off his shirt, his strong male scent mixed with bacon made her woozy.

But the red dots on his chest woke her up. "What's this?"

"The mosquitoes like me."

"Poor boy. I'll make it better." While he groaned, she kissed every pink dot. They took their time undressing each other, as if this were Christmas and they wanted to delay the surprise.

Somehow they ended up on the bed. "You are so beautiful, Lindsay."

"Not what I used to be," she sighed. "Two kids. It changes you."

But he covered her regret with his body. Did delicious things that made her forget any reservations. She felt like a teenager again. Except it wasn't like this at eighteen. Eighteen had been fumbling and giggling. This was so much more. Every kiss, every stroke, every intimate invasion—so much more.

Later, they lay cocooned in contentment. Grabbing the comforter, he pulled it up to her chin. They both flipped onto their backs

"What are you staring at?" Tanner asked.

"The chandelier."

Hands crossed behind his head, Tanner looked up. "Yeah, that has to go."

"Wasn't your father afraid it would fall on him?"

His laugh was dry. "Men do strange things for the women they love."

She held her breath. It was way too early, but the words *love* and *Tanner* merged in her mind, as if they belonged together.

Flipping onto their sides, they faced each other. Some things were certain in this life. As sure she loved chocolate, Lindsay knew she wanted this face beside her every morning. But it was way too early. She yanked the comforter against her lips so the wrong words wouldn't spill out.

"Hey, what are you doing? I liked the view. Especially those long legs."

Pleasure uncoiled inside. "Such compliments. You'll spoil me."

"I intend to. You just haven't been with the right guys." When he shook his head in disbelief, a curl fell over his forehead.

Okay, this wasn't the time to admit she'd only been with one man. She'd fallen for Rich when she was only sixteen. With him she'd felt safe.

This didn't feel safe.

This felt edgy and thrilling.

"A penny for your thoughts." He gently touched her nose with a finger.

She swallowed hard. "I like your hair longer."

"Really? Sometimes it drives me crazy." He swept one hand through it, as if he'd like to tear it right off.

"Yeah, it drives me crazy too."

Tanner chuckled deep in his throat. "Then it stays." His kiss took her right back to where they'd been an hour ago.

The shadows in the room shifted. She should leave soon. Her parents might be wondering. She'd told them she was working half a day. Church school had ended for the season.

But she couldn't help herself. "Oh, Tanner," she whispered. "We should stop." But he was busy. Yep, she was a goner.

He took her back to the office so she could pick up her car. All the way home, she tried to clear her head. Erase any trace of Tanner. That wasn't easy. She'd showered at his house. The scent curling through her car was spicy and clean. Her fingertips tingled from tracing that cobra tattoo over his shoulder again and again.

There would be no turning back. But where were they going? What were his plans? Her excitement fizzled a bit. How well she remembered waiting for Rich to come through for her, for their family. Oh, he talked about his dreams a lot but then he'd lose or leave another job.

By the time she pulled into her parents' driveway, her mood had changed. Maybe she should step back. Keep her head on straight. Slinging her purse over one shoulder, she stepped out and tucked in her top. She had to look presentable.

Rebecca and Susan met her at the door. "Oh, Mommy, wait 'til you hear. We have exciting news."

"Really?"

Her mother turned from the sink, a potato peeler in one hand. "Are you all right, sweetheart? Your face is pink. Maybe you should wear more sunblock."

"Oh it's nothing." She smiled, thinking of the stubble on Tanner's face. "Just the sun coming through the car window."

"Mommy, Mommy! Let Grandma Rose tell you our news." The girls danced around her.

"Well, what is it?"

"Guess who I just talked to?" Her mother beamed at her. "Tanner's coming for supper Sunday."

Chapter 18

The week had been a roller coaster ride. The unexpected but oh, so nice afternoon with Tanner was followed by crazy worry. He was coming to dinner. As she drove toward her parents' house Sunday, she felt they were jumping ahead. Lindsay wasn't ready for this. But she couldn't blame her parents. After all, Rebecca and Susan talked about him all the time.

Last week she'd taken the girls to the beach twice, both times with a late picnic lunch. The weather had turned warmer. After dunking in the lake and playing Frisbee with her in the shallows, all Rebecca and Susan wanted to do was skip stones. "Just like Tanner taught us," Rebecca had told her, eyes round and solemn. The two of them had contests.

Somehow he'd become a part of their lives. But was it too soon? Had she let the relationship get out of control? Each kiss, casual touch or teasing look took her to a whole new place. Lindsay felt way out of her comfort zone, as if she were plummeting down a water slide. She might struggle to slow the pace, but the rushing water swept her along.

Today, her mother was that rushing water and Lindsay wasn't ready.

"Mom, aren't you going to take us to Poppy John's?" Susan

asked from the back seat.

"Yes. Why?"

Her little girl had wanted to wear her hair down today. Soft curls caught the sun through the back window. Susan had insisted that Lindsay do the same.

"Because you just drove past their house." Rebecca held her pink plastic Barbie dolls case.

"Oh, my." Making a U turn at the next intersection, Lindsay headed back, ignoring the titters in the back seat.

"Rebecca, your hair looks so pretty." Usually Rebecca wore braids. The long curls were too messy for her.

"Her name is Becky," Susan piped up. "And I'm Suzie Q."

"Whatever you say." Lindsay didn't want to start an argument now. Mom had told her five o'clock. She wanted to get there before Tanner so she could brief her parents. Get things straight with them.

Pulling up, Lindsay parked on the street. Finn's car was already there.

As she opened the door, the smell of her mother's pot roast assured her that all was right with the world. Didn't matter that the temperature was ninety. If it was Sunday, then pot roast was on the menu.

"There you are." Throwing open his arms, her father was sitting in his favorite lounge chair, with Finn on the sofa. They were watching baseball.

"Poppy John!" Rebecca and Susan threw themselves at their grandfather.

Poor Daddy. But he loved it. Finn rose to his feet. "How's my little sister?"

They hugged. "Not so little in case you didn't notice." Her voice was muffled by his broad shoulder.

"So I hear company's coming today," Finn said, keeping his voice low. Wearing black and white capri pants with a black halter top, Mercedes was busy with the girls.

"Not my idea." She pushed away. "Mom told me after she'd invited Tanner."

"So, you two are getting serious?"

It was the tone that really got her. The same big brother, know-it-all voice he'd used while they were growing up. When he felt Daddy shouldn't let her use the car right after she'd gotten her license, he used that tone. Her parents had been more lenient with Lindsay, maybe because she was the youngest. That never sat well with Finn.

"Depends on what you mean by serious." Peeling away, she headed for the kitchen.

"There you are." Standing in the steam rising from the crockpot, her mom offered her cheek for a kiss. "I'd hug you, honey, but both hands are full." She poked the roast with her meat fork. New potatoes were nestled around the meat in the bubbling drippings that would become gravy.

"Smells wonderful in here."

"Just the same old meal." Mom popped the top back on the pot.

The green bean casserole covered with onion rings stood ready for the oven, just like always. The jitters in her stomach? They were an unnerving addition to Sunday dinner.

"I hope Tanner likes it," Mom said, pushing back her short blonde wave. "He said pot roast was fine."

"Oh, he did, did he?"

Her mother gave her a glance. "Your hair looks nice like that, honey. I wish you'd wear it long more often. You look so pretty in curls."

"Long hair isn't practical for cleaning toilet bowls. Can I help?"

With a nod toward the dining room, her mom said. "You can set the table."

Pulling open the silverware drawer, Lindsay tried to keep her mind on forks and knives. Everything, even this smallest ritual, felt different tonight. Her mind was filled with Tanner. His hands, his lips, the whispered words that came back to her at night when she couldn't fall asleep—Tanner was about all she thought about. The kids couldn't even trust her to drive two blocks to her parents' house. She was that preoccupied.

The doorbell rang and silverware fell with a clatter.

Mom turned. "Lindsay? You all right?"

"Sure." Forks pricked her fingers when she tried to pick them up.

"Well, let's just see who that is." As if she didn't know. Wiping her hands on the Join the Bingo Bus apron, Mom headed for the front door.

Lindsay followed, but Finn got there first. Opening the door, he blocked the way.

"Hi, Finn." Below that broad smile, Tanner held a bouquet of bright pink gladiolas.

Stepping around Finn, Mom said, "Tanner, how nice that you could come. Are those for me?"

"Yes, ma'am." But while Tanner nodded at Mom, his eyes veered to Lindsay. Heat crackled through her body. She was almost relieved when Rebecca and Susan fell on Tanner like a pack of puppies. "Tanner! Tanner!"

Finn stepped back, but Mercedes pressed right in with the kids. "Hey, Tanner. Good to see you."

I can get through this. Lindsay brought out the detached smile she'd practiced in the mirror that morning.

"Wouldn't miss it." Stepping forward, he kissed Lindsay's cheek.

"H-hey. Hi." Two words and she could barely get them out. Mercedes was grinning ear to ear, and the girls giggled.

Thank goodness Daddy pushed up from his lounger. "Good to see you, son."

Finn was not looking happy. The "son" thing probably stuck in his craw.

Lindsay had no idea what her dad saw brewing in that room, but she'd always told him he should run for office. He was a born politician. "It's nice outside. Why don't we go out to the back deck?" With her father leading the way, the group of them wound through the house, past the crockpot and out onto the deck.

Lagging behind, Lindsay went back to setting the table. Now, which way did the knife blade face?

From the dining room she could hear Mercedes say, "Need any help, Mom?"

"Could you put the green beans in the oven, dear?"

Mercedes was becoming part of the family. Lindsay smiled. With the table set, she wandered back to the kitchen. "This will be my culinary contribution today," Mercedes said, opening the oven. "Ta dah!"

Lindsay laughed. Mercedes didn't cook. They teased her unmercifully about marrying Finn because he owned a restaurant. Flinging open the refrigerator door, Mom handed them bags of celery, cucumbers and carrots "Could you girls cut these into sticks? I've got some ranch dip here somewhere."

Grabbing two of the peelers, Lindsay ended up shoulder to shoulder with Mercedes over the sink. "Tanner's looking fine," Mercedes said, nodding to the group outside.

"You think so?" Oh, why bother to pretend? "Yeah, he's good looking all right."

In khaki shorts and a blue polo, he was the epitome of summer casual. And now that she knew that rangy body, Lindsay felt a jolt. She knew the feel of those muscles against hers. Her mouth went dry with the memories. She had to pull her attention to her mother's garden outside the kitchen window. "So, you're going to try zinnias again, Mom?"

"Why not? One of these summers, they might not get that awful mold. I have to try." While Mercedes and Lindsay worked at the sink, Mom turned the potatoes in the crockpot so they browned nicely. Like clockwork, she knew her mother's routine.

"So, what's going on with you two?" Mercedes asked, attacking a fat carrot.

"Nothing." She wasn't about to spell it out for her sister-in-law. Strips of cucumber spun from her peeler in corkscrews.

With a low chuckle, Mercedes was hacking the death out of the poor carrot. "If nothing's going on, then something's really wrong. Ouch!"

Lindsay handed Mercedes a dish towel. "Peel the carrot not your finger."

Grumbling, Mercedes got back to work and the interrogation stopped, thank goodness.

"How's it coming, girls?" Mom asked, swirling in from the dining room.

"Almost ready." Giving each other a guilty glance, they both bent to the task.

Her mother handed Lindsay the oval platter they always used for this appetizer. Lindsay poured ranch dressing into a small bowl, set it in the center and began to arrange the vegetables. Mercedes went off to find a bandage.

Carrying the platter of vegetables outside, Lindsay set it on the picnic table. Her father and Finn had built this deck and the extra long picnic table when she was in grade school. By then Finn was in high school shop, learning how to use drills and saws although he'd rather spend time at the computer. They ate out here all the time, except when the mosquitoes were bad. Citron candles burned in the corners of the deck.

Her dad had set out the corn hole game. Tugging at his hands,

Rebecca and Susan coerced Tanner into playing. Lindsay settled at the table to watch.

"Look, Mom!" Her cheeks flushed, Rebecca swung her slender arm back and let it fly. The bag hit the hole dead on.

"My turn, my turn." Susan clamored for attention.

The commotion didn't seem to bother Tanner. Stepping up behind Susan, he helped her line up the shot. "Okay, Suzie Q, you need to take your arm back farther than Rebecca." Of course Susan did exactly as Tanner asked. Why did her children behave better for someone else?

Daddy sat down beside her.

"You taking your medication, Daddy, like the doctor said?" Finn had told Lindsay that their dad was taking a blood thinner now, as well as blood pressure medication. Lindsay felt relieved.

"Yep, you think your mother would ever let me forget a dose?"

The yard felt so peaceful, lightning bugs flitting through the bushes. "That young man of yours is great with the girls."

"Tanner's not my young man." Her father's face fell, and Lindsay felt terrible. Snugging one arm around his shoulders, she kissed his cheek. "I just met Tanner this summer, Daddy. Let's give it some time, okay?"

Elbows on the table, Dad turned to give her his fish eye. "Your mother and I met during Easter break in Ft. Lauderdale. We got married three weeks later. Time doesn't matter."

She'd heard this story a thousand times. "You were lucky. Sometimes rushing things isn't a good idea."

"Hmm." Dad turned his attention back to the kids, but it was

Tanner they crowded around. Uncle Finn was standing to the side watching. "Things were different back then, I guess," her dad was saying. "But you took your time with Rich. You never regretted that, did you, sweetheart?"

"Of course not, Daddy." Why not let her parents think she'd had a perfect marriage?

"You two sure look serious." Joining them on the picnic table, Mercedes settled next to Lindsay.

"Not at all. We're just talking about stuff."

Mercedes wasn't one to be put off. "What kind of stuff?" But she wasn't tuned into the conversation, not really. Instead, her eyes had found Finn. Her husband gave Mercedes a secret look that made Lindsay blush to the roots of her hair.

"Water buffaloes." She tossed that out there.

Still caught in her husband's gaze, Mercedes was making this ridiculous pucker with her lips.

"Dad's thinking of buying some water buffaloes." Lindsay kept going and Mercedes only nodded.

Shaking his head, her father chuckled. Mercedes swung her head around. "What was that?"

Dad and Lindsay both broke up. "Lindsay's pulling your leg, Mercedes," Dad said. "That's all."

"Hmm. Okay. Be secretive." Mercedes stretched. "Why don't we eat out here tonight? It's perfect."

A mosquito whined in Lindsay's ear. She brushed it away but in a second Mercedes was swatting at the little buzzards. "Forget I said that."

Lindsay swung her attention back to the corn hole game. They were keeping score and this was serious. Tanner caught her eye and winked as he grabbed a bean bag. Finn had joined the game. She hoped they'd get to know each other a little better.

"Come and help me dish this up, girls," her mother called from the kitchen. Mercedes and Lindsay hustled inside, followed by her dad. Lindsay scooped potatoes from the crock pot. After sharpening the carving knife, her dad set to work on the roast. Mom whipped up the gravy, which Dad had insisted upon, even though his cardiologist probably wouldn't agree. Mercedes took the beans from the oven.

"Dinner's ready," Lindsay called out. The corn hole group trudged inside. "Now wash your hands." Of course Rebecca and Susan both wanted to sit next to Tanner. Lindsay was ready to give up her place at his side when Tanner shot her a look, the kind rescue dogs offer touring visitors.

"Poor guy." She slid into the chair next to him and Rebecca sat next to her. "You okay, Tanner?"

Smiling, Tanner squeezed her hand just as Daddy said grace. "Having a great time."

When the platters and bowls were passed around, Tanner heaped his plate. One slice of beef and a few carrots were all Lindsay could handle. After too many cheese crowns and ice cream cones that summer, Lindsay was on a diet.

At first conversation flowed light and easy. Mom filled them in about the bingo bus. Dad asked Mercedes and Lindsay about Beach Vacations. Finn joined in the casual conversation but then he got down to business. "So, Tanner, as I recall you grew up here but didn't graduate from Gull Harbor?" Finn could look so innocent when he wanted to. Frustration welled inside. How dare her brother question Tanner?

"No. Military school called." Although Tanner kept his tone light, she felt him stiffen besides her.

Finn appeared to chew on that one. But he didn't find it to his taste. "Heck, why would you leave? As I recall, Coach Teegarden was pretty upset. You were the big hope for the basketball team."

"So he told me. Sometimes life takes you in another direction."

"Did you actually serve in the military after you graduated?"

Tanner met Finn with a level gaze. "Yes. Three tours. Two countries."

A muscle twitched in Tanner's cheek. Lindsay wanted to strangle her brother.

"Wow, that's really something." Finn sat back. Lindsay squeezed Tanner's hand under the table.

"Well now, I think it's fine that you served your country, son," her dad said in that slow, soft way he had when he was making a point. "Gull Harbor has a history of stepping up. Our boys have sacrificed. We should all be grateful to you." Although Daddy didn't look in Finn's direction, her brother had been put in his place.

"Can we have dessert, Grandma Rose?" Rebecca asked, bored with the conversation. Lindsay wanted to hug her.

"Well, if everyone's finished, then yes," her mother said, pushing back her chair. "Keep your forks, everybody. We're having triple chocolate cake."

Lindsay edged up from the table. "Mercedes and I will clear, Mom. You stay right where you are."

They hadn't been in the kitchen two seconds before Mercedes turned to her. "What the heck was that about?"

Sometimes Mercedes could be totally clueless. Lindsay stacked the plates in the broad farm sink her dad had installed a few years back. "You're his wife. You tell me."

"Haven't got a clue." Mercedes eyed the dirty dishes with distaste. "How about I cut the cake and you finish clearing?"

"Sure. Right." But Lindsay felt frustrated as the two of them shuffled back and forth. The tower of glistening chocolate was one of her favorites. Not tonight. She was ready to leave.

Mercedes had cut huge wedges of cake. For a couple minutes all that could be heard was the scraping of forks against the plates. "This is wonderful, Mrs. Wheeler," Tanner managed between forkfuls.

"Why, thank you, Tanner. And please call me Rose." Mom blushed as red as the clusters of English roses Lindsay's father had planted around the deck.

A soft evening had fallen. Lightning bugs lit the back garden, their blinking creating a magical design. The girls ran to get mason jars from the kitchen. Last year her father had found butterfly nets at one of the hardware stores. Now Rebecca and Susan chased across the lawn, capturing the fireflies with their nets and spilling them into the jars with a few blades of grass.

"Have you ever caught a lightning bug?" she whispered to

Tanner. They were sitting in lawn chairs. Mercedes had offered to help Mom in the kitchen. That had to be a first and Lindsay wanted to spend time with Tanner. Finn and Dad were sitting up on the deck. Lindsay could hear Finn asking Dad questions about his new medications. Fine, let him handle that.

"Can't say as I have." Taking her hand he brushed a thumb gently across her knuckles. Lindsay felt a sense of peace seep through her. "Are you going to show me how?"

"What?" She pulled her mind back to their conversation. It was so easy to lapse into daydreams when she was with him.

He chuckled. When he smiled his white teeth shone in the dark. "Nothing. You have a great family."

"Thanks. Some of them are."

He squeezed her hand. "Don't be angry with Finn. He's your big brother. I guess I'd watch out for you too."

"I don't need anyone watching out for me."

"What if I wanted to watch out for you?"

What was he saying? "I'm fine. That's silly, Tanner."

His eyes swung toward the girls. "Let me see those lanterns," he called out. The girls came screaming toward him, holding out their jars. Lindsay kicked off her sandals and the grass tickled her feet as she walked toward the house. "I'll be right back."

Stepping inside, she headed to the powder room. Finn's voice in the kitchen brought her to a halt.

"Don't you think you're rushing things, Mom?" Finn said. "After all, what do we know about this guy?"

"Finn Wheeler, what are you saying?" Mom's tone of voice

took Lindsay back to grade school. "Don't you think it's time your sister has some fun in her life?"

"I'd just like to know more about him. He hasn't even mentioned his family."

"I think his parents are both gone. Of course he doesn't want to talk about it." She rarely heard her mother this upset. "Keep your voice down, Finn."

Lindsay should get the kids and leave. But of course she didn't. That would be too sensible. She stepped into the kitchen, still warm from all the cooking.

Her mother's eyes widened and Finn froze.

"So, what do you want to see, Finn? Family photos?" She was being childish but her remark hit home.

Her brother's face turned as pink as her mother's flamingo earrings. Lindsay whirled from the room and stumbled back onto the porch. "Girls, come on now. We're leaving."

Tanner was talking to Dad. Taking the cue, both men stood. "Guess I'll hit the road too," Tanner said, shaking Dad's hand.

"Get your things together, girls." Avoiding her father's eyes, Lindsay clapped her hands. Tanner and Lindsay said goodnight to her mother.

Finn pulled her into a hug. "I didn't mean to upset you," he whispered.

"Oh, Finn." How can you stay mad at your favorite and only brother?

Herding the girls in front of her, Lindsay and Tanner left.

"Everything okay?" Tanner asked her at the car.

"I'm fine if you are." She sucked in a shaky breath.

He kissed her forehead. "I'm great. You have a nice family."

Right. The girls were busy buckling their seatbelts.

"Sleep tight, babe. I'm going to follow you home."

Lindsay took her keys from her purse. "Why? It's only two blocks away. Don't be silly."

He ran a finger over her chin line. "Humor me. I just want to make sure you and the girls get home safely."

"That's so sweet." But her thoughts right then weren't sweet at all.

~.~

Tanner drove slowly, eyes on Lindsay's taillights. Tonight had given him a lot to think about. After Lindsay pulled into her driveway and the three of them disappeared into the house, he gave a quick blink of his lights and drove off. Red Arrow Highway was deserted and he relished the darkness. Tanner wanted to just think.

A strong sense of family filled the Wheeler home. For the last several years, he'd been without family, even though his dad was still alive. Going from one assignment to the next in the service, Tanner felt on the run. He'd escaped Sleepy Hollow Lane and a stepmother he despised. Cleaning the house out with Lindsay had brought some relief.

But his house needed something. The walls of the Wheeler home were filled with pictures— family gatherings, graduations, weddings—their life was there. In stripping his own walls, had Tanner thrown away the good times as well as the bad?

Back home, he went straight to the master closet. The box

crammed with photos was still shoved into a corner. Good thing he hadn't ditched them. Dragging the box into the bedroom, he began to sort through silver-framed shots. He tossed the ones with Ursula to the side. Those were definitely going in the trash, where she belonged. But the happy family pictures with his mother and father? Those were keepers. Remembering those times brought a smile and a sense of peace.

The three of them down on the beach, Dad in the Hawaiian shirt his mother had given him for Father's Day, his eighth birthday party with Gip and some of the other guys—those were all good times. It didn't take long for him to grab the hammer from his toolkit and put some shots back on the walls. Others were meant for the tables and shelves. Maybe they'd work their mojo on this house.

Feeling emotionally drained but satisfied, Tanner sat out on the porch, listening to the night breeze high in the trees. The moon had risen and it touched the tips of quiet waves rolling onto the shore below.

Chapter 19

In the days that followed, Tanner continued to work on his house. The new chairs were great—very solid. But they weren't cozy. Girls liked *cozy*. And he didn't have a sofa where little girls could play with Barbie dolls.

Hell, Sunday had been a revelation. What planet had he been on?

But Finn was a whole other issue. Tanner couldn't figure Lindsay's brother out. What was the problem? Maybe he was being protective. Tanner could see his point. But he didn't like it.

He stewed over it all the way to Michigan City. Sure, he would have liked to have Lindsay with him, but he wanted this to be a surprise.

The day felt warm when he parked in Watson's open lot. Leaving the oppressive heat behind, he pushed through the large plate glass doors. Cold air met him. An older woman got up from a greeting desk.

"Hi, I'm Evelyn. Can I help you?" She smiled expectantly.

"Good morning." One whiff of new fabrics and formaldehyde made him hold his breath. But the doctors had told Tanner to breathe slowly to avoid an attack. He had to make this buying trip short.

Glasses hung from a beaded chain around Evelyn's neck, and now she set them on her nose. "What are you looking for?"

Time to gather his thoughts. "Furniture."

She chuckled and Tanner felt like an idiot. After all, he was surrounded by the stuff. "You've come to the right place. Why don't we just walk around?"

"Sure. Fine." Furniture crowded the large showroom. A guy could get lost.

Evelyn had a kind way of steering him, chattering all the way. "Are you thinking of living room? Dining room?"

"Living room. I already bought dining room furniture." But out of the corner of his eye, he saw beds. Tanner didn't want Evelyn to notice. He was kicking himself about that first time with Lindsay. They'd practically been on the floor, not that they seemed to notice or care.

Evelyn was rambling on about high back sofas versus low back sofas. Terms like square cut cushions or rounded were flying through the air. "Which would you prefer?" She peered at him over her glasses.

"Stuff that's comfortable," he said while Evelyn caught her breath.

"Oh, well." She adjusted her glasses with a smile. "I like to think that all Watson's furniture is comfortable. Now we have these large pits with hassocks. Part of it pulls out into a sleeper sofa."

Evelyn motioned to a massive corduroy set that could fill his entire living room. "Too big. I already have two chairs." And he was beginning to think those two had been a mistake. They were BL—before he really knew Lindsay and her children.

But Evelyn was off in another direction and he didn't want to lose her. He followed her into an area of plain sofas, none of them giant size. "Are we getting warmer?"

"It is hot in here." He pulled at the collar of his blue polo. When he felt a blast of cool air, Tanner stood beneath it.

"Color scheme?"

"What?" He couldn't help himself. The beds were still visible on the other side of the store. "Pardon me?"

"Colors. What colors do you have now in your living room?"

He thought for a second. "Brown. Wood with some leather."

For a second Evelyn looked puzzled. Then she rallied. "The sea glass palette is so popular this season."

"It is?" This was definitely over his head.

The saleswoman led him to a sofa with a leaf pattern in blue and green. The design reminded him of Lake Michigan on a sunny day. "This is our St. Lucia model."

"It looks nice." So they sat on sofas like this in St. Lucia?

"See how it feels." Evelyn gestured with manicured nails.

First he perched. Then he pushed back. "Comfortable."

Tanner tried to picture watching TV, his arm around Lindsay and a bowl of popcorn on his new coffee table.

"So you like it?" She looked delighted.

Realizing that he had his arm curled around the back of the sofa, he sprang up. "Sure, I'll take it."

That was the process for a couple more chairs. He sat. If the chair was too hard, he moved to the next one. Evelyn approved the colors and they were done. She seemed to know what she was doing.

"And I need a bed."

"Oh? A mattress set or a frame?"

"I have the mattress part so the bed."

Evelyn took off. "Nothing too big," he said as they walked. The bed Ursula ordered after she married his dad had been ridiculous. "Nothing like that sled bed stuff."

"Sled bed?" At first Evelyn looked puzzled. Then her face cleared. "Oh, the sleigh bed with the high curled back."

"You got it." Evelyn was going to have a good laugh about this later with the other sales associates. As they navigated the crowded aisles, his nose started to twitch. The searing fabric smell was even getting to his eyes.

Evelyn came to a halt. "Here we are." The beds went on forever, pieces crunched in every which way. Headboards and dressers and armoires that could hold an entire house. For a second, Tanner was right back in the home he'd just taken apart. His stomach churned. "Something simple."

So they bypassed the huge sleigh beds and anything with a footboard. "We're tall. We need foot room." But he wasn't thinking about their feet.

"Oh, so your wife is tall too?"

"I'm not married."

"Oh, I see." Evelyn pursed her lips.

Why was he using *we*? Deep in thought, he rammed right into the footboard of a bed. He should be wearing armor instead of flip flops. His big toe was bleeding.

"Are you all right?" Evelyn looked down. "My, you may need a bandage for this one."

"Thank you but I'm fine." Shopping for furniture might be worse than a mission in the Korengal Valley, where insurgents lurked behind every hill.

"Well, of course." Keeping her eyes trained straight ahead, Evelyn pursed her lips. "Maybe something in metal then?"

"Sounds good." He wished his foot would stop throbbing. But the accident reminded him of Lindsay and he smiled to himself. They'd reached some frames that looked clean and simple. The metal didn't have any girly curlicues.

"Double bed? Queen? King?" she ended hopefully.

"Big. Big enough to..."

"...move around?" Evelyn offered with a gleam in her eyes. Yes there would be conversations and he didn't give a damn. He wanted this finished, so he pointed. "That one."

She whipped a pen out and began to take notes. "Perfect. I love the greenish tint of that metal. This will go nicely with your palette. Night stands?"

A few minutes later, they were winding things up. Tanner ended up with simple birch night stands and a long dresser. No armoire. That master suite had enough closet space for two.

Lindsay's clothes in my closet. He was getting out his credit card but it slipped through his fingers. He scooped it off the floor.

Evelyn stared at him through the glasses. "How about Thursday delivery?"

"Sure." He was still thinking about his closet. Forcing himself to concentrate, he finished up the paper work. "Thank you for your help, Evelyn."

"My pleasure. Enjoy your new furniture."

He made tracks for the door, limping a little.

"Oh, and Tanner?"

He turned to find Evelyn charging toward him. "Now put this on when you get in the car." She was waving a bandage.

Why did older women always seem to have everything for emergencies? His mother always had been ready with bandages, a needle and thread or Noxzema for sunburns. But when he got behind the wheel, he ripped that sucker open and somehow got it on. It would have to be his right foot. The darn thing throbbed when he pressed the accelerator.

A Thursday delivery would work great because Lindsay came on Friday to clean. He wanted to surprise her. Tanner had been spending Fridays in the Gull Harbor library, working on his real estate course work. He wanted to stay out of her way when she cleaned.

Feeling that he'd accomplished a lot, Tanner drove home. He was creating a life here in Gull Harbor and that felt good, even though he'd hit some hiccups. Rolling down the window he let the warm summer air blow through his hair. No more buzz cuts for him. When he remembered how Lindsay's fingers felt playing with his hair, he nearly ran off the road.

Pulling into his driveway, he noticed the beige sedan in

McGregors' driveway. Leslie drove a white SUV. He'd barely turned the engine off, when Red came barreling past the mailboxes, towing a tall man with a shock of red hair.

"Tanner. Buddy! I want you to meet my dad." Red could barely get the words out. His face was flushed with excitement. Tanner walked to meet them. Red's father wore a friendly smile. His shirt was open at the neck as if he'd just taken off a tie.

"Mike McGregor." The man's hand shot out.

"Tanner Phelps." So this was the guy who was never home.

"I hope Red hasn't been bothering you. I mean, taking up too much of your time." Mike McGregor's eyes went to the basketball hoop pushed to the side of the driveway.

"Not at all. You have a great little guy. I've enjoyed getting to know Red."

"See, Dad." Red broke into an I-told-you-so smile. "Tanner and me are buddies."

Mike rested his hands on his son's shoulders. "I'm afraid it's been a long summer for Leslie and Red, the babies and all. I appreciate the time you spend with him. He's been telling me about the basketball." He raked a hand through his unruly red curls.

"Like Red said, we're buds. He was my welcoming committee." The two men laughed together.

While they were talking, Red disappeared into the garage and came back out, basketball in hand. "Look, Dad." In his excitement, Red couldn't quite make the shot but it did hit the rim. Mike caught it and bobbled it back to his son.

"My job keeps me away from home way too much, but Leslie

likes living here. The support system for Red is excellent so here we are."

Tanner's heart went out to Mike. The guy had exhaustion written all over him. "This is a great place to grow up," Tanner offered.

"Good to hear." Mike handed the basketball to Red. "Guess we should get home. Mom's making lunch."

Red dashed back inside the garage to put the ball away. Tanner watched father and son amble through the tall grass. Red must miss his dad a lot while he was gone. Leslie too. Sometimes life was just more complicated than it should be.

Feeling worn out after his shopping trip, Tanner changed into his bathing suit and headed down to the beach. Summer was in full swing. Being down here reminded him of the last time he was with Lindsay—the softness of her hand in his. Her laugh that floated on the summer air.

But the stones reminded him of Rebecca and Susan. He'd never really thought about having kids. Parenting took time and patience. Was he up to that? Would he mess it up, the way his dad had?

He didn't want to disappoint Lindsay.

~.~

Using her key in Tanner's door that Friday felt like breaking and entering. He wasn't her average client. She hauled her vacuum inside and reached behind her for the purple supply caddy. Tanner had texted her a few times that week, but both of them seemed busy. He told her he was "chilling." That was a word Rich had used a lot. "Chilling out." In the end, all it meant was that he didn't like to work. She'd cleaned three houses already this Friday. Her back was hurting and she knew she smelled like vinegar. Sometimes she thought she'd never order balsamic vinaigrette dressing again.

Except for the sound of the overhead fan, Tanner's house was perfectly still. Sunlight fell through the kitchen windows. A plate with toast crumbs had been left on the counter, a knife set across one end. Sometimes she thought Tanner might stage things. The more she got to know him, the more she realized he was very tidy. This mess wasn't like him.

Something smelled different here. She sniffed again. Yep. Leaving the sunny kitchen behind, she walked into the dining room. How she loved this table they'd picked out together. In fact, maybe that was why it felt special to her.

Another sniff pulled her into the living room. "Wow." The room which had looked so severe with the two new wooden chairs now exploded with soft, soothing colors— cool blue teamed with pale mossy green. She sat gingerly on the edge of a comfortable sofa. Okay, the furniture placement looked a little strange and made her smile. She could almost picture Tanner trying to decide how to arrange everything. Leaving the sofa, she cuddled up in one of the overstuffed chairs. He'd bought these, really?

He was getting the place ready to show or ready to rent. She wilted into the comfortable chair. The scent of new furniture gagged her. Jumping up, she opened the door to the screen porch and turned on the overhead fan. The rhythm of waves on the shore below drifted up. The day felt restless. She hadn't seen Tanner in days, only those texts. A noonday sun cast sharp shadows over the back lawn. And she could see the lake.

Going outside, she looked closer. Yep, he'd definitely been doing more work out here. Nausea swirled in her stomach. Her head pounded. She looked back at the house. The place had Ready to Show written all over it.

But she was here to clean. Dashing back inside, she started with the front bedrooms. Of course the rooms hadn't been used, so the sheets didn't need washing. The towels in the Jack and Jill bathroom still hung where she'd left them. But she'd swab out the sink and toilet just to leave some evidence of her work. After all, he was paying her. The familiar routine kept her from thinking. Saved her from feeling.

The glass-topped tables on the porch needed to be spritzed, and she cleaned the glass. Then she wiped the wrought iron pieces until the white paint gleamed. Summer filled the air and she could almost smell sunblock from the beach below where someone was playing a radio. The sounds of Donna Summer belting out "I Feel Love" carried up in phrases battered by a breeze.

Taking out her phone, she flipped through her playlist and put in her earbuds. Music could help too. Energized and distracted by the music, Lindsay opened the dishwasher to empty it. The orderly arrangement of the clean plates and cups seemed so Tanner. Did he reorganize the dishwasher after she left? She filled it again with the dishes and glasses.

After vacuuming the sand from the kitchen floor, she pulled on her purple rubber gloves and swabbed the floor with a mop. Now, this was where she really felt she was working. Some sand still remained, gritty beneath her shoes. This would drive Tanner crazy. She grabbed a broom.

He must be spending time on the beach. She wanted to be there with him.

The clock was ticking. She should get Tanner's sheets going in the washing machine. Emptying the bucket in the laundry sink, she left it there and set off to strip the sheets.

She liked the master suite. Unlike the other rooms that had hardwood floors and area rugs, the master was carpeted. Okay the carpet was a dated gold but maybe Tanner would change it one day. And would she still know him if he did?

She pushed open the door and came to a halt. He'd added a bed and the masculine metal flipped a switch deep inside. In a rogue mental flash, she saw herself gripping that metal headboard. Walking slowly around the bed, Lindsay swallowed. When had he bought this? The side tables and dresser had finished off this room. She gulped.

But no time to sit and stare. The rumpled bed waited. She should pull off the sheets, grab the towels and then start washing the load. But the bed looked inviting. Kicking off her shoes, she stretched out.

Oh my. The bed smelled like Tanner. Wonderfully masculine. Squeezing her eyes shut, Lindsay curled up on her side. The pillow felt soft on her cheek, and she buried her nose in it. Her body sprang to life. She was in his bed. But she should be working. Just one minute more. A weariness overtook her. The fears clamoring in her mind weighed her down. She closed her eyes for just a second.

Next thing she knew, someone was slipping her socks off. Her feet feel chilly and she curled her toes. The purple gloves were tugged off too. Where was she? When she blinked her eyes open, Tanner stood there, beads of water on his shoulders and chest. He was dressed in swim trunks, still wet.

God, he was gorgeous.

"What are you doing here?" she asked sleepily.

"Nothing. Yet."

He ran a warm hand up her leg and she shivered. "I shouldn't be here."

He chuckled. "Babe, you're right where you belong."

Chapter 20

"I'm having a party," Sarah told Lindsay and Mercedes when she stopped in the office one sultry August morning. A wave of hot air had followed her inside.

Mercedes turned. "Close the door. You're letting in the heat." The overhead fan offered little relief. The warped door stuck but Sarah pushed hard and it closed.

"Is it your birthday?" Lindsay asked, pulling herself away from the computer. The promotions had brought in so much business. She should be thrilled. Now they had bookings scheduled through December. But Lindsay had to recheck carefully to make sure she hadn't screwed up. Tanner was distracting her.

"Nope. No birthday. Got an email from Carolyn. She's bringing her boyfriend home to meet everyone."

Mercedes arched a wicked brow. "You mean she's showing off her trophy? I hear he's smoking hot."

"Carolyn said nothing about a trophy. But she's had a very nice summer out in Santa Fe. Hot but nice, from what she says."

"Hot. Are you talking about the man or the weather?" Lindsay couldn't help asking.

"Not for me to say." Sarah fanned herself. "I have not met Brody. But the word in the book group is that he's very good looking."

"Is this a book group party?" Mercedes looked suspicious. Lindsay and Mercedes had never joined that group. Lindsay didn't have time to read, and Mercedes didn't seem interested. She'd mentioned once that she didn't like to "tag after Kate." Must be a big sister thing.

Sarah shook her head. "This is for anyone who knows Carolyn and wishes her well."

"You are such a sweetheart." Getting up, Lindsay hugged Sarah, getting a whiff of cinnamon and sugar. "Of course I'll come. When is it?"

"One week from tomorrow. Saturday."

"Could I bring a friend?" She had to ask. The girls had slept over at her parents' house for the past three Saturdays. Saturday nights had become special for Tanner and Lindsay.

Sarah gave her an impish smile. "I'm counting on it. Tanner stops in the bakery once in a while."

"Now, *that* man is the very definition of hot." Mercedes threw Lindsay a look.

Her silence told them all they needed to know. Since that Friday with Tanner at his cottage, Lindsay had a hard time concentrating. She could think of little else but Tanner. The man who was spending summer relaxing on the beach.

She tried not to think about that part. Lindsay would not compare Tanner to Rich. She just would not. But when Tanner became evasive, she couldn't help it. All the times she'd peppered her husband with questions came roaring back. Rich would shut down. She later realized Rich said nothing because he had no answers. That didn't stop him from making joint decisions without including her. One time he bought a riding lawn mower for their tiny yard. She made him take it back. "We didn't discuss this and can't afford it," she'd told Rich.

Someone was pounding on the office door.

"I'll get it." Sarah struggled with the doorknob.

When she finally got the door open, Kate lumbered inside. The poor woman looked as big as a house. "Lordy, it's hot out there." Flip flops slapped Kate's swollen feet as she made her way to her desk. A polka dot sundress ballooned around her when she sat down.

"Well, look who's dropped in," Mercedes teased. "Did Cole finally let you out of the house?"

"Don't start." Kate gave her older sister a warning look. "I needed to get out of my home office. Natalie is with Marie so I made a break for it."

Lindsay had seen Cole's daughter Natalie around town. She was darling, just like Cole's first wife. Who could forget Samantha McGraw? She'd skipped town, leaving her husband and her daughter behind. Cole's mother and Kate's mom took turns babysitting for Natalie.

"Is Cole's little girl getting on your nerves?" Mercedes asked. "Sometimes I think she's a training experience."

"Natalie is such a sweetheart," Sarah cooed. "That beautiful blonde hair and blue eyes. She looks just like her mama." Then Sarah zipped her lip. No one in town talked about Samantha, not openly.

"I'm getting on my nerves, not Natalie. I love the dickens out of that girl. Natalie's so excited about becoming a big sister." The chair squeaked when Kate shifted. "Nope, I'm here because I needed some girl time."

Lindsay couldn't stop staring at Kate's ankles. Hers had never been that puffy. "How are you feeling?"

"Overdue." Kate cupped her belly with both hands. "Feels like I've got three kids in here."

Sarah chuckled. "Looks like one to me. When is your due date again?"

"First week of September."

Standing next to Lindsay's desk, Sarah clapped her hands with excitement. A pile of papers slid to the floor. "Oh, dear. I'll get it."

Instead of turning on her computer, Kate glanced around. "What? No bakery box?"

"Kate, did you leave a standing order?" Mercedes teased. "You should have told us you were coming."

Sarah edged toward the door. "I'll be right back."

"You don't have to do that," Kate said. "I'm fine. Really." But her pathetic tone didn't fool Lindsay.

"Sarah, I'll walk you over." Lindsay jumped up.

"I always like company." Sarah opened the door. "Be right back," she told Kate and Mercedes.

"Don't fry yourself on the sidewalk." Picking up her unopened mail, Kate fanned herself.

"Could you ask Cole to check the air conditioning in here?"

Mercedes put a hand in front of a vent. "I don't think it's working."

Picking up a pen, Kate scribbled a note to herself. "Done."

"Come on, Sarah." Lindsay led the way. She wasn't wearing much—just her usual tank top and cut-offs. Stepping into the hallway, she sucked in a breath. "It's stifling out here."

Sarah dabbed at her neck with a tissue. "The back of the bakery feels like an oven. I'm afraid it's too much for my mother. We've hired a new baker to help us."

"Where did you ever find a baker?" They were finally outside. The air was hot and still. The leaves of the oak tree hung listlessly over the parking spots.

"Jamie's brother. Do you remember Ryan? Such a nice boy."

"Boy? How old is he?"

"A couple of years younger than Jamie." Her voice softened when she said Jamie's name.

They set off. Lindsay could feel the hot pavement under her sandals as they marched across Whittaker and headed left toward the coffee shop.

"Your boys are doing all right? I mean, in this situation."

"They're doing great." Sarah's chin came up. She never seemed to dwell on the bad breaks life had brought her. "How's your dad, Lindsay?"

"He's fine." But her dad had started taking naps in the afternoon. Rebecca had mentioned it to Lindsay. "I don't know what I'd do without my parents."

"Isn't that the truth?" They'd reached The Full Cup and the bell jangled above the door when Sarah pushed it open.

"How can you work here all day?" Lindsay groaned, inhaling the undeniable sugary scent. "I'd be as big as a house."

Patting her ample hips, Sarah gave a quiet smile. "I'm getting there."

"You look fine. At least you're not thin as a stick like..." She'd nearly said Mercedes.

Lila bustled from the back with a tray of fresh loaves. "Caraway rye."

Sarah smiled at her mother. "I think we'll have ham and cheese on rye for dinner. I'll be right back to spell you, Mom. It's way too hot back there for you with the ovens."

"Not a problem." Lila wiped her hands on her apron and retreated to the back. Sarah's dad had founded the coffee shop, which quickly turned into a bakery.

Lindsay's eyes swept the glass case. "Thank goodness, you're not out of cheese crowns. Kate might kill us."

With a white box in one hand and a tissue in the other, Sarah began to choose. "Only the largest will do." Lindsay's mouth watered. She could almost taste the almond flavored ricotta and the sweet glaze topping. Lila returned to the back room.

"I have an idea," Sarah said, tying up the box with string. "About the kids I mean. Small children can wear out grandparents. I can see that with my mom, although she'd never admit it."

"Thank goodness the girls will be going back to school soon." Lindsay had been over this problem in her head so many times. "I can't afford babysitters."

"And I know other mothers in the same situation. Some work part time or they just want to do their nails without being interrupted. Why don't we form a group?" After tying the box with string, Sarah slid it over the glass counter.

"We'll asked a couple of the other mothers who need some free time during the week. Our children would rather play together than stay at home anyway. Don't you think? We could have an after school program too. Everybody takes a day."

Lindsay's mind bounded ahead. "What a great idea." Free time. And she had a flexible schedule to work around school on her day to babysit.

"Think about it." Sarah pushed away the money Lindsay offered. "And put the party on your calendar. My house. Five o'clock this Saturday."

"I can't wait to meet this Brody guy."

But it wasn't Carolyn Knight's boyfriend that filled Lindsay's mind as she went back to the office. No, it was Tanner. Her pulse pounded just thinking about him. Following her home after dinner Sunday night was so sweet. But his maple syrup eyes weren't telling her everything. Summer was ending soon. Would he stay here in Gull Harbor or close up his house like so many summer people?

After all, he hadn't used the L word. She knew it was too soon. And yet, Lindsay also knew she loved him. Wanted to be with him.

But if he left, what then?

~.~

Finally he'd get to meet more of Lindsay's friends. Tanner felt good as he parked the SUV. "Looks like Sarah invited a crowd."

A homemade banner was attached to the porch railings. *Welcome, Carolyn and Brody!* Through the slats, he could see kids' toys crowded into a corner. The small bungalow looked overgrown with lilac bushes and hollyhocks leaning every which way. Not shipshape but Sarah's house brought back memories of the old Gull Harbor before developers began to buy up property and build modern condos.

"Yep. The cars are a giveaway." Turning toward him, she laughed.

His eyes fell to her bare shoulders. Her skin was luminous. "You look beautiful tonight."

"Thank you." Blushing, she gave the sundress a tug. "I don't want to lose this."

"At least not yet." Bending his head, he had to kiss her. And he couldn't stop there. Tanner ran his lips down her long neck while she trembled. That creamy chest would probably drive him crazy all night.

"Tanner?" Lindsay's fingers threaded through his hair. "What are you doing?"

"Doing a taste test." She tasted as delicious as she smelled.

"Not now. Please. We need to join the party."

"I'd rather create my private party," he whispered against her skin.

She groaned. "Just not now."

How he hated to stop. But he did.

"Whatever that perfume is, it's got me going."

"You know I don't wear perfume with you. That's soap."

"Seems appropriate, right? After all, you started as my cleaning lady."

"Aw, that sounds so romantic."

"It was, in a weird way." He couldn't stop looking at her. "There isn't one thing about you I don't love."

Love. The word hung in the air.

Lindsay dropped her eyes. Had he spooked her? A blast of music came from Sarah's house. "Maybe we should go inside. Meet your friends." He pulled himself upright.

"At least I don't smell like vinegar." She gave her dress another tug.

"On you vinegar smells sexy." If only she knew.

She looked at him with disbelief. "You're kidding, right?"

"No. In fact, I'd like to wait here a second, just so I don't embarrasses myself walking in there." Then he spotted Finn's car. "So, your brother will be here?"

Lindsay shrank. Why had he opened his big mouth? "Well, yeah. I guess so," Lindsay said. "Mercedes knows Sarah. Do you have a problem with Finn?"

He didn't want to ruin the evening. Maybe he'd have a chance to talk with Finn. Get to know him better. "Of course not. Why would I?"

Her gray eyes clouded. "Oh, I don't know."

Tanner didn't want this to get complicated. Another car pulled up. He cracked open the door. "Let's party."

Laughter and music poured from the house. Ringing the doorbell was useless. He followed Lindsay inside. The place was packed. "Do you know all these people?"

Sarah waved to them. "Lindsay. Tanner. Come and meet Carolyn."

An attractive blonde looked up and threw them a shy smile. "Hi." The guy with an arm around Carolyn was wearing a bolo tie and boots.

Sarah nudged them forward. "This is Carolyn. Tanner, maybe you knew her in school? She taught English."

They began to play the name game. Finally they figured out that Carolyn had taught seniors when he was just a freshman. Getting to his feet, Brody was tall. He looked familiar, but then so did half the people in Gull Harbor. "I think you might have been a year ahead of me." They shook hands.

"Yep, we played basketball together for a while," Brody said. "What happened to you? Coach Teegarden planned on us going to state finals with you. Then you were gone."

Tanner hated hearing this again. "I chose the military."

"Wow. Well, thanks for that." Brody grinned. "Don't take this the wrong way, but I remember your mom coming to watch practice sometimes. Coach Teegarden didn't like it."

"I didn't like it either. And she was my stepmother, not my mom." He could feel Lindsay's eyes on him. Time to change the subject. "So you came back to visit?"

Brody leaned closer. "Dude, I'm being checked out and so are you. If we don't pass, we're out."

Tanner smiled. "I'm not used to failing."

Brody just laughed and hugged the pretty blonde closer. "I am.

In fact, I flunked Carolyn's class ten years ago or so. Just ask her."

Giving Brody a playful sock in the arm, Carolyn said, "Stop it." Then she turned. "He made things miserable for me my first year of teaching."

"I was just toughening you up." Brody came right back at her. "Figured you'd need it."

Tanner exchanged a look with Lindsay. This couple had their own way of communicating. Private jokes and secret smiles. He wanted that with Lindsay.

"So how did you two meet?" Carolyn asked.

"I was cleaning his house," Lindsay said. "It was very romantic."

The memory of that first meeting made him smile. "Right. She called me an idiot."

"My way of flirting." Lindsay batted her eyes and they all laughed.

"Food this way." Sarah motioned to them. Tanner was hungry and they joined the line circling a table in the dining room.

"This is not a fancy meal," Sarah said, handing out paper plates. "Sloppy Joes, potato salad, canned beans—like those high brow restaurants. Beverages in the ice bucket. Tables outside in the yard."

While they were filling their plates, Mercedes appeared with Finn in tow. He gave Tanner a quick, curt nod. Coming closer, Finn kissed Lindsay's forehead. "Mom told me the girls were sleeping over tonight."

"Yep." Lindsay didn't look up. "They enjoy babysitting for

Rebecca and Susan."

"Need anything?" Sarah circled back. "Has Lindsay told you about our collaborative venture?"

"No." Mercedes looked as puzzled as Tanner felt.

"Babysitting," Lindsay said with a smile in his direction.

"I have two more mothers who might be interested," Sarah told Lindsay.

"Glad to hear it. School starts pretty soon for Rebecca but I'll still have Susan."

Sarah gave Tanner an apologetic look. "Don't we sound terrible? But it's hard to work when you have small children."

Mercedes had fallen silent. Then she nudged Finn along, as if she didn't like the turn in the conversation.

"Let's see what's going on outside." Lindsay said. Tanner was all for it. This room had gotten way too small.

Card tables had been set up in the yard. Lights were strung through the trees and small candles were placed strategically. Lindsay sank into one of the chairs. Tanner had just sat down when Finn took the chair opposite him.

He was halfway through his sloppy Joe when a very pregnant woman appeared at the top of the stairs. Her husband took both plates, put them on a table and then went back to give her a hand.

When Tanner looked over at Lindsay, she had a glazed look on her face, as if she'd just checked out. "What's wrong?"

"Nothing."

But she wasn't fooling him.

Chapter 21

That look of concern on Cole Campbell's face touched Lindsay's heart. She didn't know why, but it was so sweet. Cole seemed so aware of his wife and how she might be feeling. Tears brimmed in her eyes and she blinked them back. Had Rich looked at her like that when she was expecting Rebecca? She didn't think so and couldn't believe how bad that made her feel now.

"Lindsay, what is it?" Tanner repeated.

"She told you." Her brother's voice cut the air. "Nothing. She's fine."

"Finn." Mercedes voice held a warning.

Finn visibly took a breath. What was going on with her brother? But Lindsay wasn't about to ruin the party and ask.

Cole and Kate took the next table. "You sit right here, Kate." Cole pulled the chair out and Kate sat down. The food on Lindsay's plate had become tasteless.

"You feeling all right?" Tanner asked softly, tilting her chin up.

This was silly. "Everything's fine." But she was still shaken.

The back yard had darkened except for the tiny white lights strung through the trees. Tanner stroked her bare arm. "Let's take a walk." He got up.

"Okay. Sounds good."

Tanner whisked their paper plates from the table into the trash, giving a nod in Finn's direction. "We'll be right back."

Skirting the crowd was easy. Everyone was focused on Kate and Cole. Tanner led her down the side of Sarah's house. The huge trellis of clematis brushed her shoulder when they passed the front porch and she shivered.

"Are you cold? Come here." Tanner tucked her close to his side. She wrapped one arm around his waist. Totally in sync, they walked together down the dark street. Intersection illumination was all that was needed in Gull Harbor. "What's up, babe?"

"Nothing." She didn't want to have this discussion tonight. She wasn't ready. The answers might be too painful. Instead, she gave herself to the summer air, so soft on her skin. A cool breeze from the lake enticed them.

He kissed the top of her head. "Look, what bothers you bothers me. That's just how it works. Every breath you take. Of course I notice."

No use holding back. With every kiss, every comment, Tanner was unlocking her heart. The release felt wonderful. "Okay, seeing Kate with Cole touched something off in me. Stupid really."

"What kind of things? I thought women were always happy when a friend is expecting a baby."

"Oh, it's not that. Of course I'm happy for her. It's silly."

"Why is that? Can you explain this to me, please?"

Sharing was easing the hurt. "Looking at Cole made me realize that Rich never fussed over me when I was pregnant. Silly, right?"

"How old was he? You both were young, so eighteen?"

She nodded.

"Huge difference between a guy who's eighteen and one who's thirty. Cole's older and he has another child. Don't sell Rich short. Sounds as if he did what he had to do back then."

Maybe it was time to let that go. Time to forgive Rich for his shortcomings. She'd had her own back then and still did. Feeling as if a weight had been lifted, she smiled up at him. "How come you usually make so much sense?"

"Usually?" He smiled and she grinned up at him.

"Aw, babe." His lips were soft on her cheek. "Hey, you taste salty."

Wrapping her arms around him, she snuggled into his arms. "I *am* warm and sweaty."

"I know. I like it."

She felt his smile against her cheek. "You can be so bad."

"You don't know the half of it."

Desire stirred deep inside. Tanner could turn her on without even knowing it. "We should keep walking. This is a family neighborhood." When she broke away, he caught her hand and held it tight.

The smell of the lake grew as they got closer. She'd never get tired of this scent. It was rooted deep in her soul.

"Here's the path." And she led him through the tall grass that tickled her bare legs.

Lindsay turned. He was lagging behind, and the rising moon cast shadows over his eyes. "Come on. What is it?"

He closed the space between them. "Funny but I still don't like to walk through an area when I can't see what might be hidden there."

She slowed her steps, trying to see the dune grass rippling under the moon through his eyes. "Do you need your inhaler?"

Tanner patted his pocket. "Got it. But my asthma hasn't been giving me any trouble lately."

"Good, I'm glad."

"I like it when you say stuff like that." He nuzzled her.

"Like what?" She looked up at him.

"You know. Words that show you care."

"Of course I care."

Other words bubbled to her lips. Serious words. But she didn't want to break the mood. Tonight the lake sounded almost seductive. When they reached the sand, they kicked off their sandals. "Let's walk." Tanner steered her toward the shoreline.

"Was the party getting to you?" she asked. He sure hadn't seemed comfortable.

"Your brother's getting to me."

"Aw, Tanner." She stopped and turned. The water pooled at her feet. "I don't know what's going on with him. He's looked after me for so long."

"And I get that. But I want your family to like me."

The breeze lifted wisps of her hair. She smoothed them back. "But they do. My mother adores you and so do the girls."

"Not your brother. I can't put my finger on it, but I know it's there."

Frustration bubbled up inside. "Then ask him. Why can't men

just ask questions?"

Tanner looked at her as if she'd just fallen from a tree. "Because we're guys and supposed to know everything."

They walked for a while, and it felt as if they were the only people in the world. The homes up on the bluffs were dark now. A few decks were marked by lights.

"We should probably head back." Tanner came to a halt. "Sarah will wonder where we are."

"I guess." She hated to leave the beach.

"We can come back tomorrow night."

"But I'll have the girls."

"That's fine, isn't it?"

Her shoulders relaxed. "If you can put up with them."

Tanner stopped. She looked up.

"Lindsay, I love you. I'm still getting to know your children. But I hope someday I'll love them too. And I sure hope Rebecca and Susan will feel the same about me."

She was stuck on his first three words. "Oh, Tanner. But..."

He pulled away. "There's a but?"

"Not really. But I have some questions. What does this mean?" She had to ask.

His shoulders lifted. "Can we give it time? Does it have to mean anything right now?"

He was right. "No, it doesn't. I love you with all my heart." There. What relief to finally say those words. "But does this mean you're staying in Gull Harbor?"

"Of course I'm staying." Pulling her to him, Tanner folded her against his chest. "How could I ever leave you?"

The words touched and amazed her. For him it seemed that simple. Still, she needed more. "What will you do here? What if you do decide to move on? You're un...unattached." She'd almost said unemployed.

"Do you want me to go down on one knee?"

"No!" How horrifying.

The rumble of Tanner's laugh rippled on the night air. "Okay then. I have a plan. Don't worry."

But she'd heard the "don't worry" thing before. Apparently Tanner could see it in her face. "What?"

"It's just that I've heard the promises, Tanner. Good intentions are great but that doesn't mean they will happen."

His flashing eyes could have toasted marshmallows. "Look. I don't know what your experience has been," he finally said. "I don't just talk about things. I do them. And I wanted this to be a surprise. But here's the plan."

Now she'd hurt his feelings. Lindsay pressed a hand to his chest. "You don't have to tell me."

"But I want to. You're looking at the proud owner of a real estate license. I've put out a call to all the numbskulls I once hung out with. Some have inherited family homes. A couple want to sell them. Remember the big place where we parked that first night?"

She nodded, amazed and wordless.

"Gip lives in Naples, Florida now. Tells me he had no intention of returning to Gull Harbor." Tanner was grinning. "I assured him that I wasn't the idiot I was in high school and he laughed. Said he wasn't either and wasn't that too bad."

By this time, Lindsay was laughing.

"So Gip's house is going on the market next week. I'm the listing agent. The plan was to surprise you. Take you past the Phelps Realty sign in front of Gip's place. The house includes several lots so it's a high ticket item."

How totally amazing. Amazing and wonderful.

"You stinker." She covered his lips with one hand. "You've said enough. I believe you. I believe *in* you."

Taking her hand away, he kissed her until she pushed away, breathless. "Maybe we should be getting back. Finn might send out a search party."

~.~

They'd settled a lot tonight but Tanner still had to clear the air with Finn. As they drew close to Sarah's house, the place was blazing with lights and the backyard was dark.

"What happened?" Lindsay picked up her pace.

"Let's find out." The front door was open. He took the steps two at a time and she was right behind him.

The front room was bedlam but it seemed like happy excitement. Sarah pushed her way through the crowd of people. "Hey, where have you been?"

"Why?" he asked. "I told Finn we were taking a walk."

"What happened?" Lindsay took Sarah's arm.

Sarah's face creased into one huge smile. "Kate's water broke."

From the look on both women's faces, this was a good thing.

"But she's early. How exciting." Lindsay scanned the crowd.

"Where's Mercedes?"

"She went with Cole. You know, to be with her sister."

"Of course."

This was turning into a hen party. "I'll be outside," he whispered to Lindsay.

"Tanner, could you help Finn clean up?" Sarah asked. "He's in the back yard."

"Sure. No problem." Just the chance he'd been waiting for and he slipped out the kitchen door. Sure enough, Finn was dragging a trash can from table to table.

Finn looked up. "So you've heard the news?"

"Yeah." Tanner swept some discarded plates from a table and dumped them into the can. "I've never been a father so I have no idea what the guy's going through."

"Neither have I, so ditto."

Well, at least they had that in common. Tanner had to choose his words carefully. The last thing he wanted was to tick Finn off. "I've never been good at saying what I mean," he began.

Tossing an empty can into the trash, Finn nodded. "Glad to hear it."

Heck with being polite. Tanner blocked Finn from the trash detail. "No you're not. But you're going to listen to me."

Finn set the can down and waited. His tolerant expression made Tanner even madder.

"What's up with you, dude? I'm in love with your sister. She thinks the world of you. But you're not exactly doing a happy dance about us. Why?"

"I don't want her hurt, Tanner."

"Good, neither do I."

The wary look in Finn's eyes? He'd seen it on the faces of villagers who hoped the American soldiers had really come to help them. They wanted to believe. "So what's the problem?"

Finn exhaled. "Look, I remember how ripped up those fields were after you and your friends took your joy ride that night. I was the guy who got kids together to help old man Garrett."

Now, that made Tanner feel even worse about that night. "Trust me, I was fifteen and didn't know what to do with my anger. My friends went along for the ride." Thinking back, sometimes he still got steamed about the whole thing. But he was only mad at himself. And Ursula.

"Finn, my dad didn't send me to military school. I asked to go. And I needed a reason that would convince my dad."

"Why? You wanted to fight in the war?" Finn didn't look convinced.

Well, if this is what it took. One glance at the house told Tanner they were alone. Finn waited, arms crossed.

"My stepmother came onto me."

He didn't need a flashlight to see how pale Finn had gotten. "No way."

"Exactly. After five years of watching me grow up, I guess she liked what she saw. She was sick, man." He looked up to where the trees were dark against the sky. "But my stepmother was about the only thing holding my dad together after my mother died. At first she was okay. Fake charm, all of that. But as I got older, her attitude toward me changed. I locked my door at night. Avoided her, even when she came to basketball practice. She enjoyed that especially."

"Good God." Finn's astonishment somehow made it easier to tell the story he'd spent years trying to forget.

"Up to that point, I wasn't exactly a wild child. But that night? I can't even tell you what she did. I took my dad's car, no license of course, and set out with my buddies. We ripped through those fields. I still can feel the tears on my cheeks. Gip and the guys in the back were too drunk to notice."

Maybe he'd gone too far. Finn looked beyond shocked. "There was no other way?"

"I was fifteen. I could never tell my dad the real story. Yeah, I wrote Garrett a letter and apologized. Eventually I paid my dad back for any restitution he had to make. There was a lot of collateral damage that night. I pretty much ruined things for Gip. His parents sent him to a prep school he hated."

"I'm so sorry." By this point Tanner and Finn had both collapsed into lawn chairs. The fire had gone out of Finn's eyes. "How did you handle it later? When you came back to visit?"

"I avoided coming home and when I finally did, my dad was sick. My stepmother was a wreck by that time. Wanted nothing to do with my dad's illness. She just waited. Everything was divided equally in his will. She took off right after the funeral. I just came back to purge the place. It feels more like an exorcism, although Lindsay knows none of this."

They stood there in the darkness and Tanner wondered if he'd blown it.

"Man, I've been a real jerk." Finn finally said with a dry laugh.

"You've got that right." Relief made Tanner's head swim. "The war gave me lots of opportunities to take out my anger. Your sister? Lindsay is the best thing that's ever happened to me."

"She's had a rough time."

"I can see that and I appreciate what you and her parents have gone though. But I'm in the picture now. And I'm not leaving anytime soon."

"Suits me fine." And Finn gave him a brotherly grin.

"You can never tell your sister what I've told you," Tanner added. "The whole thing still makes my skin crawl."

But Finn wasn't cool with that. Tanner could tell. "Look, this is your business," Finn said slowly. "But if you want a relationship that means anything, you have to tell her. Don't keep stuff from the woman you love. Lindsay's tougher than that and she'd be hurt if she ever figures this out."

Tanner didn't know what to say. "You're sure?"

"Just my two cents, but yes, absolutely."

Just then, Lindsay appeared on the deck. She looked fresh and wonderful, the night breeze playing with the skirt of her sundress. "What are you two doing out here, making trouble?"

They looked at each other. "Nope. We're cool."

With Lindsay's help, they finished cleaning up the yard while Tanner's mind spun.

When they reached his house that night, Tanner turned to her. He knew in his heart that Finn had been right. "Lindsay, I've got something to tell you. It's hard to say and might be harder to hear."

She took his hand. "Any time you're ready."

Epilogue

"How do I look?" Lindsay fussed with her dress.

"As pretty as Cinderella." Rebecca looked at her mother in awe.

"You do, Mommy," Susan chimed in.

"I feel like Cinderella." And she did another spin in front of the mirror.

Both girls looked darling in their petal pink, tea-length dresses. Mom called the color rose pink for herself, of course.

"Such a beautiful dress." Sarah fussed with her veil. "That Meghan Markle who married the prince? This might be the same design, but you look better. Really."

Lindsay didn't believe that one bit but she'd been thrilled to find the knock-off at Second Hand Rose.

Mercedes poked her head in. "Ready?" Stylish in a black cocktail dress with cap sleeves, Mercedes was a knockout. Sarah's dress was also black and showed off the results of her latest diet. How she managed that working at the bakery, Lindsay would never know.

"The wedding cake is so beautiful, Sarah," Lindsay whispered. Topped with pink roses that matched the bridal flowers, the cake had been Sarah's wedding gift. "I hate to cut into it. Thank you."

"Oh, it's not every day that we get to prepare a wedding cake for a close friend." Careful not to crush the veil that cascaded to the floor, Sarah gave Lindsay a hug. "I'm so happy for you both."

"And you're marrying the right guy," Mercedes joked. "He's bringing us all that business."

Since opening his real estate office in September, Tanner had managed to score at least four properties they could use as rentals. The football season strategy had worked. Chicago people bought the homes and rented them out for the winter and some of the summer and fall months. And to top it off, Edna Willoughby, Lindsay's long-time customer, had decided to sell. Of course Lindsay steered her right to Tanner.

"You've been a great partner." Lindsay smiled.

"Someone's got to help me since Kate likes staying home with that baby."

"Who can blame her? Quinn's darling."

Mercedes went to the door of the dressing room and opened it slightly. "I think it's time." The wedding march was playing. Lindsay had found a harpist and she smiled, listening to the beautiful string version.

"Are you nervous, Mommy?' Susan asked.

"No, she's fine, silly," Rebecca said. Lindsay's oldest had settled down considerably since Tanner became part of their lives. The bickering had eased, to Lindsay's relief.

"Okay, troops." Sarah flung open the doors. "First Mercedes, then me. And then you two little ladies get to go. Use the handrail and be careful not to trip." She handed each girl a basket of rose petals.

Standing at the top of the stairs of the Inn at Gull Harbor, Lindsay waited. Sometimes this felt like a dream. Tanner had encouraged her not to wait and he was right. They wanted to start on their forever.

The late November wedding made good business sense too, as Mercedes had reminded her. A June ceremony would have played havoc with their rental schedule. And the wedding had to happen before her parents left for Florida. After a great deal of coaxing, Poppy John and Grandma Rose were renting a place in Florida for two months this year, beginning right after Christmas. With the support of the new babysitting group, Lindsay's parents weren't constantly on call anymore.

Sarah slipped out the door, followed by Mercedes. Blowing dramatic kisses, Rebecca and Susan were next. Then it was her turn.

One hand on the rail, Lindsay slowly went down the stairs. But it felt as if she were gliding. Everything about this wedding felt so right. And she knew Rich would approve. He'd be happy that Tanner had stepped up to parent the children he had to leave behind. There was an intake of breath from the small group of guests when she reached the bottom step.

Daddy was waiting with a wink. She took his arm.

"You look beautiful, little girl."

"Oh, Daddy."

"You're always my little girl. Don't you forget. And you better come down and visit us this winter with your husband and the girls."

My husband. Standing next to a crackling fireplace, Tanner looked so handsome in the tux he'd insisted on wearing. He wanted everything to be right. Standing next to him was Finn, his best man, along with Gip. His childhood friend was in town to close on the house Tanner had just sold. And next to Gip was Red, giving Lindsay a thumbs up. The little boy was beaming and with reason. Without Red, Tanner may never have realized how much he had to give to a child.

The minister opened his book.

Sitting in the front row, her mother dabbed at her eyes. Of course she was wearing a rosy pink dress and pearls. She'd insisted on wearing a fascinator, since Lindsay had found a dress like Meghan Markle's. "We'll be our own Royal Family," Mom had said, so darn cute in the tiny hat with a tilt.

The time was here. Tanner lifted her veil and settled it behind her shoulders with Mercedes' help. "You look beautiful."

"Take good care of her, son," Daddy said. With a tear in his eye, he kissed Lindsay's cheek. In his eyes she was moving away, even though it was only a mile farther up Red Arrow Highway.

Tanner chuckled. "You know I will. After all, I'm outnumbered."

Adoration in their eyes, Rebecca and Susan gave Tanner a small wave before joining their grandparents. After all, they each had a bedroom now at the front of the house, where they could hear the waves at night. They thought that was magical.

Together they stood in front of the minister, eager to begin their new lives. But glancing over Tanner's shoulder, Lindsay knew this was a family wedding, a joining of all their hearts and hopes.

THE END

Other Books by Barbara Lohr

Man from Yesterday series

Coming Home to You
Always on His Mind
In His Eyes
Late Bloomer
Still Not Over You

Windy City Romance series

Finding Southern Comfort
Her Favorite Mistake
Her Favorite Honeymoon
Her Favorite Hot Doc
The Christmas Baby Bundle
Rescuing the Reluctant Groom
The Southern Comfort Christmas

About the Author

Barbara Lohr writes heartwarming contemporary romance with a flair for fun. In her *Windy City Romance* series, the Kirkpatrick family and friends are based in Oak Park, Illinois, a suburb of Chicago. However, these adventurous girls take readers on exciting jaunts to Tuscany, Guatemala and Savannah. They travel wherever their hearts take them. The *Man from Yesterday* series is set in Gull Harbor, Michigan, where the boy you left behind might be the man you want forever. The charming, small beach town actually exists but under another name.

Family often plays an important role in Barbara's stories. "No woman falls in love without some family influence, either positive or negative." She feels strongly that dark chocolate should be an essential part of the food pyramid. Good food often figures in her work. She lives in the South of the United States with her husband and a cat that insists he was Heathcliff in another life. Visit her Facebook page and be sure to sign up for her newsletter for new releases, great giveaways and a fun group of readers who enjoy Barbara's work. She loves to hear from her readers!

www.BarbaraLohrAuthor.com
www.facebook.com/Barbaralohrauthor
www.twitter.com/BarbaraJLohr